To Gaze Upon a Darkened Cloud

A Race Against Climactic Armageddon

N Joseph Glass

Monocle Books

eBook ISBN: 979-8-9907484-3-9
Paperback ISBN: 979-8-9907484-4-6

Part One
Cloud Storm

One

As Michelle studied the front door through her windshield, the vegan leather seat gave no comfort to her squirming bottom. While it looked like every other farmhouse she had driven past, this one held *her* memories, *her* secrets, *her* hopes and ambitions. A time capsule.

In a moment of recantation, Michelle had decided not to revisit this memory. Some things were better left in the past.

Yet, after tearing herself from the office, she came. It had been too long, and the climate crisis had taken its toll on her parents. On everyone. If only her family would finally recognize the importance of her work, especially since the dark clouds came.

A glance at the path beside the barn summoned memories of childhood boredom broken only by bike rides to the riverbank. Trips to the mall had always required a drive her father seldom took in his Chevy Suburban, no matter how much his teenage daughter had begged.

The riverbed had dried out last year—another casualty of the dark cloud storms. Michelle had outgrown any desire to go to the mall.

Arms folded over the steering wheel, she thought of what she'd left behind in that house. Her thirst for a life not defined by birth and circumstance had dragged her from that nurturing environment. Though Michelle didn't doubt her parents' love, she knew her brother received more of their affection. Those two concepts often blended, but she knew the difference. Since her tumultuous departure for university sixteen years ago, the idea loitered in her parents' eyes and slid into subtle comments. Her detachment from the family had left scars on the aging couple.

After a deep breath, Michelle tucked a lock of amber hair behind her ear and summoned the fortitude to pull herself from the seat. She grabbed her roll-aboard bag from the trunk and plodded toward the front steps. No breeze dared challenge the crease in her pressed black trousers. "One step at a time—you can do this," she said, encouraging her hesitant feet. A silent reminder of her father's speeches on how much safer it was here than in the big city twisted in her palm, and the door swung open. He didn't need to speak the words, as the memories shouted in her mind. Those words would be spoken, nonetheless, as always.

A smile filled Bobby's face, his eyes shining at the sight of his big sister. She wondered how long he had stood there, waiting for her to build up the nerve to open the door. After a hug that lifted her feet from the wood floor, he took her bag and said, "Hey, sis."

The musky scent in the room filled her with recollections of her life in this place. Any freedom she'd enjoyed, the independence under which she now thrived, had vanished the moment she entered.

Nothing had changed in decades, except for signs of aging. Each wooden step sagged a little deeper. The scruffs and scratches had grown in number. Fractured light peeking through the tile windows outlining the front door played with swirling dust motes. Michelle exhaled and slipped out of her Converse All Stars.

"I'll take this to your room. Head into the kitchen—Mom's there." Bobby scurried up the stairs two at a time in his faded, mud-stained Wrangler jeans.

Michelle inched down the hall. The living room to the left showcased a new television facing the same plaid cloth sofa her little-girl bottom had sat upon for Saturday-morning cartoons on the old tube TV. Her mind brought forth an image of a younger man on Dad's empty chair and her on his lap, bouncing and giddy.

To the right, a wall of memories rose with the stairs to tell a one-sided story—more photos of Bobby than of her and only one of Daniel. A family history as the family wished to tell it. A facsimile of reality. No one wanted to remember childhood punishments, adult arguments, teenage groundings, or those horrific "I hate you" moments every parent endured.

The familiar sight of her mother's back and the rumble of flowing water awaited her across the island her dad had built a few years ago.

"Hi, Mom."

Her mother turned from the sink, her bubble-laden hands dripping. After peeling off her yellow gloves, she closed the tap. "Hey, darling."

A warm embrace filled Michelle with the reassuring feeling of *home*. She surrendered to the thought that this would always be that for her, no matter how long she stayed away or what she made of her life.

Falling into an old pattern, Michelle took up the drying rag while Mom handed her clean dishes, one at a time. Preliminary catch-up talk filled the spaces between clatters of porcelain and clinks of silverware. Bobby entered and grabbed a Coke from the fridge. The towel snapped against his rear like a horsewhip, and his big sister told him to make himself useful by putting the clean dishes away.

Michelle inquired about the horses. "How many do you have these days?"

Bobby splayed his fingers. "Five, counting our two. Been slow these last couple of years. With water so scarce, not many keep horses anymore."

"It's enough. And we've got plenty of well water." Their mother closed the tap. "Five horses is a lot of work for the two of them."

Michelle tried not to infer contempt in the words. "Is the money enough from only—*Hey*!" The pop of her brother's towel slap made Michelle's buttocks clench.

Bobby said, "Five's basically the same work as eight, but for less money."

"Eight's probably too much for Dad. How's he been?"

"Your father's as strong as ever," her mother replied. "You know how he loves caring for those horses. Treats the customers' ones as good as our own."

Bobby added, "He's slowed down... 'cause of his heart. Our clients are good folk, and they understand."

"*Clients*? How do they know more than..." She couldn't finish the question.

"Dinner's almost ready. You kids go set the table."

How old would they be before she stopped calling them kids? It fit Bobby, half his sister's age. He pursed his lips and shrugged as he schlepped the stack of dishes into the dining room.

"When Dad comes in, we all want to hear about your work on cloud forecasting. We won't understand it much, but we're right proud of you for it."

Michelle beamed. "Don't be too proud, little brother."

Bobby rolled his eyes with his *yeah right* look.

"I was part of a team that worked it out. I... I mean *we*... have a long way to go, and I hope to improve predictability to more than a few hours."

When their mother lugged the serving tray into the dining room, a wave of gravy crawled over the edge and splashed onto the floor. Bobby reached to take the tray from her. Refusing his help, she heaved it onto the edge of the table with a plate-rattling thud. As Michelle bent to wipe up the spill, Bobby centered the tray on the table. When Michelle's father came in, they all sat, and he said grace.

"You should tell Mom and Dad how you worked with a team on your cloud-storm forecaster alert thing." A juvenile smirk ran across Bobby's face.

Her dad raised an eyebrow. "They teach teamwork at that fancy college?"

Swallowing before having fully chewed, Michelle readied herself for a snide retort. Bobby's snickering poured fuel onto the fire.

Their mother patted her husband's hand. "Hank, stop. This is supposed to be a nice family dinner. First one we've had in quite some time. Michelle's here now—that's what matters."

"Well, I suppose we oughta be grateful our daughter spared a little time from that important job of hers for a visit."

Red-faced, Michelle tried to control her volume. "My job *is* important. More so now that these cloud storms are here. I'm needed in DC. I think trying to save our environment is worthy of my time. As the leading authority on cloud storms, I can—"

"My world-famous daughter. I'm not saying we ain't proud." Her father's tone softened. "It'd be nice to know you were proud of where you come from. Proud to be part of this family."

A storm alert on everyone's phones muted Michelle's explosive comeback.

Two

Under a cloudless Ghanaian sky, Juliana had crossed the farms and open fields again today. She needed to help her younger sister, a widow with a newborn, who couldn't handle motherhood alone. Though not a mother herself, Juliana skillfully burped her nephew, swaddled him, and put him to sleep just before Jonah phoned to warn her about the cloud-storm alert.

"Yes, I saw it on my phone," she replied.

The clouds wouldn't come for four hours.

"I'll finish here and be back in plenty-plenty time."

Her husband said, "If you are delayed, *abeg*, stay there and let it pass."

"Of course. I'm almost finished—I'll be home soon. I love you."

"I love you more. See you soon." Jonah hung up.

Unsure whether she'd settled his mind, Juliana let her smile fade into a sigh. Burying the prick of guilt she felt for neglecting Jonah, she dismissed her sister's inquiry. That would only transfer the guilt to her sister, whose time of need had kept Juliana from her husband.

More than thirty years into a good marriage, they'd never argued as much as they did over the amount of time Juliana spent helping her sister—more time than she spent with her husband. A kind, gentle man, the hardworking farmer needed a woman's care. Juliana's mother, who lived in the same house, had picked up the slack.

Carrying such heavy thoughts, Juliana headed home with sufficient time to beat the clouds.

Or so she thought.

She shouldn't have run. In her haste, Juliana hadn't seen the creature under the pile of weeds and leaves. It must have been a carpet viper. A sharp pinch had buckled her leg, and she'd fallen hard.

The "sizzle" of its scales alerted her to the snake's defensive posture. As it readied itself to strike again, Juliana rolled away, the tussle with the weeds ripping the phone from her hand. For more than two hours, she sat exposed, with nothing to protect her but her faith.

Everyone knew not to be caught outside when the dark clouds crowded the sky. But prayers to the Celestial Maker would carry her through this. Heralding the Glorious Transition, the storms meant salvation. No member of the Order had yet been lost to their fury. Since adopting this religion, she'd tried to convince her husband to embrace it as well. Although he supported her decision, Jonah held to none of the faiths he knew.

As an unearthly darkness descended over the field, hope dissolved from view. Juliana's leg began to swell, and the bleeding wouldn't stop. Overwhelmed by an irrational desire to look up, to see what no one had yet described, she pressed her eyelids closed. The whirring howl of fierce wind announced the narrow dust funnels spiraling around her.

The deadly rain would soon come.

"Look after my dear Jonah," she implored the dark heavens.

Three

Sheltered in their Norway cathedral, the twelve elders gathered.

With great care, the group had documented each occurrence since the first majestic clouds had filled the sky one hundred and eight weeks ago. As the storms increased in frequency and intensity, evidence of the nearing Transition had manifested. At this point, according to sacred tradition, those who wavered in their faith were to be cast out. There was no place for those lacking the resolve needed for what would come.

Cloaked in robes of crimson, the elders knelt in a circle outlined by candelabras in the center of the cathedral. They dropped their hoods to expose their shaved heads. Twelve voices vibrated through the musty air of the otherwise empty inner sanctum of the marble-block building.

"We welcome the Transition."

The elders bowed, palms on the cold, hard tile.

"We welcome the Guide Couple."

Twenty-four arms stretched toward the clouds beyond the ceiling.

"We welcome our glorious future."

The chairperson reminded all of what they well knew—they needed to record accurate storm data for their clans. Each elder represented their clan and carried the charge to preserve their bloodline. Collective certainty said the Guide Couple had been born and would soon manifest their divine presence. No one knew which of the seven and a half million members of the Glorious Transition group, commonly called the Order, would be the couple to lead them through the nearing Final Days.

Silence battled the flickering light to dominate the room as the Twelve filled pages of their paper notebooks. All logged the details of the storms, from the exact time of the first sighting to the time it took to blanket the globe in darkness and how long they lasted. Each storm caused disappearances and deaths, but casualties never mattered unless a clan member died by direct cause of a storm funnel or its deadly rain. No clan members had been lost to the clouds.

By strict interpretation of the ambiguous Code, the elders met during every storm. While Elder Ferguson repeatedly wrote the same details, some new developments had occurred in recent storms. *There has been no rain in the last seven months except when the dark clouds come. Their rain now burns the skin of humans and certain animals, and no one knows why.* She doodled some clouds. *Droughts continue to cause health and economic problems. Loss of life and crops are worsening the global financial crisis. Increased environmental decay exacerbating global warming and climate change has accelerated in recent months.*

In addition to tracking cloud activity, these gatherings allowed them to discuss the status of their clans and address any issues or crises of faith among the believers. Elder Ferguson called the first point to order.

"What is the status of the alarming rise in teenage marriage?"

While no one elder held authority over the others, each meeting needed a chairperson, and they rotated the assignment every five years. The woman holding that position now had the distinct honor of being the one who would lead the group in welcoming the Guide Couple to usher them through the Transition.

Eleven elders said their clans had seen increases in teen marriage.

"Reduction in Clan Tartagni." The youngest of the group led a clan from Italy that had spread into France, Spain, Croatia, and Greece.

All parents hoped their son or daughter would be part of the Guide Couple. Many of them arranged marriages to orchestrate fulfillment of the foretelling. Member couples parented many children, hoping to bestow upon themselves the honored title of Guide Progenitor. Rumbles among the others led the chairperson to conclude many doubted the veracity of Tartagni's claim.

Elder Ferguson cleared her throat to stifle the murmur and collect the attention of the room. "I think we all find that hard to believe. Your clan has had some of the highest numbers among our people."

"My people respect the Code." His reply brought more grumbles.

While some saw the practice as a violation of the Code, it had a centuries-long history. Some parents subjected teenagers to marriage before the children reached their respective country's legal age. Religious freedom laws gave some leeway, but several key court cases had brought unwanted notoriety to the Order. The most infamous came from Italy, when a nineteen-year-old boy married a girl of only thirteen.

Tartagni ignored the others. "And I believe we have found the Guide Couple."

Four

Everyone behaved with exceptional calm despite the alert. They had some time before the storm set in and ate mostly in glorious silence. The roasted chicken was dry and the potatoes hard. Unlike her mother, Michelle didn't cook much and wasn't good at it. But never had Michelle eaten such a disappointing meal in this house. To not have both parents on her case, she decided to hold her tongue under the orange mush of overcooked carrots.

After confirming his father had latched the barn door, Bobby eagerly related how he had taken over the bulk of the work with the horses. Their father mostly did lighter work, such as the nightly brushing. Mom cracked a joke about him combing her hair too. The mood turned somber when she mentioned how Daniel used to like playing with her long curls.

A spectator of her older brother's degeneration, misdiagnosis, and the illness that took him from them, Michelle couldn't imagine the emotional toll it must have taken on her parents. In her younger eyes, her father had been a superhero—the strongest person on Earth. Her mother had always had such fortitude and the wisdom of her namesake goddess, Sofia. Daniel's death had drained those personas, leaving empty shells in their place.

The passing years shed light on aspects of her childhood that had been impossible to illuminate at the time. Daniel, originally thought to have developed Tourette syndrome when the twitches and spasms started, hadn't received the help that could have saved him from the brain tumor. When the vomiting, memory loss, imbalance, and constant headaches began, the progression had already killed him. The body took a little longer to expire.

She didn't know why they had Bobby—a comfort or a replacement, perhaps. But her inextinguishable fear for her little brother saw his future predetermined. He'd be the one to run the family horse stable and become their parents' eventual caregiver. An inheritance or a life sentence—Michelle had gladly given up her birthright.

To change the subject, Michelle asked, "None of you are worried about the cloud-storm alert?"

"Why, sis? Never been anything to worry about since *your* early-warning system went online."

"People still die or disappear. After every storm, we get reports from around the world... and my system isn't perfect."

"Angel, look." Her dad hadn't used that nickname in ages. Assuming he was trying to make up for earlier, she silently accepted the apology. "The only thing wrong with your warning system is that they didn't call it the 'Anderson Alert System.' Maybe if you'd been a man. You say you worked with a team, but I know my little girl. The way you talk about it, that system was mostly *your* doing."

Taking Michelle's hand, her mother said, "We're right proud of you. No more crashed flights, and such a reduction in traffic accidents since your warning system's been alerting people."

Though considered the world's leading expert, Michelle's mind raced over how little she knew about the cloud storms. A task force had recently been proposed in DC. If they had any chance of comprehending the magnitude of the storms' impact on the environment and counteracting it, she knew a united global effort was needed. Her early-warning system, which had been shared with all governments in agreement with every communications company around the planet, was so far the only thread uniting the world against the dark clouds.

"It's not *my* system. And I think you're missing my point. The warning system is only that—a warning that a storm is coming. We haven't found any way to protect people from its effects. And they're only getting worse. That's why my work's so important."

"Look, sis, I know it may be unfamiliar territory, but take the win. In their Mom-and-Dad way, they *both* said they're proud of you."

Michelle shook her head at her little brother. "Mom, dinner was fantastic, as always. Thank you. Now I think we really should prepare the house. We have…" She checked the wall clock. "Maybe an hour."

As Bobby rose to his feet, the chair's legs screamed against the wood floor. His mother's face cringed.

Smirking, Bobby said, "I'm Chewbacca," and bellowed a gurgling squeal. "Come on, let's do as the famous meteorologist says."

***

With the storm shutters closed, candles and camping lanterns ready, and jugs filled with water, the family sat together in a scene from a memory.

As she lit a candle, Sofia said, "Isn't this wonderful, Hank, all of us together?"

In his *almost*-smile, Michelle saw the love she knew her dad felt but struggled to display—more so in her adult years, when she became a visitor in this house. When Bobby asked Michelle if her office would publish more detailed data on the increasing impact of the storms on climate change, her father grumbled, "Fake news."

"Don't tell me you're still listening to those stupid AM radio pundits," Michelle said. It was bad enough when he dismissed global warming as a liberal hoax. Seeing the country divided, even on this issue with evidence over their heads darkening the sky, twisted Michelle's face into a grimace.

"I listen to FM radio," her father replied.

"And I work for the US Climatological Society. Trust me when—"

The lights went out, ending the unpleasant discussion. Bobby lit more candles, and Michelle readied the camping lanterns. Flickering illumination encased them like an igloo, draping the corners in dark seclusion. An hour later, Dad rose and announced he would go check the generator, saying it should have kicked in automatically.

"Don't look at them," Michelle shouted as he opened the door.

"You ever tried?" Bobby asked. "To look at the clouds, I mean."

"Please tell me you'll never try it. People go mad. I mean, you're already nuts—and stupid... so please don't go mad on top of that."

He whacked her in the face with a throw pillow, and the siblings burst into laughter. "I miss you, sis."

"Me too."

"Really? You miss *yourself*?"

Michelle threw herself onto Bobby and pushed the pillow into his face. He giggled as he'd done as a child.

The rattle of wooden shutters fending off the increasing winds crept up beside them in the living room. It hinted at the relative safety of the old farmhouse. Cloud storms still frightened Michelle, especially here, "in the middle of nowhere." In her Washington, DC, apartment, she barely felt them pass.

"Bobby, why don't you get the fireplace going?" their mother asked.

Bobby hopped to his feet and went for the logs. In no time, he had a roaring fire. Its warmth wrapped around Michelle like a tight hug. Realization that her dad hadn't returned pulled her from its consolation.

"What's taking Dad so long?"

The clang of the shutters loudened and became constant.

"It's crazy old," Bobby said. "And Dad's too cheap to buy a new one. It never works when we need it, right when the storms come."

"Because the storms knock out..." Michelle exhaled a long breath.

She couldn't explain again how the storms impacted all machinery. The effect could last an hour or more, while the power grid stayed dark for the duration of the storms.

"Forget it," she said. "I think the funnels have started. The rain comes next. It's not safe out there. We should go get him."

In the mudroom, Michelle hastened her legs through rubber pants and pushed her feet into rain boots. The oil-thirsty hinges on the screen door squealed as Bobby pushed it closed behind him. With only a jacket on, he took off without her. While fishing her second arm through its sleeve, Michelle thoughtlessly thrust the door open. The flimsy wood frame flung against the side of the house with a sharp pop, and its spring shot off into the storm.

As she took a straight line to the generator shed, she reminded herself to keep her head down. Throughout her studies of the clouds, she had never been outside this far into a storm, and this was a big one. As howls of twisting funnels played an ominous soundtrack over the blackened backdrop, Bobby's cries fought the onslaught of the roiling winds.

"Dad," he shouted. "Dad!"

Five

Flames danced on candle wicks, projecting a stop-motion film of Jonah's pacing. Maame sat near him in a puddle of worry. Her daughter had been out too long. Jonah tried not to say it—his mother-in-law had been repeating it more than enough for them both.

"I hope she wasn't outside," she said again.

It reminded him of his old record player. It always skipped. Scratching the curly white whiskers of his close-cropped beard, Jonah could do nothing until the storm cleared. Despite knowing the futility, he checked his mobile again. No service.

When the lights went out, the funnels started. Jonah had to hope his dear wife had stayed in her sister's home. A prayer shared with his mother-in-law asked to find her safe there in the morning. He knew his wife prayed to a "newer god," as he called it, but he didn't care who answered. Tribal gods, the Christian God, or the Celestial Maker of the Order—he'd happily worship whichever one brought his wife home safely.

Rain bombarded the corrugated metal roof like an enthusiastic drummer beating a steel pan. Deep inside, in a place he buried for Maame's sake, he wondered if Juliana had tried to come home. If she had, and the rains fell... No, he couldn't think of it, couldn't imagine her in that. It had been at least a year since anyone in the village had been caught in the unholy rain brought by those dark and unnatural clouds. To picture his beloved like that burned corpse...

Though he'd quickly dismissed it when Maame had brought it up, Jonah mentally reviewed the stories of those whose loved ones had gone missing. Which would be worse, he wondered to no avail, finding Juliana's dead body or never finding her at all? Never knowing. He had to believe she stayed with her younger sister for the night. Rubbing his sandpaper-dry hands, he paced around the small living space. Belief alone wouldn't let his mind rest, and not even the dense darkness allowed exhaustion to overtake his dread.

***

When Jonah woke, only silence fell upon his roof. He stumbled off the chair, tipping it onto the floor with a clang, and relit the oil lamp on the table. Pushing his legs through his pants, Jonah hopped onto his feet. A foot stomp prevented him from falling face-first as he pulled on the jeans.

Maame stumbled in from her unlit bedroom. "Has it stopped?"

"Yes. I'm going to find Juliana."

"I'm coming with—"

"No. The storm has passed, but it is still dark." Hurried and erratic movements carried him through his mental fog into the bedroom to grab a shirt.

"Do find her, my boy."

As Jonah rushed out while pulling on his shirt, he banged his elbow on the doorframe. Keeping his eyes on the dirt below his feet, he scampered to the shed to fetch three torch lights. In his middle-of-the-night desperation, Jonah rapped on the door of his closest neighbor. Three of his cousins still lived with his aunt and uncle. The eldest had moved to Accra city a few years ago. He had only to ask, and Michael and Antony pulled on boots and joined his search. The commotion stirred their sister, and she caught up with them, insisting on tagging along. With some convincing, Jonah sent her to look after his mother-in-law.

The blackness of night absorbed the beams reaching out from their torches. Booming voices were their only search tools, so they used them liberally. Heading in the general direction of his sister-in-law's home, they spread out until their repeated yells of "Juliana" became distant echoes.

Such dense darkness, even in the dead of night, was unusual after a cloud storm. Seeing no moon, no stars, Jonah called his cousins to him. Howling winds rushed in, and Jonah knew he had made a terrible mistake. A tree line lay just ahead. The canopy would provide some cover, and the thick trunks would lessen the wind's fierce grip.

The rain fell.

As they ran, Jonah felt the fiery drops strike his neck. Wet blades of grass lashed over the top of his boots, stinging his shins.

One of his cousins screamed—he didn't know which.

"He fell," Antony cried.

The two stopped, retraced their steps, but didn't find Michael where he had gone down. Scurrying this way and that in a frantic search, the burning raindrops pelted their exposed skin. Antony's calls for his brother became moans. After the moaning silenced, Jonah's foot hit something soft and hot. The torch caught the last of the light in Antony's eyes. Riddled with agony himself, Jonah fell over the young man.

His search for Juliana had sacrificed two of his cousins to the storm he thought had passed. With eyes unable to focus, he couldn't see what pain receptors shot to his brain. His exposed skin boiled with each drop that pinched like acid. Remarkably, the rain hadn't ripped through his clothes, but when they became heavy with its moisture, they burned his skin.

He rose, and while in a full sprint for the trees he could barely see, Jonah pulled off the shirt. A light broke the dense darkness ahead. Swirling dirt and leaves danced around a glowing faint-blue patch of ground. Not recalling the last steps, Jonah stood in the center of a strange bubble of blue electricity, wide and tall enough to envelop him. Whatever had taken hold of him, it wouldn't let go. Not even the searing rain dared enter the unhallowed space surrounding him.

The darkness blackened and engulfed his eyes, and he collapsed.

Six

The chairperson stared again at the one photo of Alexandar—forbidden for her to possess—that she kept on her phone. Her marriage at eighteen had been arranged by her parents, but she'd had to renounce her husband and any claim of them being the Guide Couple to accept her role as elder-elect. In her experience, most arranged marriages lacked the bond hers had forged.

The price of salvation.

A side effect of faith.

Only in the solace of her chamber did she allow the name Ameilia into her mind. Alexandar had called her Amy. The name was shared only between them, and she'd grown to love it. Three decades ago, whispers had made their way to her ears and summoned a single tear. Alexandar had remarried. Not arranged—perhaps his marriage was born from choice. From love.

Chairperson Ferguson had called a fifteen-minute recess to use the restroom and stretch their legs. She now sat on the bed in her room, surrounded by cold marble walls. Hung tapestries failed to enliven the space or add warmth. Too many belief systems—she found the word "religion" repugnant—pushed a somber and morbid ambience not only into their places of worship, but also into the lives of their adherents. Amy didn't know why. Most of these faiths touted hope and salvation, glory and honor, redemption from sin and misery. So why did they languish in despair of the now rather than bask in the rays of the glorious future they promised?

The next agenda point would address the growing concerns of waning faith among the youth and, alarmingly, those who've waited for this moment for decades only to falter at the dawn of their salvation. Most days, Amy felt like one of the latter. Would she have been in the former group if not for Alexandar's firmly rooted faith? No matter. She had shed her former life—as symbolized by the shaving of her head. Eldership was an identity-consuming role that defined her. No longer Cynthia Ameilia Ahlquist Ferguson, she would be known forever more as Elder Ferguson of Clan Ferguson.

Wearily, she pulled herself from the mattress, a task that had become considerably harder in her declining years. Leaving *Amy* on the bed, Elder Ferguson trudged to the bathroom to splash cold water on her face.

***

As the storm raged on, the Twelve again formed the circle. The meeting room, a circular space orbited by the elders' chambers, could hold a few hundred worshipers yet operated at full capacity with a dozen. Her clan's cathedral was home to the Council of Twelve for her term "in office."

"Now…" She sighed. "Next on the agenda, we must address the losses. We are losing—"

"Excuse me, Elder Ferguson. I hate to break protocol," Elder Tartagni said. "You ignored my statement about the Guide Couple."

Tartagni never hesitated to butt in. All eyes fell on Ferguson. Power flooded into her, strengthening her bones and emboldening her tongue—the only positive aspect she'd found in being chairperson for her first and only term. To her relief, Tartagni would succeed her successor. With any luck, she'd die before then. Unless, of course, the foretelling of the Guide Couple found its fulfillment—as the others believed it would.

"I dismissed your outlandish statement because it was as baseless as your claim of not having the same issue with teen marriage as the rest of the clans."

"I am prepared to offer proof. I have seen the signs."

This would be a lengthy process, and she would have to lead it as part of her sacred duty. No one dared refuse the honor of assuming the position as their clan's spiritual leader when the preceding clan elder passed on. As *Amy*, she'd never comprehended where they passed on *to* or why everyone celebrated the death of their respected elder. As *Elder Ferguson*, she still couldn't be sure. Would she pass *on* or pass *away*?

Trying to read Elder Sato's expression here was impossible. He played the zealot much better than she did. Though they knew they could be cast out, they often conversed in each other's quarters. Rumors had spread about a love interest between them. Amy figured that was better than anyone thinking the platonic friends exchanged doubts about the Twelve's interpretations of the Code.

"Elder Tartagni," chairperson Ferguson said. "You may present evidence to substantiate your claim of identifying the Guide Couple in Clan Tartagni."

A bluish holographic globe filled the center of the circle as Tartagni called up the first of many eyewitness testimonials. An interview with the couple came next. As Ferguson had speculated, their arranged marriage had happened young. She couldn't help but feel a measure of gratitude that her parents had waited until she turned eighteen. The bride in question, Isis, had married at sixteen—with judiciary approval—before the standard legal age in Greece. At nineteen, her husband Nickos had needed no such consent. To Ferguson, it seemed the young—too young—couple wore their smiles like masks. No part of the Code indicated the couple needed to be happily married, only legally so.

On her notepad, Ferguson wrote a checklist. Begrudgingly, she checked off her boxes. The couple had been married for more than one year and had no children. Check. They were born on the same day, no more than six years apart. Check. Since cesarean-section births had been made admissible, parents had begun orchestrating matching birthdays for prebirth arranged marriages. The idea made the chairperson wince. The couple married on their birthday and had the marriage legally registered. Check.

Harder-to-orchestrate attributes of the Guide Couple included details of their physical characteristics, matching birthmarks, and their pure lineage traced back to the original Twelve. The couple passed every item on the extensive list—closer than any other she could recall in her tenure as an elder. She had to accept all preliminary foreshadowing as satisfactory.

***

Internal conflict caused Amy to toss throughout the night. Her two personas met in heated combat, a war between mind and heart on the battlefield of faith. Alexandar had been a pillar—if not of faith, of normalcy. He'd provided stability and love as she had not known before and would never know again. She'd been pulled away from him and their sixteen-year marriage annulled when she began her elder training at thirty-four. A violent twist slackened the tucked corner of her sheet.

Sacred texts and foreshadowing ran through her mind. Fabled to have been delivered to the only faithful men on an earth steeped in darkness and chaos under the Ur III Dynasty of ancient Mesopotamia, the Code had endured for millennia.

The basis of the faith of millions germinated from those original twelve. Once enlightened, they emigrated to distant lands and, mostly through procreation, grew the membership of the Glorious Transition Order. Like a worm on hot concrete, she contorted herself but found no relief.

As she stared at the darkness suspended over her bed, she had to admit this couple's genealogy looked clean. The Code clearly specified that the Guide Couple must come from pure, traceable bloodlines. Nothing stipulated whether the couple could share the same ancestry. This couple did—a little too closely for Amy's liking. But Elder Ferguson said nothing about the couple being second cousins.

History raced around the track her mind had paved. She considered the power of faith. Of zealotism. Some of their clans had been responsible for horrific deeds in the name of the Celestial Maker and of welcoming the Transition for the descendants of the original twelve. The goal of producing the Guide Couple had fostered pure-race ideologies that plagued humankind and had led to some of its greatest atrocities.

Clan Ferguson's proud Scandinavian history was told now without mention of their professed Nordic racial superiority—nor of the clan's significant impact on nineteenth- and early-twentieth century notions of nationalism. No living Ferguson would ever comment on how such propaganda and self-aggrandizement had fueled the Nazi "Master Race" ideology and the horrors it spawned.

Having passed the initial stages of verification, the pedigree couple had been summoned to the cathedral to stand before the Council of Twelve. If the elders agreed they were the Guide Couple, would that substantiate Amy's faith or undermine it? The next question her mind conjured couldn't be answered even by the most faithful.

What lay beyond the Glorious Transition?

Seven

The flapping of her plastic jacket in the gusts of wind became a deafening rumble as Michelle reached for Bobby's arm. He hunched over their father, who was on the ground with his back against the generator shed. The skin under the aged man's chin was stretched taut as he stared into the endless cover of darkened clouds.

Michelle's flashlight found eyes from a memory, looking at her from a younger version of her father. Wide and full of wonder—she hadn't seen that spark in twenty years. Not since Daniel. He looked blissful and at peace. She yelled for Bobby to help get him back to the house. Each taking an arm, the siblings heaved. Though not a large man, he felt heavier than expected.

"He's resisting." Bobby's shout fought to penetrate the storm's acoustic bombardment. As if yearning to ride the wind and join the tempest, their father's thin gray hair fluttered wildly. His eyes rolled upward to steal another gaze of the black heavens above that reminded Michelle more of hell. Instinctively, she looked up and immediately pulled her eyes down.

"Stop! Dad, you can't look."

Bobby tugged again. "Why's he fighting us?"

"Just help me get him inside."

In protest, their father's legs flailed against the dirt and gravel. "No," he muttered loud enough to be clearly heard. "It's so beautiful. Can't you see? You must look. So beautiful."

Again, Michelle's eyes stole a forbidden glance and withdrew immediately.

The three steps up to the house rose from the earth like Mount Everest. They scaled it against gravity's oppressive tug on their father. To keep them from pulling him inside, he became increasingly frantic and tried to free himself from their grip. The closer they got to the door, the more he struggled. The first drops fell. Although she and Bobby were giving the task all they had, Michelle yelled for them to hurry.

As Bobby pulled the door closed behind them, their father said, "So beautiful."

When she locked eyes with him, Michelle felt a renewed connection.

He added, "Do you see?"

With strenuous effort, they hoisted their father onto the sofa. The back of his neck was blistered where the first drops from the malevolent clouds had splattered on his skin. But he seemed to have been touched in another way—one filled with even more treachery and dread.

Their mother crept closer, and the dim glow of the camping lantern she held fell over her husband. "Hank. Hank," she said repeatedly, the word working itself into a shout on her last call.

Blubbering incoherently, he occasionally said, "It's so beautiful. Do you see? You must look." His unsettled pupils shrank and widened in the flicker from a distant candle. *Distant*, Michelle thought. Her father's sight wasn't there, his gaze finding neither the room nor his family.

"Is it...?" Bobby didn't say what they both knew.

As if the sound would rouse him to his senses, their mother continued saying her husband's name. While Michelle hadn't read much about the cloud madness, she knew no one had recovered. No one knew what caused it. Looking at her father, once so strong, her superman, her eyes fell upon a frail reflection of the man she once knew.

"He didn't get the generator going?" her mother asked.

Before she said something unkind—her mind shouting, *How could you ask that?*— Michelle took a breath.

"No. We found him at the shed, sitting on the ground."

"Looking at the sky," Bobby added.

"Hank. Hank. You need to get the generator going... Hank."

"Mom, forget the stupid generator."

Bobby's outburst caught in his mother's trembling eyes. Michelle's outburst would have been more explosive.

"He means we need to focus on Dad. He's in no condition to go back out. Besides, it's raining now."

After wiping her husband's brow, Sofia mopped up his drool. As far as they could tell, he'd fallen asleep. Through an exchange of knowing looks, Michelle and Bobby expressed their concern without words. Sitting on the floor beside her mother, Michelle clutched her hand until the haggard, aged woman nodded off in the chair. Michelle nudged her awake then helped her to her bed upstairs, but only after Bobby said he would sleep in the living room with his dad. Michelle needed a bed.

Her head hit the pillow with a greater weight than she had anticipated for this night in her old room with the same bed overlaid with the same pink sheets and white comforter. The same pillow now supported a troubled mind no longer filled with childhood dreams. The burden of her independence crushed her skull into the soft foam. A mind wired and racing kept her eyes fixed on the ceiling, even though they couldn't see for the darkness of the quiet room.

Quiet. No shutters rattled. She heard no whirring of wind. No pattering of rain. The storm had abated. Hoping her dreams might offer more tranquility than her conscious thoughts, she drifted into a fretful sleep. Tossing like a colicky baby, she forced her eyelids closed as soon as they startled open. The shutters rattled, but her exhaustion didn't care.

*****

When she finally awoke, she thought first of her phone, of its battery and the cornucopia of messages and missed alerts it held in waiting. *How is Dad?* should have been her first thought. As she swung her robe on and raced downstairs, she mentally chastised herself.

Along with Bobby, her father slept beneath the brightness of the wall sconces left on before the storm. Michelle thought the bulbs were too bright for sconces, but her parents had told her they needed them to see well.

Face down on the coffee table, Michelle's phone taunted her. With this "leash" that went everywhere with her, she was never off the job. She'd never wanted to be. But at eleven past six Central time, she ignored the leash a little longer. The office wasn't open yet. Not even she started work by seven Eastern. After a steaming shower, Michelle decided to make breakfast for everyone. The sight of her phone, caught out of the corner of her eye, reminded her of her other life. The life she'd chosen.

For the first time, she felt relieved to see her battery had died. Normally, she would have cursed at it along with everyone she could remember who worked at Apple for sacrificing battery life to make it so thin. In the kitchen, she plugged her iPhone into the charger and prepared breakfast. The others would be up soon, and no doubt as hungry as she was.

Along with Michelle's "Good morning," the stimulating aroma of coffee greeted Mom when she staggered into the kitchen. When they sat to eat the scrambled eggs and toast, Bobby refused to say grace, so their mom said it in her husband's place. A reluctant "Amen" from Michelle encouraged one out of Bobby.

With a piping-hot second cup of coffee in hand, Michelle slid back into the role that defined her. The phone screen popped with alert messages: emails, iMessages, missed calls. Never had Michelle seen such numbers in those app notification bubbles. Over three hundred unread emails. Knowing the iMessages likely outweighed them in importance, she'd get to the emails later. Missed calls carried the greatest urgency. No one called anyone unless they were elderly or needed an immediate reply for words too numerous for messaging apps.

Thirteen calls from her boss had gone unanswered. One from Brian. He had been distant since the pause. A greeting here or there at the office, but he hadn't called once since she responded to his proposal with a request for *space*. That space had been larger than she'd expected.

Several more missed calls had come from workmates and friends. The names listed in her call history kept her eyes locked on the small screen. Her phone divided contacts into only three categories: work, family, blocked. Starting with a voicemail from her boss, she went one by one. All included the same two points of "Are you alright?" and "That was the biggest storm yet, and it had a second wave." Her boss had added a third: "I need you back here ASAP."

While debating whether to call him or send a message, the ringtone on her phone screamed for her attention. The same obnoxious song snippet, that classic from Shania Twain about feeling like a woman, beckoned more ominously now. Unknown number. Why she touched accept when she almost always rejected those, she didn't know.

"Hello?"

"Doctor Anderson, this is Raymond Barnes."

When Michelle's early-warning cloud-storm system had gone online, she'd received a signed letter of commendation from Vice President Barnes. As he compensated for background noise, his voice came through the tiny speaker like a hushed yell.

Barnes started with the same two points. After assuring him of her well-being, she shocked him by confessing she hadn't followed the storm or learned the details of its magnitude. Slamming a fist on her thigh, she chastised herself for allowing such distraction from her all-important work. As she expressed her amazement about the second wave, V.P. Barnes interrupted her with a shocking revelation of his own.

"We need your help."

Eight

Something hummed. Not human or animal, it sounded unlike any mechanical noise Jonah had ever heard. It tingled; he felt it underneath his body. Where he lay or why eluded his hazy mind as he vacillated between feeling drunk and hungover. A blue sky carved sharp edges around the leaves of the treetops.

After dragging his weary body to his house, he wilted in defeat. His mother-in-law sat with his cousin Gifty, and it hit him like a jolt from a nightmare. He had to tell this young lady her brothers had been killed by the storm. Jonah's ears weren't prepared for the guttural moans and sobs that flowed like lava from his cousin's mountain of pain. She ran out, taking upon herself the unlucky burden of informing their mother.

Respectfully giving a minute's silence for those poor boys' demise and the grief the girl carried to her family, Maame and Jonah stared blankly at each other. At nothing. Antony and Michael had been like sons to him. Thinking of them made the curly gray hair on his chest itch. No amount of scratching drove away the irritation. He couldn't imagine the impact on those boys' parents.

Jonah's uncle had a few years over him. They had grown up together, and Jonah had shared in rearing his younger cousins. He and Juliana couldn't have children—an unspoken ostracism in their culture. So they were "Auntie" and "Uncle" to every child in their village.

Examining the boils over his flesh, Maame unscrewed a glass jar. "You said the storm had passed. How is it you found yourself with your cousins under its rain?"

Never having heard of a second wave of wind and rain in a single cloud storm, Jonah wept as he told her how he called Antony and Michael to join his search. With that guilt washing over him, he guzzled two glasses of water. As he explained the mysterious blue electricity, he tried to understand what his mother-in-law couldn't believe. For some reason, that spot in the dirt had protected him. That fact gave him renewed hope that his Juliana had been spared as well.

As she spread a greasy ointment over his burns, Maame said, "You believe whatever spared you has saved my Juliana from the storm?"

"Why else would it save me? She is out there. I'll find her."

***

With eyes full of desperation, Jonah scanned the countryside, fearing Juliana might have wandered from the path in the dense black that had loomed under last night's darkened sky. Every footfall pounded conflicting notions into his mind. Left—*she's fine, stayed the night with her sister.* Right—*she tried to get home, died in the storm.* Left, right, left, right...

Perhaps his wife's newfound faith held the answers. To distract his mind, Jonah considered her commentary on the clouds. "Evidence of the coming Transition," she had said. "Salvation is near," she often chanted. Juliana welcomed the dark clouds. She said the Guide Couple would lead them to the other side. Jonah never understood where that was or what they hoped to find there. Could she have been taken to this "other side"? Married young and used to working as a team for decades, he couldn't imagine going on without her. As none of his faiths provided hope, he looked to hers.

The top of the house peaked above the next hill. Its rust spots hid in the shade of the massive baobab tree leaning over the home. Jonah hoped this "tree of life" had sheltered his Juliana for the night. It had failed the job of protecting their brother-in-law.

The door flung open with a thud, and the suckling baby squealed.

His mother covered her morning face in surprise and horror. "Where is she?" she asked.

Jonah had the same question. Hearing it echo in his ears rather than escape his lips hit him with a possibility he had tried to bury. Juliana had left but didn't reach home before the storm.

"You will find her, Jonah. Have faith."

Having spoken no words, communicating with only a wide-eyed stare, Jonah spun and ran out the door, leaving it open behind him. I fire ignited inside him—a raw hatred for the widow nursing her newborn. She was the reason. No, this was not the time for blame. He needed to act.

In the distance, a dozen men approached.

Jonah ran to meet the villagers—men he knew well. Everyone knew everyone in the little farming village. The feeling of family and its strength overwhelmed him. As if he could embrace them all at once, Jonah spread his arms. His hopes of finding his lost wife increased exponentially, and their eager support clouded his eyes.

Now they had sunlight, and that made all the difference. Juliana would be found; Jonah was sure of that. They'd find her on another circle, protected by the blue light. He directed the men to spread out in three directions, as the hills behind the home would have prevented Juliana from going that way, no matter how dark it had been or how disoriented she was.

Hours given to the search yielded no results. Last to return, Jonah met the men at his home. His heart sank at the sight of the solemn faces worn by each. The group's consensus came with nods and hands upon Jonah's shoulders—acceptance, which led to the first stage of mourning. Shoving the grief back down his throat with a gulp, Jonah refused to accept anything.

With tears in her eyes, Maame supplied *fufu* and water to the dozen hungry and weary men who'd left before breakfast and returned well past lunchtime. Tolerating the pause for sustenance, Jonah repeated his call to resume the search. Like warding off blows from enemy fists, he deflected each verbal jab that claimed no one could have survived such a storm and blocked every objection thrown.

"Don't tell me my Juliana couldn't survive the storm! I survived it."

The commotion brought more neighbors to the scene, halting their post-storm cleanup. An aged man in a technicolored shirt, the village chief, invited Jonah to meet with him and several respected ones of their tribe. Jonah didn't want anyone to talk sense into him or try to convince him of what he could not—would not—accept. But in Juliana's voice, he heard the words he knew she would say. "You must never disrespect our village chief or your elders. You will soon sit among them."

As he entered the chief's home, what he saw surprised him beyond expectation—the village lunatic. The moniker was what people called the elderly woman. Miss Ashanta had been caught in a storm two months earlier. After ranting for a couple of days, telling anyone she saw to look up, she had not said a proper sentence since. "It's so beautiful," she had kept repeating. Now, only gibberish fell amid the drool from her cracked lips. Most villagers thought her speech juju, but no witchdoctor's spell ever caused such madness.

After expressing his sympathy, the chief simply asked where Jonah thought his wife could be. That sage man asked a sensible question, but it implied something Jonah didn't wish to think of and refused to acknowledge. Doing so would lead to the conclusion he had been mentally pummeling into surrender through the night and into the afternoon. She had to be safe, protected in a ball of blue electricity. As he said it in his head, he heard how ridiculous it sounded. He kept the words there for now.

"Storm victims have but two fates." The wise old man quietly observed the thought process projected through Jonah's eyes.

Not finding a corpse scorched by the blistering rain reduced that to one. The funnels must have taken her. If so, no one knew to where.

"I know it is difficult to accept, my son." Weakened by age, his voice carried confidence and warmth. "And we pray she is cared for by arms stronger than our own."

An interesting way of *not* saying, "she's with God" or "in a better place," Jonah considered. The chief had chosen his words with deliberate caution. He then asked one simple question about people who had disappeared in the storms, presumed to have been carried away by a funnel. Jonah knew the answer. They all did.

No one had ever been found.

Silently, Jonah answered with a lowered head and eyes full of tears he could not blink into submission. Giving them the time they needed to fall, the men sat without words. When his glossy eyes focused, Jonah noticed the strange old woman again. His pensive gaze toward her asked the obvious question.

"The third outcome of the storms," the chief said. "If we do not find a body desecrated by the rain and the storm's prey was not ripped from the earth to the next life, we find this." Contending with the forces of gravity, he raised his arm to point at Miss Ashanta. "The only one from our village. Many more like her around the world. Be glad we did not find your Juliana like this."

As if on cue, the wild woman rose and darted out of the house. Instinctively, thoughtlessly, Jonah sprang to his feet.

Nine

Awake but not up, Amy felt like she was lying in her own filth. The night's mental exertion had submerged her in guilt manifested as perspiration drenching her body, nightgown, and sheets. Sins of the past had converged with those she committed through the uncertainty of her faith. Sins of omission. Sins of concession.

A hot shower failed to wash away the lingering doubt about the Guide Couple. With nothing to do but wait for them to arrive, the Twelve would doubtless engage in unofficial banter over the nomination. Amy wished she could hide in her room all day. Unless they called a meeting, no one needed Elder Ferguson to take part in such idle gossip—as she considered it. Not wishing to be alone either, Amy called for Tilda.

Each elder had one personal assistant. Other servants cared for the laundry, did the shopping, and shared their time on common tasks around the cathedral and its grounds. Only Tilda spent time with her in her chamber. A personal aide, chef, head shaver, and cleaning lady, her greatest service was conversation.

It took continuous effort to get her to open up, and after almost two years, Amy was starting to get to know the Tilda beneath the zealot.

Each time, Amy had to first cut through the wall of reverence every cathedral servant had had ingrained in them since their training began at age thirteen. Semantics—Amy considered it indoctrination. With her white-blond hair and fair skin, the thin-as-a-rail girl of seventeen years arrived minutes after being summoned. The servants' quarters were on cathedral grounds, just across the withered side garden.

After Amy enjoyed the breakfast prepared for her, Tilda cleaned the pans and dishes. As always, she did not speak until spoken to. As elders were forbidden to talk about their past lives, Tilda was only to know Elder Ferguson. In time, traces of Amy had seeped in, though with the delicate caution of sifting whey through a cheesecloth. The curds never penetrated. Unlike Sato, Tilda was an impressionable young zealot who couldn't know the true condition of her elder's faith.

"That was delicious. Thank you."

"Thank you, your reverence. It is my honor to serve."

"Please, in here you may call me—" An incautious slip of tongue. Amy hadn't realized how relaxed she had become in the young woman's company. "You may call me, um, call me Miss. Yes, I rather prefer Miss."

The young lady studied the floor as if it held some revelation of truth. "With respect, I must address you honorably."

"Quite right, dear." She patted the girl's shaky hand. "I don't wish you to be uncomfortable in my presence. My position as elder is an honored one, and I value the respect you show it. But I am just a woman filling a role... as are you."

"Mistress, I am but a lowly servant. I am grateful for this honor and am humbled by it."

Amy could see a true believer standing before her. This teenager didn't seem likely to suffer a crisis of faith and leave the Order. Yet, she had leaked droplets of truth about the hardships of her life of servitude. Always quick to course-correct, Tilda seamlessly spoke of the honor to serve and her gratitude for her parents offering her for such a privilege.

"Tilda, my dear, are you promised?"

Only her eyes rose to address her elder. "Since before I was born."

"C-section?"

She nodded. "We have the same birthday. He is twenty and we will be wed this autumn."

More than a mirror, looking at Tilda was looking at herself from a memory. That young Amy couldn't have imagined accepting being sacrificed for cathedral service. A flat palm offered the young woman the other seat. Tilda looked at it with a puzzled brow and continued standing.

"Do you know this young man you will wed?"

"We met once, before I began my training."

"Please, sit."

Reluctantly, Tilda sat and squirmed uncomfortably. Amy knew the girl would take a knife and jab it into her own hand if Elder Ferguson asked. "Thank you. I, too, was promised, even married for a time before becoming our clan's elder-elect."

The young lady cupped the sides of her head. "Please, Elder Ferguson. My ears may not hear such things. I must not know of your life before. You are my elder."

"I am." Amy wrapped her fingers around Tilda's wrists and pulled her hands down. Setting them on the table, she held those delicate little hands in her own. "And I'd like to know your answer to a question. We have strong candidates for the Guide Couple. If the Twelve confirm their nomination, will you still wed?"

Revealing a face full of wondrous confusion, her head drifted upward. After a pensive pause, Tilda said she would still marry if their parents wished. Her words overflowed with conviction, while her unsettled eyes spilled doubts over the table.

After a sigh, Amy said, "Our faith doesn't completely remove freewill. If the Guide Couple is confirmed, you do *not* have to marry this boy."

"Do you think I would displease him?" As though it were its default position, Tilda's head hung again. "You have never requested me."

"As I have told you... You never have to do *that* for anyone. Not for me or the next elder after me. No one has the right to ask you for that, to rob you of your dignity. Or your individuality."

Amy squeezed the young lady's alabaster hands and asked, "Do you understand me?"

Tilda said nothing.

Lifting the girl's chin to look sternly into her innocent eyes, Amy said, "You have the right to make your own choices."

Although she didn't reply or even nod, her youthful gaze showed understanding. A spark of hopefulness electrified those brilliant blue irises.

****

An interview or an interrogation—it depended on who asked the questions. The Twelve took turns scrutinizing the couple against the signs the Guide Couple must fulfill. The process exposed the hopes and intentions of the elders. Elder Ferguson needed to be careful, to choose her words and intonation carefully.

"Your clan, and especially close members of your family, Nickos, are known to have participated in recent acts of terroris—"

"Objection," Tartagni shouted. "Personal opinion aside, when our more zealous and committed members act on directives in the Code, they are just and loyal warriors. We do not call them terrorists, Madam Chairperson." He spat the last two words with contempt.

Ferguson hadn't been careful enough. While those so-called "just and loyal" actions found no direct justification in the

Code, many, including the majority in the room, interpreted it that way. Most in the Order hailed them as heroes, "righteous warriors" defending them from their most outspoken opponents.

"Of course. Such worldly terms have no place here. Thank you, Elder Tartagni." She hoped that would be enough. "Still, by clear stipulation in the Code, we must learn if Nickos has partaken in any such activity. Righteous as it may be, no Guide could be entangled in such dealings. They must be pure in heart and clean of the blood of all, including the unrighteous and unworthy."

Sato said, "Once again, Elder Ferguson, your insight into the Code is admirable."

With Tartagni placated for now, she repeated her question to the twenty-one-year-old candidate. In her eyes, Nickos was a boy trying to be a man. After his adamant denial of any involvement, she continued her inquisition with more probing questions. Foreshadowing quotes from the Code followed, each met by the couple to a reasonable degree.

DNA tests had already confirmed their pure stemmata. Neither showed signs of crossbreeding impurities. As the Code was written thousands of years before humans could perform genetic tests, it mandated physical verification. Ferguson completed the examination of Isis, and Sato took the role with Nickos. While no one expected the Guide Couple to be physically perfect in the truest sense, they were to be closer to perfection than "ordinary" humans. With excellent muscle tone under clear skin and healthy hair and nails, Isis and Nickos were.

Ferguson considered the final and most critical foreshadowing that phase five of the trial would reveal. These would erase all misgivings from the most doubtful, as they could not be faked—at least, no one thought they could.

Ten

FROM THE FIRST WHISPERS of a cloud-storm task force, Michelle had assumed she'd lead it. Being consulted because of her education and position made sense. Plus, she'd led the team that created the early-warning system. No one knew the dark clouds better. And the V.P. had called her personally—someone often described as a glorified TV weather forecaster by envious peers. A silly notion since, as a serious scientist, she had never been on TV before the countless interviews about her detection system.

"We need you at the Pentagon right away."

"I was just called into work. My dad is—"

"Doctor Anderson, Michelle, this is a national emergency—no, a global crisis. I think a presidential mandate should quiet your boss. The president herself has requested you on the task force. You're to report to the Pentagon immediately."

"I need a couple of days, sir. My father was in the storm. He has the…" A forced cough steadied her voice. "He's sick and I'm gonna have to take him to the hospital. Then... I'm a day's drive from DC."

"We can help your father. And don't worry about the transportation."

As his words trailed off, a thunderous and pulsating roar bombarded the wooden farmhouse almost as fiercely as had last night's storm. Bobby's shout confirmed Michelle's guess. He described it as "a honking-big chopper with an official United States emblem on the side."

***

When Vice President Barnes told her not to worry about her father—poor choice of words, as it had sent Michelle into a rage-induced internal tirade—he said he'd arrange her father's transport to the hospital where he would receive the best care. No medical care, not even what the best money or the government could buy, had thus far helped any cloud-madness sufferer.

As her father's indistinct mumbles gave way to those same words, "It's so... beautiful. Look. You must see," a new thought entered her overactive brain. She had to know what he saw in those clouds. Why had no one else said those words? As far as she knew, no one said anything even halfway intelligible after going cloud mad.

Although she couldn't explain it, Michelle felt convinced her father's condition held the key to understanding the storms.

The president wanted her to help "fight the storms," as the V.P. put it. She believed someone suffering cloud madness could help her unlock the mysteries churning in the black clouds—clouds her dad said were beautiful. Michelle's stolen glimpse hadn't taken her mind. But it hadn't shown her anything beautiful, either.

Bobby insisted their father stay home, where he would be most comfortable. Mom didn't speak, didn't seem to blink. Michelle had seen her like this only once, with Daniel.

"Comfortable? Does he *look* comfortable?" Michelle took her brother's hand and a desperate breath. "Look. I don't know about you, but when I was a kid... Dad was..." A tear interrupted, and she fought it with a series of spastic blinks. "He was the strongest man in the world, you know? He was—he was Superman. Like every child, I... I mean, I grew up, and he wasn't any more. He was just a man. A good man... A strong man... But just a man."

"Okay? I guess. He was a bit older for me."

"You're right. But seeing him like *this*... If we could ask him if he would rather stay here a blithering mess drooling on the sofa or... or come with me for a chance to save the world, which do you think Dad would choose?"

If she asked, the soldiers outside would forcibly remove her father without the family's consent. She could never do that to them, not on a weak hunch that his presence in Washington would make any difference.

"I want to see him as Superman again," she said.

Eleven

Grabbing Jonah by the arm, the chief said, "Let her be. There is no sense to be found in following the senseless."

While the logic resonated in Jonah's mind, other forces motivated him. "I must find out what she knows. Miss Ashanta is the only one who has been out in the storm."

With deadpan eyes, the chief looked Jonah square in the face. "Why do you not look to yourself for the answers you seek?"

"I have no time for your riddles."

"I have spoken no riddle. You are the only one who has been caught in a storm and come home unscathed. Why do you seek the words of a lunatic who shares them willingly, but without meaning?"

"She knows something. She must."

"There is nothing for Miss Ashanta out there but for the *Zangbeto* to get her. As with the others lost to the storms, he will end the poor woman's suffering and lead her to a better place."

A forceful headshake brought Jonah down from the tower of rage erected by the mention of such superstitious folklore. Although he couldn't articulate why, Jonah believed that woman was the key to finding Juliana. To his knowledge, no one had ever passed unharmed through a storm by being encased in blue light. Plus, no vanished body had ever been found, so no missing person could be confirmed dead. Since Jonah had been saved, he found reason to hope his lost wife had also.

Huffing as he ran, Jonah caught up with Miss Ashanta along the same path he'd staggered along after his awkward nap in the ghostly blue glow. Assuming a connection between Juliana and Miss Ashanta, this spot of dirt under the trees filled Jonah with confidence. The answer to finding his wife lay in the ramblings of this woman's jumbled mind. He was sure of it.

The circle of hard-packed earth where he'd woken hours ago looked perfectly round. Not a leaf or twig dared lay upon it. Eerily silent, Miss Ashanta held a blank stare when Jonah approached and examined the geometric anomaly. He studied the strange markings around its perimeter, taking photos with his mobile. Miss Ashanta said nothing. Death lurked behind her lifeless gray eyes.

Those eyes rounded, and the woman's chin dropped. Arms that had hung loosely at her sides shot upward, and she cast her gaze upon the empty sky beyond the tree canopy.

"So beautiful. You must look. Do you see?" she cried, slurring the words. "It's so beautiful." She collapsed to the ground before Jonah could catch her.

As Miss Ashanta's life fled its host, Jonah felt his hope extracting itself, its marrow sucked from his bones.

***

Hunched over the laptop in the open space that was the kitchen, dining, and living areas, Jonah pored over every article and watched every video on the clouds and disappearances. Even if he knew how to operate the computer half as well as Juliana, it would have taken years to read and watch everything. As he feared, none of the missing had yet to be recovered. Juliana would be the first, no matter what, he silently tried to convince his now-doubtful inner self.

To his surprise, he found no records of cloud madness victims saying those few words Miss Ashanta had spoken through all the gibberish. Every report he found stated cloud madness victims never uttered a distinguishable word. Jonah found no mention of a circle of steel-hard dirt with blue electricity. It seemed he was the first to survive by such a means. Unless, as he hoped, he was the second.

One name recurred on several pages he read—that of a woman who had been interviewed on all the major news platforms. Doctor Michelle Anderson, a meteorologist, had led the team that developed the early-warning system for cloud storms. Her work had saved thousands, maybe millions of lives. Perhaps, Jonah considered, she could help save one more. Maybe she would know what those markings in the circle meant. Though not enough for a resurrection of hope, it gave him a microdose of the optimism the last 24 hours had drained from him.

Futility dominated the next hours as he tried everything to contact Doctor Anderson. She worked in Washington, DC, at the Climatological Society. The next thirty minutes saw email after email fly to the *Contact Us* addresses on the websites of every weather, cloud-storm, and climate site he could find in the Washington, DC, area.

Shoving back Maame's protests, Jonah did the only thing he could think of. He booked the flights. While most crossed the Atlantic by ship, spending his savings on airline tickets would get him there much faster. Transatlantic sailing had longer waiting lists, as a fear of flying propagated around the globe after the hundreds of plane crashes in the first months of the cloud storms.

After a seven-hour bus ride to Accra, he would fly from Ghana to Senegal and on to Morocco. He would continue to Barcelona after a layover. The next hop would take him to London Heathrow. If the weather aligned with his itinerary, he'd take the longest flight remaining in service, only possible because of the five-to-six-hour early-warning system created by the woman he needed to meet. From London, he'd make it to Newfoundland in just under five hours.

Boston next, then on to Washington, DC. Though he'd never used it before now, he thanked his Juliana for insisting he get a passport when she got hers for her upcoming pilgrimage to the Order's cathedral in South Africa. That had sparked the greatest argument the couple had had in their thirty-two-year marriage. Now Jonah wished more than anything his dear wife would be able to take that trip next summer as she had planned.

With a kiss and reassurance that he would get this woman to help him find her daughter, Jonah bade farewell to Maame, hoisted the backpack over his shoulder, and boarded the bus.

Twelve

By the third day, Michelle had put faces to the names and stopped calling her teammates by the wrong titles—an insult to anyone with a doctorate. Her esteemed colleagues were scientists at the top of their respective fields. No longer out of place, she belonged in this room, the one they needed to get this task force moving in the right direction. That direction had not presented itself.

General Nathan Tucker took the lead—at least until the technical jargon sailed so far above his head that he relinquished the chair. Figuratively. He still sat at the head. Michelle thought it kept him out of the line of fire as she and the others shot theories and speculations across the long black conference table. No one acted as team leader, so Michelle took that upon herself, despite some pushback from Doyle.

Repetitious grumbles from Doctor Brendon Doyle, a fellow meteorologist, carried obvious resentment toward her presence. Only their field of science was represented by more than one "renowned expert" on the team. He also hadn't been invited to join the research group that worked on the storm warning system—a team Michelle had assembled and led.

Doctor Wilma Jones had published several papers and was considered the leading astrophysicist in the United States. Michelle had looked her up on the first day. Doctor Natasha Kournikova, on the other hand, had needed no introduction. An accomplished and equally vocal climatologist, the world had known her long before the clouds came. She and Michelle worked in the same office. Ecologist Samuel Brockmann, whose name she had heard of but whose reputation she hadn't, had entered the "brain trust" a day after Michelle had.

Try as she might, Michelle couldn't accept the addition of Patrick O'Malley. He'd arrived late the day before to meet the team, and today was his first time contributing to the volley of ideas and wild guesses. She believed an exobiologist had no place on her team.

Welcome quiet came when everyone went deep into research on their laptops, their elbows bent, heads down. It became clear early on that the level of knowledge and expertise afforded by the array of scientific studies hadn't begun to unravel the mysteries hiding within the unusual clouds. Two years of independent monitoring, testing, and studying produced few conclusions and piled question after question onto the mountain of unknowns ascending from the table before them.

When Michelle suggested her father could hold the answers, some in the group scoffed. While extremely irritating, it chased some of their android-like personas away, and Michelle finally saw some of them as human. Wrong, but human. For a second, she wondered how they saw her. Having acquaintances—even romantic connections—with only her colleagues at the Climatological Society, she contemplated the chance of these people becoming new "friends." A new love interest certainly wouldn't be found among this group.

***

As she did every morning, Michelle checked on her dad. When no hospital could help him, they put him in the room next to hers at the Double Tree Hotel. Nurses looked after him 24/7 and fed and bathed him. Sometimes, they chased him down the corridor. Once, when he'd made it outside and ran across the street, he'd caused a traffic accident. Michelle spent whatever the conference table left of her evenings in that room, eating her takeout and engaging her dad in one-way conversation. In the five days since saying goodbye, she had daily FaceTime chats with Bobby and regular updates by text.

When Bobby called, Michelle set her Coke Zero on the table beside her dad's bed and pulled her eyes from her laptop. After Michelle updated them about his status, her mom asked, "Is your father comfortable?"

"You can see him, Mom. He stays in bed. Walks around. Eats and sleeps. And he hasn't said an actual word since we got here."

Sucking in her bottom lip, Michelle's mother dipped her head. From weekly video calls that dwindled into monthly ones when she was in college, Michelle knew that look of restrained disappointment well.

"You said he would help you in your research. It seems he can't do that. I don't suppose we can expect you to come, but I think it's time your father came home."

"I'm doing important work here, Mom. And I believe Dad can help."

"Has he helped at all so far?"

The answer to that was a resounding "no." And Michelle had no logical reason to expect that to change. With nothing else to show for her work on the task force thus far, she couldn't let go of the possibility of being right. Her gut churned with the idea that her father was the key. She simply hadn't found the right lock. Yet.

"He will. And he's getting the best care here. I just need a few more days."

***

In time, the more intelligent ones on the team seemed optimistic—or at least willing to see it out after Michelle's insistence—about her father's value to the task force. Her dad's inarticulate mumbling eroded that sentiment quickly.

"Has he said anything coherent in the last two days?" Wilma asked.

Michelle's head-shake reply cast dense silence over the table. After another round of everyone staring at their own laptops, Michelle had to vocalize a question no one wanted to hear again.

"What do we actually know about the cloud storms?"

Fondling his coffee cup, Doyle exhaled. "A week's worth of nothing."

"Almost two years of nothing," Natasha said, correcting him.

"Okay, everyone. Just to get us all on the same page and focus our research and attention..."

When Michelle shared her laptop display on the wall-filling screen, the group grumbled.

"Let's review, shall we?"

She understood the complaints. They had done this at least a few times, and no one seemed to want to start the morning this way. Charts, graphs, and weather maps transformed the wide display into a macabre mosaic. Michelle summarized the unusual electromagnetic frequencies in the clouds. They came without predictability, and their best detection systems allowed up to a six-hour warning. Since the storms had started, there had been alarming changes in natural weather patterns, warming of Earth's median temperature, and interestingly, no severe storms—other than the cloud storms, of course.

The climatologist stood—tall and looking through thick glasses framed by straight black hair—and pointed at the line graph of global temperature gains. "This may be the result of our doing. We've done an *outstanding* job of attacking our ecosphere and destroying our environment."

"We'd made tremendous progress before the clouds came." Doctor Brockmann pointed a finger and an angry scowl at Doctor Natasha Kournikova. "We were on our way to recovery."

"True. I believe... it was too little too late. These clouds are likely the result of ground-level ozone combined with the imbalance our industrialization has caused in the atmosphere." Natasha raised a hand to silence an oncoming objection from Brockmann and continued in her Eastern-European accent. "Whatever the cause, Sam, everyone... recent storm escalation proves this will have an extinction-level effect."

***

They had been at it for almost a week, and the result of their efforts amounted to a collection of data they'd already compiled into reports nonscientific minds (politicians) could read. The only photos and video they had of the clouds were grainy and indistinct. Recording equipment wasn't immune to the storms' effect on electronics.

Proposed hypotheses had all been readily debunked. The group even entertained O'Malley's alien-invasion theories. When Michelle called those "science-fiction nonsense," some of her colleagues pointed out that a true alien encounter would certainly reveal technological discovery beyond the current limit of human scientific knowledge. Despite Doctor Kournikova's encouragement to keep an open mind, Michelle restated her position.

"Natasha, your own explanation about how we did this to ourselves is the most plausible." Looking around the room, Michelle added, "I agree with Natasha, Doctor Kournikova. We need to keep an open mind. I also happen to think we'll find our answers right here on Earth."

That sparked an intense and somewhat entertaining debate, with most affirming their support for O'Malley's ideas as worth considering. When Michelle tried to counter, Doyle reminded everyone that the president was interested in all proposed explanations, terrestrial or extraterrestrial.

"President Carter just wants an answer from this task force and a way to reverse the storms' devastating effects," he said to drive the point home.

General Tucker slipped in during the ensuing silence. "People, doctors. Time's running out. The worldwide drought situation is only getting worse. We're getting reports daily of a rapid decrease in staple crop production and depletion of livestock. And the storms are becoming more intense."

"The last one was the first to have two waves, each of the highest magnitude we've registered." Michelle scrolled through notes on her laptop. "And we've seen an increase in cloud-madness cases reported."

Sharpening his gaze upon her, Doyle replied, "We haven't seen anything to suggest that has any relevance, Michelle."

"I still believe my father's situation *is* relevant. I've scoured the web, used every A.I. chatbot out there, and no one has ever reported a madness sufferer saying anything close to intelligible."

"And since you brought him here, neither has your father."

Scowling at Doyle, Michelle took a long breath. "He did. Right after and the next day. He saw something in those clouds. Something he said was beautiful, and that we needed to see. I know he believes something he saw will help me in my research."

Thirteen

Sitting at the small table in Amy's chamber, the stoic Japanese elder shook his head at her. A shared disbelief in the events of the last few days swirled in the air surrounding the pair. In Sato's eyes, she saw hope rising like the morning sun. Conviction brightened his irises, when doubt and skepticism had dulled them over for decades. For the first time, she saw *him* in his eyes and worried her friend had been swayed by the trials to a renewal of faith.

For the last two hours, the round wooden tabletop had absorbed the evidence and trial results. To even the less faithful, Nickos and Isis looked genuine. Physically, genealogically, chronologically, and with every *-lly* word she could think of, they had passed diligent scrutinization.

This young couple had endured standing for twenty-four hours in that room. No signs of fatigue exited the antechamber with them. Like film stars from their dressing rooms, made-up with perfect hair and ready for action, they looked like they were in perfect health. Neither asked for food or drink. Again, Tartagni had bowed before them.

"The Guide Couple is upon us. All hail the Celestial Maker. We welcome the Glorious Transition."

One final test remained. Picturing it, Amy's shoulders shivered. Since the coming of the cloud storms, creative interpretation pointed to a foreshadowing in the ancient writing for the final days. The ultimate trial would prove or falsify any claim of Guideship. The two would lie on their backs in a storm and do what the elders had agreed for the final phase.

While not specifically referencing the Guide Couple, the sacred text said, "In the final days, they will gaze upon the darkened clouds." That solidified the modern dogma of the cloud storms heralding the final days, as the Order now officially taught. Only the true Guide Couple would endure that trial without succumbing to subsequent madness. Only then would the Ultimate Truth to lead the faithful through the Glorious Transition be revealed through them.

Amy couldn't imagine these children remaining outside once the storm's danger presented itself. The next storm would provide the answer she sought. But at what cost?

***

Sometimes, Amy couldn't look at the cathedral servants, couldn't stomach how they acted around her. Any of them would lick her feet if she asked—without question and with absolute reverence. It felt like worship. Worship she didn't think anyone deserved, least of all her. At fifteen, these children had been given by their parents as an "offering" to live in servants' quarters on cathedral grounds and serve their masters for twenty years—a prison sentence, in Amy's mind.

"Thank you, Tilda," she said to the teenager gently lifting the cloth napkin from her elder's lap and clearing the table. Her eyes said *you're welcome* without the words—round pure white eyes with deep aqua-blue wells around wide pupils. The dim lights helped Amy relax and enjoy her meal. "You're an excellent cook."

Saying nothing in reply, Tilda began washing the dishes, and Amy rose to stand beside her.

"Nickos and Isis are very strong candidates. Have you met them?"

Sheepishly, Tilda nodded.

"Do you believe we may have found the Guide Couple?"

"I believe they have been born, as the Code teaches, and the cloud storms prove. If I am not part of the Guide Couple, then I rejoice to welcome the true Guides."

"You know, don't you, that they will be left out in the next storm?"

"I believe in the Code and must trust my elders' interpretation of it."

"So you realize it is only one of many possible interpretations?"

Dipping her head again, Tilda failed to hide the reply her eyes disclosed.

***

Amy knew better than to reveal her doubt to anyone. With Elder Sato she risked exposure. He had become a trustworthy confidant and helped preserve her sanity, allowing Amy to function as Elder Ferguson as needed. Confiding in Tilda came with no such assurances. The ears of the youthful, innocent zealot could not bear the impact of the words that would assault them—from her spiritual leader. Yet the expected shock in response to Amy's question did not blanket her features. Instead, the young aide appeared to give her thoughts freedom to ruminate.

Before Alexandar had propped Amy's faith upon his own, it had wavered. Back then, she had every reason to believe her predecessor's devotion to the Code and to the Transition had been rock-solid. Now Elder Ferguson needed to be that for the next generation of the Glorious Transition Order. If she couldn't be that for herself, she knew she'd not support the faith of almost a million others in her clan, the largest of the twelve.

Amy had never aspired to become Elder Ferguson.

Now poor Tilda had had a spiritual and moral dilemma unfairly thrust upon her by a foolish old woman tired of playing the role of leader. Tired of pretending. Tired of waiting for a transition to something she'd never understood or fully believed in. Her abdication would be the first in the history of the Order. The first in over three thousand years. There would be repercussions.

Of course, Elder Ferguson commanded silence from her loyal servant before dismissing her. The one time she had been demanding, used her power to restrict the rights of another, made her feel dirty. A morning shower's scalding abuse and all the soap Amy had couldn't wash off the guilt from her reddened skin.

As the day passed, many of the elders followed the couple like sheep. Amy wondered when they'd reach the slaughter. The next agenda point was set by the cloud storm's timetable, not the chairperson's whim. She walked about the grounds as the evening fell over the cathedral, the shadows growing and shifting to find their resting place in the earthen-colored stones. Amy gazed up at the innumerable stars. Since the storms had started, the air tasted different. It smelled sterile—no longer carrying the fragrances of the surrounding flora. The cherry blossoms hadn't bloomed since the dark clouds had arrived.

Strolling the long way around, Amy passed each of the elders' chambers as if to say goodnight. A pause outside Sato's chamber brought an onslaught of contemplation. He was the one person, the only thing she would miss about her life as an elder. It felt like a goodbye. Like at any moment the guards would seize her. The elders would convene a special counsel to remove her and cast her out into the world. She mused over whether that would be a bad thing.

Without remorse, Amy felt Elder Ferguson dying.

Fourteen

Tires screeched, and the plane bounced on the runway of BWI. After a grueling six days of travel, Jonah had arrived. The "welcome to Baltimore" announcement said the weather was ninety-six and sunny. After a rush of anxious panic, Jonah remembered they used Fahrenheit in America.

Now the hard part began—finding and getting to speak to Doctor Michelle Anderson. His backpack pulled from under the seat and tossed over one shoulder, he stood and waited with his head cocked under the overhead compartment above the window seat. It took *forever* for the door to open and the people in the long line to finally move. Hope glowed in his eyes as he pushed through the crowd of passengers, strolled past baggage claim, and followed the signs for ground transportation.

A bus and two trains and an hour and a half would get him to George Washington University, where the Climatological Society's dark cloud research center had been established. There he would find the meteorologist who knew the clouds and would loosen his Juliana from their grip. The doctor must have known where those taken had gone. Perhaps there were more of those circles of blue electricity, and one had saved his dear wife.

On the second train, the business suit-clad woman seated beside him hadn't said anything. Her face had remained buried in her phone, her earbuds in the entire time. She must have noticed his fidgeting, and she asked if he was nervous or suffering from motion sickness.

"No, I'm fine. Thank you. I'm anxious, that's all. It's urgent that I find someone in Washington. She will help me."

"Well, I hope so, for your sake." She raised her hand to free one earbud from her ear. "You're not from around here, I assume?"

"The accent? I'm from Ghana. First time in America."

"That too. Also, no one around here calls it Washington. It's 'DC.'"

"Um, thanks. Do you happen to know Doctor Michelle Anderson?"

"Of course." Her face shone with surprise.

"You do? Oh, what luck. She is the one I need to find. She will help me. Please, how do I get in touch with her?"

"I don't *know* her know her." Jonah puzzled over the lady's words. "I mean I know *of* her. Doesn't everybody?"

"I found her on the internet. I must meet her."

"A little advice..." She leaned close to whisper, "Don't go around saying you must find someone you stalked online, especially a woman. That might not go so well for you."

"So you don't know how to find her? All I know is that she works at the Climatological Society at Washington University. Sorry, at *DC* University."

The friendly lady giggled, but Jonah didn't know why. She said, "If you go looking for her there, let me give you one more bit of advice..."

***

At the entrance to the Climatological Society, guards made him empty his pockets and place his backpack onto the conveyor belt to be scanned or x-rayed or something. Not even in Accra had Jonah been in a building like this. A buzz stiffened his neck as he edged through the metal detector. On the other side, one of the guards waved a flat paddle over him.

Another guard shoved blue-gloved hands into Jonah's bag. All it contained were a few clothes, a toothbrush, a travel-sized tube of toothpaste, his mobile phone and charger, and his passport. The guard flipped through that before placing it back into the bag. Jonah took his backpack, put his belt back on, slid his wallet into his pocket, and went to the reception desk. Following the train lady's suggestion, he explained he had some information about the cloud storms he thought would be helpful and wished to speak with Doctor Michelle Anderson. While this didn't bring him the cautionary response of a suspected stalker, it didn't work either.

"I have something important to share regarding the dark clouds. I must speak with Doctor Anderson," he repeated.

Each time Jonah tried to explain, the man behind the desk restated his directions to fill out the submission form on the website. As Jonah's volume increased with each request, the directions upgraded to demands, and one of the guards laid a hand on his shoulder. His "Sir, I think you need to leave" was not a suggestion. How had Jonah thought this would go? The optimism he tried to keep alive inside him gasped for breath in the thickening air of desperation.

As Jonah turned to leave, a new male voice said, "Have a good evening."

The man at the reception desk replied, "You, too, Brian."

"Excuse me, sir," Jonah said to stall the man's exit.

*****

Without international mobile service, Jonah had to be creative to find a place to check his email. Everything in this city brought new sights to his eyes. As Jonah wasn't even familiar with Accra—he only went there when needed and left when finished—any city would be unfamiliar territory to him. But he was not in just *any* city. He was in America's capital city, the seat of the most powerful person in the world. With all her power, President Jessica Carter couldn't help him find Juliana. Thanks to Brian's kindness, the one person who could help would soon contact him.

Having exhausted most of his trip money on transportation from BWI to DC, Jonah couldn't afford a hotel. As he wondered where to find somewhere safe to sleep, the answer rolled up in front of him. With a roundtrip ticket for $4.99 each way in hand, Jonah climbed aboard a Flixbus bound for a place called Richmond, Virginia. The journey was three hours there and three back. He could get six hours of sleep and end up back in DC bright and early tomorrow morning.

***

As they neared the destination before the bus would turn back for DC, Jonah used the impossibly small restroom. The whiff that assaulted his nostrils when the door opened snapped him wide awake. By the time Jonah came out, the passengers were all gone, and the driver asked him to get off. After showing his return ticket, Jonah wondered what time it was and when they'd head back to DC. When he reached inside the bag he had left on the seat, all he pulled from it was sheer panic. He checked his pants pocket and every pouch in his backpack.

Taking everything out of his bag, he found nothing but dirty clothes. No phone. No wallet. No passport. The bus rolled away, leaving Richmond and all of Jonah's hope in the rear-view mirror. Of all the problems this meant for him—no identification, no money, no mobile—one sat foremost on his mind. He had no way to check his email.

Chants and memorized prayers exploded like firecrackers in his head, as useless as the ashes after a pompous fireworks display. Since his desperation attached itself to his wife's newfound faith, he beseeched the Celestial Makcr Juliana trusted with her life.

Fifteen

As she watched her father drool away most of the liquid dinner the nurse spooned into his mouth, Michelle wondered what those trembling eyes had beheld that no other cloud-madness victim had seen. The answer hid inside that closed mind—she was certain. So far, all the tests and studies done on him had yielded no tangible results.

Her emotional state, which she'd never considered anything but *functional*, had her at a constant low she didn't recognize. Added to the worries about the effects of the storms, improving her detection system for more advanced alerts, and now "saving the world" from the dark clouds, she had worry over her dad's condition to fill every morning and evening—that and constant pestering for updates from Bobby.

"Sharp mental focus of a high-efficiency brain," Brian had termed it. He had a way of describing her... *quirks*. She wondered for half a second how he was and what he might be doing at the office since she last saw him. Since the massive storm, he had phoned her and sent messages. She hadn't replied. Now her ability to focus had faded, and her brain had lost its proficiency.

After putting the laptop down beside her father, she answered her brother's daily FaceTime call on her phone. During the chat with Mom and Bobby, Dad muttered noises no one could understand. Her mom had convinced herself he was speaking in tongues and attributed his ramblings to communing with God. Michelle and Bobby thought it preposterous—they weren't even Pentecostal—but had stopped trying to tell their mother otherwise.

After the normal how-are-you exchange came the updates about her dad, with him included on the video chat. Michelle didn't know if he heard or comprehended anything they said, if the incoherence worked one way or both, so they all spoke to him. The medical and mental professionals caring for her father had learned little about cloud madness from him.

"Some guy called, looking for you," Bobby said.

Returning her eyes to her phone, Michelle asked, "What guy? He had your cell?"

"Said he got my number from the reverse directory after Brian told him you had come here. He seemed desperate to talk to you, so I said I'd let you know."

"*Bobby*. He could be any kind of crazy. Please tell me you didn't give him my number."

"Course not, sis."

"And why'd you even talk to him? It's not like my name's not all over the cloud-storm reports and websites." In a brief pause, she subdued her sarcastic tone. "I bet he found Brian outside my office. He's probably some nut looking to make a name for himself."

"Or a stalker. Hey, if he's into you, maybe you *should* call him. You must be lonely since, um, you know."

Sometimes, Michelle had to remind herself of how young—juvenile—her brother was. He seemed to understand the silence that conveyed her annoyance at his mention of her breakup.

"Sorry, just kidding. But really, he seemed desperate. Said he had some crucial information for you about the storms."

"See, just another nutjob thinking he cracked the mystery and 'figured out' the clouds." Holding her phone in one hand, she put single-handed air quotes around *figured out*. "Going to save the world and get their fifteen minutes."

"I think you should call him. He said he had information about the madness. And he found something in the ground related to the storm he called blue electricity."

Michelle's back stiffened. "Blue what? Forget that. What did he say, *exactly*, about the madness?"

"Only that his friend died after being a drooling zombie for a few months. Said the old lady kept saying, 'So beautiful, you have to see it,' just like Dad."

"Give me his number."

"Oh, actually... he's not from here. Came from Africa or somewhere. Said Brian let him use a phone in the lobby because—"

As if she could reach through it and grab her brother, Michelle shook the phone in her hand. "*Bobby*. His number?"

"As I was about to say, he doesn't have cell service. Only he said *mobile,* like a Brit. He left his email address."

As soon as she ended the call, Michelle pulled up her email and sent this man a message. Taking a chance, she included her cell phone number and the name of her hotel. She considered it might have been the stupidest thing she had ever done.

***

After checking her email and ignoring any *not* from a guy called Jonah Blankson, she rushed through breakfast at her father's side. For a second, she thought he looked happy to see her. Whether the saying was true for babies, she couldn't say, but she'd discovered that her dad's gas did make it look like he smiled at her. Part of Michelle hoped he didn't recognize her and had no awareness of his condition or surroundings. Or the pungent odor he released into them.

Was her Superman still in there somewhere?

This morning, she would make her strongest case yet for the need to understand cloud madness, its cause, and the effect it had on people. If she got her way, the general would approve of the use of military equipment to attempt to record a video of the clouds. Previous attempts with the best cameras had recorded static or had been so badly damaged that they saw nothing. The electrical outages affected battery-operated devices as well, so recording equipment had a short lifespan under the clouds.

As her father mumbled on, Michelle pored over web articles and official reports from her office and the mountain of data released to her for the cloud-storm brain trust. Why did no one else mention the "So beautiful" statement? No one else told people they had to see it. Every report said the sufferer mumbled indistinctly. None listed actual words in their mutterings. How did her father and someone in Africa say the exact same thing? She hoped to have corroborating evidence from this Jonah Blankson to present in her briefing.

"Why won't you reply?" she said to her phone, again shaking it violently.

***

As expected, her colleagues had moved on from the idea of getting any useful data from cloud madness sufferers. While everyone agreed they would like to know what they saw, and that such knowledge could be useful, they now considered it unattainable. Doctor Doyle cited Hank Anderson's test results and reports from his examinations as proof it was a huge waste of time.

"I admit, the tests on my father have thus far not yielded much."

"Zero isn't 'not much,' Michelle. It's zilch, nothing," Doyle fired back.

How she wished the team had only one meteorologist. He clearly wanted the same. Directing her next point to General Tucker, who had mostly been there to stop arguments with his commanding voice, she made her case for the military recording gear to capture a glimpse into the darkened clouds brought in by the next storm. He agreed.

"Thank you, Nathan," she said to the general. "I can't believe the military hasn't already done this. I mean, you agree this is a global emergency. Why haven't you put a soldier in a rain suit out there to get a camera working after the initial power outage?"

"I never said we didn't. You have records of what we tried to capture. As you pointed out, the electromagnetic disturbances wreak havoc with equipment. Fries even the most shielded stuff we've got. From our Doppler stations to cameras, from our most advanced AI climate monitors to old fashioned weather balloons, noth—"

"You mean UFO's," Patrick O'Malley said. "The military's been using that lame weather balloon excuse since Roswell."

Everyone looked at O'Malley in shock. Not only had he interrupted the general, but he also did it to spew his UFO and alien mumbo-jumbo. When he smiled, the others realized his joke. Even Patrick thought some of his flying saucer conspiracy nonsense was funny. A much-needed chuckle chased the overbearing seriousness from the room.

"I bet he's been *flashy-thinging* us this whole time too," Patrick added, collecting more laughs around the otherwise boring conference room table.

When the laughter subsided, Nathan said, "Very funny, O'Malley. As I was saying, we've been revamping some of our equipment and I'll approve its use. We can have it brought here and secured to the helipad outside."

Finally, Michelle thought. Some progress. A glance at her laptop found no email from Jonah Blankson. Undeterred, she mentioned the reported use of the same words her father had repeatedly uttered. While that piqued the group's interest, they were far from convinced.

Natasha adjusted her thick glasses. "None of the thousands of cloud madness sufferers have been able to enunciate a single word, and now two people, on different continents, said the same exact thing. That's too randomly specific a detail to rule out."

Her friend and colleagues' logical intellect drew Michelle's lips into her first smile in days. It was about time these people shared Michelle's confidence in herself. Wilma Jones, the most silent of the group by far, questioned the source of this newfound information. Stammering through an answer that wouldn't have convinced her if someone else said it, Michelle reported the phone call to her brother and the second-hand message.

"And where is this Jonah Blankson?" Wilma asked.

"When he arrived from Africa he had no cell service, so he left me an email address. I'm waiting for his reply."

Some debate ensued over the hearsay testimony of the mystery man from the "dark continent." When Sam called it that, Natasha pointed out how all continents were dark under the clouds and would eventually stay that way if they didn't figure out how to stop them. Get a group of brilliant minds together in one room, Michelle noticed, and they can bicker and argue like four-year-olds, same as anybody. Basic human instinct fought its way out, always triumphant over intellect.

After lunch, the group fell into its pattern of silent research with occasional private conferring among the cliques that had formed in the little group. No one ever shared in such whispered collaboration with Michelle, and she had no problem with that.

Once again, she appreciated how respectfully General Tucker carried himself. They worked together on the list of storm-tracking and camera equipment. With it, Michelle would prove herself the most valuable part of this team. While she needed no convincing, she thought her task force teammates might. With renewed momentum, she focused on the current task of setting up the equipment, securing it to the cement, and waiting for a storm.

They didn't have to wait long. An alert from Michelle's early-warning system blared on every screen in the room, from cell phones to the giant wall display, flashing the warning.

Cloud-storm activity detected. Estimated time for cloud fall: 4 hours, 37 minutes.

Part Two

Superstorm

Sixteen

CRINKLING A COPY OF his report in his hand, Jonah left the police station with nowhere to go and nothing but a sack of smelly clothes. With no money, no documents, and no phone, he had no way of knowing whether that doctor had emailed him. If he had to guess—and that was all he could do—he figured he would never hear from her. His village elder's voice echoed from a dark corner of his mind, telling him to face a reality he wasn't ready to accept. So he forced his optimism to resurface.

After finding the embassy and applying for a new passport, Jonah was struck with a last-ditch idea. Sure to be arrested if he tried Doctor Anderson's office again—plus he knew she wasn't there—and with no identification or money, he would go to the White House. A brochure he found on the bus said the tour was free. He could walk into the home of the most powerful person on the planet. If anyone could get in touch with Doctor Anderson, people working there could.

The plan had a fatal flaw—well, two. After an hour-and-a-half journey on foot, the tour office sign read Closed. Without the meager fee for a bus, he had nowhere to sleep and nowhere to go. His stomach growled angrily to remind him he had forgotten one other basic need. What he did next, he had sworn he would never do. It was why he had repeatedly warned the young men in his village not to follow many of their countrymen on a foolhardy migration to Europe.

The jobs and prosperity in those places didn't exist. Too ashamed to return home, many of the African men that paid human traffickers to cross the desert faced the horrors of Libya. Those not among the thousands of lives claimed by a Mediterranean Sea crossing to Italy ended up begging on the streets.

Standing outside a supermarket in the warm evening breeze of a cold, heartless city, Jonah extended his hand and asked for a small gift to get something to eat. Hard looks chastised him for the low he had sunken to, and many snickered. One man mumbled, "Get a job," as he hurried by. After some time, a woman with almond-shaped eyes full of kindness handed him two quarters. Stingy with her words, she made eye contact and walked away. A few more quarters landed in his open palm between the glares and snide comments.

After buying something to eat, he sat on a bench in a nearby empty park. He ripped mouthfuls off his loaf of bread with his teeth and scooped tuna from a pouch with a tiny plastic spoon. He hadn't known about sales tax, and with just enough money—or so he had thought—to cover the bread and two packages labeled Tuna Kit, he had to leave one fish pouch with the cashier. That would have been his breakfast.

A playful little dog ran up to him, wagging its tail. Jonah pulled a small pinch off his loaf and held it out in a lowered palm. The little creature with curly white hair and big eyes assessed the giver. Apparently deciding to trust him, the pup eagerly snatched the bread and gobbled it down. For the first time in a week, Jonah found a smile on his lips, and that smile brought comfort.

"Sorry, sir. I'm so sorry if he's bothering you." The soft, feminine voice sounded apologetic for no reason. The woman stepped around from behind Jonah's bench and apologized again.

"Do not worry," Jonah replied. "He just wanted to share a little of his happiness with a lonely man."

"Oh... It's you."

"Always."

"I mean, the man from the store. I... I gave you some money." She eyed the stump of bread and empty tuna pouch. "I'm glad you were able to get something to eat."

"You are very kind. You were the first to help me. I was about to give up, and then, more than the money, you gave me hope."

"Well, I'm happy to have helped. I heard what some of those callous jerks said to you. I don't judge people or presume to know their stories."

The woman's head tilted as she watched Jonah pull another small piece from his depleted loaf and share it with her dog.

"Oh no. Please don't give what little you have to my dog. Bad Buddy. Bad dog, taking this nice man's food."

"No, your dog—did you call him Buddy? He shared with me... his energy and joy. I'm merely returning the favor. I thank you Buddy, for your uplifting friendship." Buddy's ears lifted, and he panted with his tongue out as Jonah rubbed his head. "We have the same hair."

The pup's owner chuckled. "Dogs do have a way of making us feel good." A raise of her wrist lowered the woman's brow. "We don't have much time. Do you have a place to stay... um, mister?"

"Blankson, Jonah Blankson. I think I will stay right here. I hope to have an appointment in the morning to straighten things out. I came from Ghana to meet someone and was robbed on a bus. I have already applied for a new passport at the Embassy." In case she doubted his story, he showed her his papers.

"I'm sorry to hear that. *People.* They don't care how their selfishness affects anyone. But... you can't stay here, Mister Blankson. You must find shelter—soon."

"Please, I am Jonah. But don't worry for me. In Ghana I spent many nights under the stars."

"Under a cloud storm?"

Jonah's face sprang to life, full of wide-eyed surprise, and the kind stranger noticed.

"You didn't see the alert? A big one, they said."

"Thank you, um..."

"Christina."

"You're an angel, Christina. Thank you. I will find someplace to take shelter."

Jonah reached to give one more pat to the dog's soft coat and offered him his last morsel of bread. Once on his feet, Jonah tossed his backpack over his shoulder and wished Buddy and Christina a good and safe night.

"Wait... Jonah, please wait." Her pause contradicted her earlier statement for him to find cover as soon as possible. "My friend works at a shelter. It's not far from here."

***

After a bowl of soup and a communal shower, Jonah felt a little of his humanity settle back into his bones. Christina's friend Matt was as kind as she had described. When she promised to return in the morning before going to work, Jonah assured her she had already done enough. Only when she said she volunteered here often and would help serve breakfast to the guests did he bid her a goodnight and add, "See you in the morning."

As they ate, the storm came. Matt brought out a few decks of cards for the men to play in the dining area. When the lights when out, Matt told everyone to stay calm and lit a few candles. After a while, small but bright lights mounted on the wall dripped a dim glow into the room. Jonah cocked his head.

"You don't have emergency lights, I take it," Matt said.

"There is no electricity or running water in our village huts," Jonah said flatly, letting the stereotype hang between them.

The Americans looked at him with blank faces. Perhaps they did think all of Africa was tiny villages with thatched-roof mud huts and scantily clad savages dancing wildly around bonfires. Jonah let out a hearty, bellowing laugh.

"Oh—you got us."

***

After serving all the guests a modest breakfast of creamy oats, Christina called Matt over to sit with Jonah. When she asked about his journey to America, Jonah told the whole story. Matt expressed skepticism about the meteorologist's ability to help him and told Jonah to accept that his wife was most likely dead. Adamantly refuting the idea, Jonah explained his wife's new faith and how the dark clouds were to usher her through some kind of transition, not kill her.

"You've gotta be kidding me," Matt said, leaning back and deflating in his chair. "We've had a few of those nut-jobs here. Some even tried to go out in a storm."

Never having publicly defended his wife's faith, Jonah searched for words to make sense of what he hadn't accepted. Rubbing his dry hands, he said, "I didn't believe but never mocked my Juliana's faith. I was saved from a storm. *Me*, without faith. I know she isn't dead."

Pulling her lips to one side, Christina studied him. "No one really knows what happens to those taken by the storms. I don't think any have been found."

"Yet," Jonah said. "My Juliana is alive. I will find her."

"How can I help?" she asked.

"I'm expecting a message from Doctor Anderson. Without my phone, I have no way to receive her email."

After pulling a laptop from her bag, Christina opened it and slid it in front of Jonah. He pecked at the keys for a moment, but he didn't find his email.

"I've never used an Apple computer. I opened the Mail application. There are many emails, but they are not mine. The top one says 'Singles Match: Click for your next date.' And there's—"

With flushed cheeks, Christina ripped the laptop from Jonah's grasp. Matt chuckled. She told Matt to shut up and clicked on the trackpad a few times before setting it back in front of Jonah.

"Use the web browser. What email service do you use?"

Jonah replied with a blank face.

"Do you have Gmail? Yahoo? Hotmail?"

"My wife set it up. I press the Email button on my phone, and all is there. The browser is for websites."

Pushing out pursed lips, Matt tilted his head. "Do you know your email address?"

"Of course. Jonah dot Blankson twelve at west African post point G H."

Matt pulled the laptop in front of him and clicked the keys for a few seconds. "Okay, I found the login for their email host. I'm entering your email address. Password?"

"Yes, of course. Everything must have a password."

"What is *your* password for your email?"

When Jonah squinted, Christina asked, "Do you have a common password you use?"

"There is one my wife made for me. She told me not to forget it, or she would divorce me. I know she was joking. She used our anniversary. This is why she said I must never forget it."

Christina's face brightened. "Good, we're getting somewhere. When were you married?"

After Matt failed with combinations of "Juliana" and their anniversary, Christina tapped her palm on her forehead. Looking at Matt, she said, "They use British dates. Switch the month and day."

"Yes! That worked... Oh crap."

Christina craned her neck to see the screen. "What?"

"It sent a one-time code to his cell."

Seventeen

With her equipment enroute, Michelle knew they would be cutting it close. Only eight days after the last storm, the gap between them had never been this short. Natasha had pointed out the increased frequency and predicted seeing a similar rise in their severity. While Michelle's system mostly looked for the atmospheric pressure and electromagnetic activity preceding a cloud storm, it also provided a prediction of its intensity based on an established baseline and historical data.

For Michelle, the severity of the coming storm exacerbated the issue of the devastating impact on the climate. The truck drove up the ramp to the elevated parking lot and along the access road to the helipad. Four soldiers jumped from the vehicle as it stopped and moved quickly to unload the cargo.

Two industrial cameras in metal casings with thick glass windows on top landed at Michelle's feet, and she took to setting them up. Doyle joined her a few minutes later to set up the infrared camera. Several other boxes contained weather trackers, radarscopes, barometers, and monitoring stations. Using a power-actuated fastener bolt gun, one of the soldiers secured each of the crates to the cement landing pad.

With all the equipment affixed to the concrete base, the men climbed back into the truck and left. As twilight receded, Michelle and Doyle continued in haste to finish calibrating and preparing the equipment. When the general questioned the crate labeled Samaras Tornado Station, Michelle explained that it might help them measure the funnels. If they got lucky, the turtle would release sensors and capture a host of metrics.

Each system had a military-grade flash memory drive believed to be impervious to the storm's electromagnetic wavelengths. With the mysteries of cloud storms not classified into one category of interference, Michelle knew the systems would falter. How long they would capture data and record was anyone's guess.

By nine o'clock, when the work and rechecks were completed, Michelle stood to stretch a spine unhappy to have been bent over for so long. The cracks sounded like a chiropractic adjustment, and she thought she might need one after all that squatting. When she asked for the time, Nathan replied, "Ten, fifteen minutes, give or take."

While the alert broadcast the estimated time of cloud fall, it used the low end of the scale to make sure people reached safety in time. As Michelle rechecked one of the cameras, Doyle headed into the building.

"We need to finish up and get inside," Nathan said.

While that was obvious, Michelle pondered the brief glimpse she'd sneaked in the last storm. No madness had come. Nor did she see or learn anything. Speculations had raced through her mind for days about there being a tolerable limit to gazing upon the clouds. Surely her father didn't wish her to go mad. Yet there was something in the clouds he wanted her to see.

An eerie calm surrounded them. A noiseless vacuum of tranquility consumed the United States defensive headquarters (complete with a Starbucks) in one of the most bustling cities in America. As Michelle and Nathan scampered along the path from the heliport, the clear sky captivated her. A false sense of peace had spread across the uncluttered expanse. The natural water cycle had been disrupted by this relatively new phenomenon. The sky had never held a single cloud between storms. Somehow, the sky seemed even emptier now—the calm before the storm. Its nearness tingled her skin.

Outside the north entrance, the two stared out at the vastness waiting for the clouds to roll in. Michelle knew they didn't *roll in* from anywhere. That had presented a huge challenge for their prediction. Weather patterns, winds, airstreams, moisture, evaporation—none of it had helped them forecast a cloud storm. When it started, the clouds simply formed, filling the sky as far as the eye could see. They commandeered the entirety of the heavens the world over. A global darkness under the menacing clouds.

The stars went out. The moon disappeared. Silvery gray at first, the clouds blackened and carpeted a darkness over the

US Capitol. As unwelcome as the clouds were, they had made her famous. Despite the technology not being named the "Anderson Early-Warning System," every alert that saved lives had been credited to her. She hadn't realized how widespread that notoriety had become until someone came all the way from Africa to meet her. And he still had not replied to her email.

Something pulled against her arm.

"Come on Michelle... *Michelle*... Doctor Anderson!"

Nathan tugged on her arm, beckoning her to safety, but a stronger pull kept her there. She needed to see. Perhaps she could learn the secrets hiding in plain sight. In what the world saw as ugly, deadly, and even the harbinger of the end, others saw unspeakable beauty. Resisting the constant yanks on her arm, Michelle stood her ground, lifted her chin, opened her eyes, and began counting.

"One."

The clouds thickened and churned, consuming the night sky. Never had Michelle stared more than a second into the turmoil above. No one had seen the dense blackness of fully settled clouds without going insane. But something had made her father's experience different.

"Two."

The beauty he spoke of summoned her, enticing her eyes to keep looking, to see what couldn't be seen. The curtain slowly pulled back—the scene would soon be revealed. Michelle continued to shrug off the tugs on her arm. Needing to gaze upon the forbidden clouds, she ignored the call of her name.

An electro-metallic odor swirled in the air around her. Like the aftereffects of a lightning strike, a sharp, pungent scent of ozone filled her nostrils.

"Three."

The curtain closed. A new darkness covered everything. Was this what it felt like to communicate on a transcendental level with this malevolent and inexplicable force of nature? Her thoughts drifted to O'Malley's theories. Something had taken hold of her. She was no longer in control of her body. The powerful sensation surging through her matched what so many self-professed alien abductees claimed to have experienced.

"Doctor Anderson, you need to get inside."

Pulling against the force wrapped around her chest had no effect. Her body was being dragged, and she kicked her feet helplessly. As she struggled, her pinky toe struck something as hard as steel.

"You mustn't look. We need you sane."

The secret to understanding the clouds, to stopping the storms, swirled just above her head, and Nathan Tucker was hiding it from her.

"I need to see. The answers are right above us. Let me go. I need to see it."

Once she'd been pulled inside, the door slammed behind her, the thud slapping her ears. Her sight returned. Her pupils adjusted to the florescent glow of the lobby. The glass in the doors had been shielded with metal plates since the storms began, and shutters had been lowered over all the windows. Thanks to her early-warning system, the entire building had been sealed, blocking all views before the storm came.

Her shoulders heaved, and her chest swelled. Deep breaths came from frustration and the physical exertion of resisting the general as he'd wrangled her inside. An unfamiliar fire raged within her, heating her bones. Throbbing pain in one foot caused her to lean her weight onto the other. She couldn't remember the last time, if ever, she'd felt such anger reaching for hatred's blind fury. An echoing pop rang in her ears and stung the soft flesh of her palm.

Eighteen

Elder Ferguson directed her fellows not to neglect the necessary step of chronicling the storm and to be thorough in their notes. When Elder Tabashi protested, stating they should be getting the couple ready for the final test, ten others nodded. Some voiced their agreement. Ferguson had to admit this was the moment their order had anticipated for generations. If the storms were the sign of the apocalypse that the others assumed, as her Italian counterpart said, "the Guide Couple must be revealed."

While she did have her reservations and certainly didn't trust Tartagni, resisting this process would expose her to the others and get her cast out. True, she desperately wished to be free of this burden. But the idea of starting a life on the outside, at her age and with no money or possessions, made her wince worse than any cloud storm ever could. But as far as epiphanies went, she realized dying in her ridiculously pompous elder robe wasn't something she hoped to experience.

After lifting herself to her feet, Ferguson walked to the podium on which the Code was displayed like an idol. She flipped the pages under the ornate gold-accented cover until she found her place.

"At Phidias seventeen, verses nine and ten, we read, 'And the faithful shall suffer further tribulation once all elemental trials have been successfully traversed. The Twelve shall send them out into the tempest of the world where they shall be shielded neither from its wrath nor its beauty. With eyes wide to the truth and the coming transition, they will gain insight and full enlightenment and shall lead the people to glory.'" Ferguson closed the book. "We have interpreted the 'tempest' in the verse to mean the cloud storms."

"What else could it be? The meaning is clear," Elder Mmoledi of South Africa said.

"On this we twelve have agreed. Yet I remind you, before the appearance of the clouds, we had a very different interpretation of the tempest and had been expecting the Guide Couple to come."

Tartagni slapped the floor. "Elder Ferguson, I must point out that foretelling is best understood when the signs present themselves. The Code says as much. We didn't apply the tempest to the cloud storms because we had never seen them. Now, as you said, we all agreed this is certainly the correct understanding."

"On this I do not disagree. I'm merely pointing out, as chairperson, the need to follow the text we hold sacred. 'The Twelve shall send them out into the tempest,' it plainly states." All nodded. "Do we also agree, then, that in order to send the couple into the tempest, or cloud storm, a storm must be upon us?"

Shouts of "Yes" and "Of course" signaled full accord among the elders.

"Then, as I pointed out earlier, we have time. The only preparation required for the couple is to summon them from their chamber, open the door to the garden, and send them out into the tempest."

***

The final trial of the Guide Couple couldn't be avoided or even postponed. Amy pondered for a moment if the possibility of proving the foretelling true caused the twisted knots in her stomach. No, she feared something far worse than her fate. To send that young couple into the storm to lie on their backs, eyes wide open, was to condemn them to madness or death. Such zealots—she believed they would lie there, skin blistering, the feeling of fire in their bones, and watch the sky to receive their enlightenment. She lamented what blind faith had made her people become.

The clouds formed. While madness seemed like an awful thing to subject this couple to, the rain would be worse. Better to send them out now, get it over with, Ferguson concluded. No matter how much she wished to stop this, she knew she could not. The chairperson did her duty and sent Tartagni and John-son to summon Nickos and Isis. At only twenty-one and eighteen, whatever happened here would change—or end—their lives forever.

Out they came, escorted by the two elders, and took position in the center of the circle. Johnson and Tartagni sat, closing the ring around them. The chairperson had the *honor* of making the final preparations and sending them outside—hopefully not to die or go mad. To her aged eyes, they looked like children, standing silently in their ceremonial robes. Ferguson stood to anoint the couple. A spicy scent like that of chai tea filled the space as the gold alabastron spilled its perfumed oil onto their heads.

"It is done," Ferguson stated as she set the vessel on its stand.

Eleven elders prostrated themselves, stretching their flattened palms over the cold marble on which they sat. Lowering their faces to the floor, they chanted the sacred words in unison.

"We welcome the Transition. We welcome the Guide Couple."

They raised their heads, arms stretched toward the clouds.

"We welcome our glorious future."

As Elder Ferguson walked the couple toward the garden door, her crimson robe wafted around her thin frame. The chanting continued as they made their way to face the storm's scrutiny. The couple stepped out into the garden. Tartagni stepped beside Ferguson. A fear of the unknown swirled in Isis's eyes, dilating her pupils. How Amy wished to grab her and run her out of this frenzied ritualistic sacrifice.

"The Celestial Maker be with you," Tartagni said. "Blessing and enlightenment be upon the Guide Couple. We welcome the Transition."

As much as she knew the Code, studied it as all the elders had, Ferguson didn't know how long after the confirmation of the Guide Couple the Glorious Transition would occur. Did they have hours, days, weeks, or years?

After a circumspect pause, the young couple centered themselves in the circle of stones said to have been brought from the ancient city of Ur. According to legend, not the Code, the original twelve had sat upon those rocks to receive the first revelation of the Glorious Transition. Holding hands under the gentle illumination of the garden lights, the couple lay on their backs. No funnels swirled, and the rain hadn't yet come. The only danger roiled in the sky above, in the churning clouds shedding the last of their deep silvery sheen and fading into the dense black that would bestow either insight or madness.

Amy couldn't help but wonder whether these kids believed they were the Guide Couple. Had they been pressured into this against their will? Or had they been persuaded by propaganda, swayed by the passionate pleas of their clan's revered leader? Did this young couple display deep-seated faith or staggering foolishness? Amy didn't see a difference.

The young lovers looked into each other's eyes longingly then turned their faces to the sky. With eyes rounded and full of wonder, they gazed into the unknown in search of enlightenment.

Nineteen

Out of focus and slightly spinning, the room didn't look familiar. In the days she had spent at the Pentagon, Michelle hadn't been in General Tucker's office. Or had she? Her brain was a hand groping for thoughts in the dark. When they came, murky and incomplete, she couldn't know if they were correct.

She remembered being outside, working on the sensor equipment and camera. The silver clouds had hovered above, and they ran toward the safety of the building. She had planted her feet and stopped outside the door. Had the clouds revealed an unspeakable beauty? A pain in her toe registered.

"Doctor Anderson, are you alright?"

"So beautiful," she said groggily.

"No, please no. We need you. *Michelle*?"

"General Tucker? Nathan?"

The madness hadn't come—she had not seen the mysterious wonders of the black clouds. The general's hand had indeed been fast enough to save her mental faculties from ruination.

Michelle fumed, angry enough to hit someone. A memory came into focus. She had hit someone.

"Nathan, I... I think... Did I slap you? I'm sorry."

"Don't worry. You were a bit hysterical. I thought the clouds had taken your mind. We need you to figure this out, and no matter how much you resisted, I had to pull you inside."

Still needing time for her brain to process, she said nothing. Decision-making lingered on the border of impossibility. Questions rattled around in her skull. She could feel her brain working—the headache proved that much. Yet her mind was a stranger, someone she needed to know better before she could trust it.

"When you muttered the same words as your father, you really scared me. The think-tank is full of brainiacs, sure, and most of everything I hear in there goes way over my head. But I'm smart enough to know you're the one who counts. Without you, we'll never figure this out, never stop it."

"Stop it?"

Impossible, she thought. Why? Why could they not stop the clouds, the storms, the funnels, the rain? Some more thoughts rushed in. Could she trust them? Yes. Memories from her research surfaced. Time was running out. Climate change had shifted into high gear and raced along at unprecedented speed. The little efforts they'd made, the improvements that had given humanity a glimmer of hope, had died, absorbed into the darkened clouds.

"You ruined my only chance for that, *General*. We've been at it nonstop for days, and we've accomplished nothing. Until we understand the clouds, how can we possibly hope to stop them, stop the effects on our environment, our crops, our future?"

"That's why we need you to stay with us. You're the only one who guides the group, keeps them focused. You sift through their ideas and proposals. The vice president didn't appoint a chair for your group, but you've naturally slid into that role."

Had she taken control of their group of scientists—and one alien conspiracy nut-job—as Nathan had suggested? Idiots, all of them. She'd had to do it. Michele always believed in the adage, "If you want something done right, do it yourself." She had built her career on it. And yes, she realized her father had been correct when he said they should have named her work after her. The "Anderson Early-Warning System" had saved countless lives, prevented traffic accidents, and kept airplanes from falling out of the sky.

The mental fog had lifted considerably, though not completely. Perhaps the first stage of the madness had started to take hold. Had she discovered a window of opportunity? Could she gaze into the clouds for a time before madness entered her mind and find the answers she desperately needed? The world needed her to be brilliant. Michelle knew she was, yet so far, she had failed. The vice president of the United States had sought her out, trusted her, and she had nothing.

"I need to try again."

Nathan's eyes widened. "Are you crazy?"

"No, not completely. I think I may be a genius—or at least I've got an idea." She stood and limped around the small office as Nathan looked on, a puzzled look over his face. "I think I started to feel the effects. I said the words, but my brain was trying to push itself somewhere it hadn't gone. Not quite. I didn't see anything beautiful up there, only the emptiness of our looming destruction."

The general remained quiet as Michelle stopped circling and leaned toward the man's kind face. She hadn't considered that until now—Nathan Tucker had a kind face. How had she not seen it before? She shook her head to clear it.

"I looked, for a short time, and I'm fine. Mostly. I believe we've discovered a... a grace period, we can call it. There's a window of time before the madness sets in. In the next storm, we extend my time a little, then more the next, and so on until we breach that barrier just enough for me to see what's there before going crazy."

"Doctor Anderson, is that scientifically sound?"

"Don't 'Doctor Anderson' me. You said it. I'm the one taking charge here. If you want something done right..." After taking a deep breath under a long blink, she continued, "It's all we have. Let's just hope the next storm isn't too far off. They seem to be happening more frequently."

"Please sit. I think your look into the clouds affected you more than you realize."

With a forced sigh to be sure Nathan understood her annoyance, Michelle sat. He folded his hands on the desk and leaned onto his elbows in a fatherly posture. She had no idea how old he was.

"What about your friend from Africa? We have two cloud-storm survivors now that had the same reaction. Both said the exact same words." Leaning closer, Nathan stopped her from rubbing her hands by taking them in his. His were warm, and the safety they radiated settled her fidgeting. "I think their experience is common. I suspect others who suffered the madness saw the same thing."

"Okay, Mister Army-Man-Not-a-Scientist," she said, baiting him sarcastically. "Enlighten me."

"Since you told me about the message from that man, with the same words your father spoke, I've been searching through reports of others who've gone cloud mad. Stupid name, I know. It's used in a lot of the articles and videos."

"I've done the same, obviously." Michelle pulled her hands from his. It had started to feel weird, holding them like that. "No one else reported those words. No one called it beautiful. That's what has me so interested, desperate even, to contact this guy. Still no reply to my emails. Maybe he's just another dead end."

After an emphatic nod, Nathan froze. His eyes glowed with the reflection of something on his computer screen that had his full attention.

"What is it? You look almost... frightened."

"A report on this storm. It's more intense than any previous."

"How's our equipment doing out there?"

Twenty

The two stayed so motionless they looked dead. Ferguson wondered if they blinked when she did and tried to keep her eyes open to verify. A tear climbed the corner of Isis's eyelid and rolled toward her hairline. Mesmerized, Ferguson watched it snake its way to the girl's ear. She looked so beautiful lying there, her youthful skin glistening under the dim garden lights.

Amy snuck into Elder Ferguson's thoughts and reminded her she, too, was once young and beautiful. Her mind's eye superimposed herself and Alexandar over the young couple. She held his hand, looked into the eyes she had fallen in love with as a child, and they both gazed into the storm. Would she have done it if they had been called for the trials? Had they had the faith needed to lie there facing the clouds, confronting madness or death? Had she ever had that level of faith? Every time she dug into herself for that answer, she found the same reply.

Even now, Amy's doubt consumed her. The girl was just a teenager with her life ahead of her. It took every fiber of self-control Elder Ferguson could muster not to run into the garden and drag Isis back inside to safety. To freedom.

To be free, she mused longingly...

In Tartagni's eyes, Ferguson saw conviction. Of course, she knew it may have been the fervor of the moment, of wanting the Guide Couple to be from his clan. If they somehow passed this final trial, their elder would ascend to council chair, replacing Ferguson. That didn't bother her at all, except that she knew he'd be even more of a pompous twit as chairperson.

But even if demoted, she couldn't quit. Clan elders served until they died. Unfortunately for her, the Code held the definition of "death" to a strictly literal physical end of life. Inside, she'd qualified to leave the council years ago.

The couple disappeared until her eyes adjusted. For the first time, Ferguson wondered why every power grid on the planet went dark when the clouds came. Every storm greedily took the world's electricity. The blackouts lasted from minutes to hours with no observable pattern—even portable electronics went out. Something struck her as different in this storm.

The wind blew harder this evening. Larger funnels appeared in the distance. She could just make out their forms in the darkness over the outer wall of the compound. No expert on dark clouds, she had dutifully logged the details of each storm since they began and knew of the mini tornadoes that produced those slender funnels. She often wondered how they had the strength to lift people from the ground, never to be found again.

The rain would soon come. It always came after the little twisters. Perhaps the three-meter-high stone walls, more than the Celestial Maker, protected the couple from the funnels. The walls wouldn't stop the rain from falling upon them, eating away at their flesh and killing them if they didn't flee to cover. That would be a true test of the depth of their zeal for the Code and their place as the supposed Guide Couple. Would they lie there and die or escape the pain pelting them from the clouds their people practically worshipped?

The intensity of the storm felt like pressure in her chest. How must it have been for those poor kids on the grass? Ferguson looked again at Isis—her form hardly visible under the cover of dense darkness. From eyesight or imagination, Amy saw tears pouring from both of her eyes. A face drenched in unimaginable fright.

A new pressure squeezed her. Forgetting about Nickos completely, she couldn't look away from Isis. Part of her blamed him for doing this to that child. Amy squinted, demanding all the focus her eyes could give. Isis appeared thinner, her small breasts flattened, as if a thick sheet of glass pressed down on her body, pushing it into the dirt and grass.

Tartagni had a grip on Amy's arm. Did he suspect her skepticism, see the doubt in her eyes, her longing to save these children from this senseless sacrifice? Did he, perhaps, feel the same? For only a second, Ferguson turned to look at him and couldn't believe what she saw. His usually stoic face held wide, stirring eyes. Never had she seen anything on that rugged Italian exterior besides confidence and pride.

"So beautiful." The wind carried the sound to her ears. They heard the weak voice again. "It's so beautiful. Look and see."

"*Isis*," Ferguson blurted. She looked at Tartagni. "Did you hear it? What did she say?"

"It is enlightenment." As he shouted the words again and again, the elders still holding their place in the circle on the floor joined their voices to his declaration.

A splash landed on one of the stones around the couple. Another and another and another. The sound sparked the memory of a gentle springtime sun shower from before those had stopped occurring. Ferguson knew the trickle would become a torrential downpour—they always did. In seconds, that couple would suffer unbearable pain as their skin blistered and boiled with every drop of rain that assaulted it.

Thoughtlessly, she tugged her hood over her forehead and raced through the doorway unhindered. No hand clutched her arm. No one held her back. As Amy bent over Isis's motionless body, she saw Tartagni digging his arms under Nickos. Their eyes met in solidarity. Her fellow elder had the boy in his arms and hauled him out of her periphery while she struggled to lift the girl's limp body. Blisters dotted her previously unblemished skin, and her eyes swirled beneath a glassy glaze.

The aged elder almost had Isis up when the girl's loose body found strength, and Isis used that strength to resist as she continued repeating, "So beautiful." She struggled to remain on the ground. Knowing she'd never be able to lift her, Amy grabbed her under the arms, spun her around, and heaved her backward toward the door. Isis swung her arms and kicked her feet, repeating those same words and telling Amy to look at the clouds.

A drop of rain found Amy's hand and sizzled on her skin. With nothing to protect her, boils now peppered the girl's face and arms. The path to the cathedral's garden entrance stretched as Ferguson pulled with all her might to drag the young lady against her will. Tartagni returned. No—it was Sato who wrestled the girl's ankles into his hands and lifted her, making the job of getting her inside doable when Amy had failed to manage it herself.

A hefty thump hit her ears and startled her. As they held Isis still, Nickos ran through the inner sanctuary. Fumbling over the elders, his frantic movements knocked over one of the candelabras. Tabashi jumped up. The edge of his robe sparkled with yellow fire. A few waves of the fabric chased them away. The fallen candles dripped pools of quickly hardening wax onto the stone floor. Their flames flickered out.

Without forming words, Nickos mumbled incoherently. Tartagni again subdued him and dragged him to the couple's chamber. Amy and Sato hauled the still-resisting Isis to the room and sealed themselves in with Tartagni and Nickos. When the two finally stopped physically struggling, they lay on the floor as if each were unaware of the other.

Elder Ferguson summoned all her might to keep her inner Amy suppressed. Her look at Sato told him they would discuss this later. What bounced in her mind now, she struggled to comprehend. Did this validate decades of faith, brittle as it was, or had she lived a lie all these years for nothing?

She felt... empty.

More so than usual.

Until an idea sparked to life.

Twenty-One

CHRISTINA PULLED HER FACE from the pale illumination of the computer screen. The post-storm sun breaking through the window set her hair aglow like it had caught fire. Her face dissolved in the aurora as the light shining on her back turned her into an angel. Jonah's angel who had offered that first gift toward his success. She'd gone above and beyond anything he had expected from an American.

"I found her," Christina said.

"Sort of," Matt said as he rose and went back to the kitchen.

"Sort of found who?" Stretching his arms behind him, Jonah yawned.

Matt set three mugs onto the table and filled them from a carafe. Clanking dishes hit the metal counter as other guests, homeless or otherwise unfortunate people, placed their breakfast plates and cups down. One of the men asked for and took the carafe from their table to his. Observing the amount of sugar Jonah piled into his mug, Christina rounded her eyes. He had to suck in a sip not to spill it. When Matt said something about having a little coffee with his sugar, Jonah chuckled politely.

"Sort of found who?" he repeated.

"Doctor Michelle Anderson. She's here, in DC."

Jonah said, "Yes, this I know. It is why I'm here. But I have been to the University where her weather office is, and she wasn't there."

"I mean, she's here, just not in her office. It took a while—it's not like they're advertising it or anything, but I found her name in an article buried deep in a subsection on the us.gov website." As Christina pulled a full sip from her cup, she looked at Jonah like a child waiting for permission to continue. "She's working on a task force for the V.P."

"I told you she was the one who could help me."

"Um, how did we prove that?" Matt looked up from the coffee cup he cradled in two hands. "All we learned is she's working with the administration."

With the pop of a single clap, Jonah said, "You see, she *is* the world's leading expert on the clouds. Even the government looks to her for help with the storms."

"He's not wrong. Her credentials are impressive. She designed the early-warning system and knows more about the clouds than anyone."

"Yeah, Chrisy. And she's working on the V.P.'s special task force."

"Yes," Jonah agreed. "As Christina said."

Letting her shoulders sag, Christina said, "What Matt's saying is it will be even harder to reach her now."

"I have a plan. What you found makes it an even better plan now. I will go tour the White House this morning and ask for her there."

"Yeah, not sure how things work in Gambia, but you're not getting close to anyone important."

"He's from Ghana." After spearing Matt with a fierce glare, Christina turned to Jonah. "I'm afraid he's right. You won't see anyone important. And not to be pessimistic, what makes you so sure Doctor Anderson can help find your wife? It's just... I'm afraid you might be setting yourself up for disappointment."

Matt grimaced. "And when I said it, you snapped at me."

"I told you about how I was saved from last week's storm. That proves someone can survive. My Juliana could have survived. I'm sure she did. Whether from our ancestral gods, the God of the Christians, or the Celestial Maker of my wife's faith, I don't know. But whatever saved me might have saved her as well."

"Right. Your wife belonged to the Order." Looking off at nothing, Christina continued, "They believe the clouds are a sign of the end times. Why would any god save you, Juliana, or anyone, only to wipe us all out?"

"As my wife told me many times, their sacred Code states the end times will result in a Transition. The faithful will be delivered. You see, the clouds wouldn't destroy her or any member of their faith."

Matt slapped his forehead. "The name of that cult is the Glorious Transition. Now that makes sense... I mean, not that I believe in any of this. I just never got that before."

"Yes. My wife was prepared for that transition. I will find her."

"But..." Lifting her chin, Christina paused. "You said it's not *your* faith."

"I am not one of the faithful, no. But if my Juliana is, and I can find her, her deliverance is enough. She is all that matters."

"That's so sweet."

After a cynical smirk, Matt said, "Yeah, really touching. But there's another problem with your plan. Weren't your wallet and passport stolen?"

"I'll buy him a bus ticket."

"No, Christina. You have already been too kind. I can go by leg. It's not far at *aaall*." Jonah showed her a smile with a small space between his front teeth.

"Yeah, not what I meant." Still fondling his now-empty coffee cup, Matt turned to watch the carafe being drained by a man two tables over. "He has no ID."

Twenty-Two

AFTER THE STORM'S WRATH, the clouds left the sky empty. The morning sun spread a spectacular array of yellow and orange like silk sheets over a luxurious bed. Michelle slogged along the walkway thinking her exhaustion must have made her picture the dazzling show above as a comfy bed. How long had it been since she'd slept on her own mattress—the perfect balance of firm and soft—in her apartment? It was just across town in Colombia Heights.

General Nathan Tucker had escorted her from the makeshift accommodation (a cot in a cleared-out office) in the Pentagon building to the rear exit and out to the heliport. Every other step hurt so she tried to walk on the heel of that foot.

All the equipment had died. While dutifully doing their jobs on battery power, the scanners logged their findings to internal storage disks before they failed. The cameras saved their video and still frame photos to flash drives as well.

At *too early* past seven, they were joined by Doctors Kournikova and Doyle. The two walked like they had "the right stuff" and would embark on setting humanity on a new course to a glorious future. Optimistic about the data herself, Michelle fought off a more realistic expectation about its impact.

Nathan was as accommodating as ever, but she couldn't let go of her resentment toward him for covering her eyes and pulling her inside. To her, he had blown the best chance the task force had to make headway. As she told him, repeatedly, the first step to solving a problem was understanding it. Perhaps the sensors and videos would give them something.

Four holes outlined in chips of broken cement betrayed anchor points not strong enough to keep the crate secure when the funnels had barreled through like semitrucks. With a quick inventory check on his tablet, Nathan said the crate had held the Samaras Tornado Station, so they'd lost any "tornado...*y* readings," as he put it. With an eyeroll, Michelle recalled his earlier confession of not following her science jargon. No argument there—a fact Michelle welcomed after having exhausted her reserve of pompous indignation at her team members all week.

The first to get started, Doyle took a power screwdriver to one of the crates. Her rival meteorologist was a daily nuisance, and Michelle nearly salivated watching him reach into the open metal box. He had applied for her job a day before she'd interviewed and would have had it if not for Michelle being much more qualified. That was how she'd interpreted the meaning of "you are our preferred candidate" when they offered her the position.

After a girlish yelp, he fell onto his backside with a dull thud. Michelle considered that a pretty good description of Brendon Doyle and his career. She decided to give him a nickname that would only be spoken by her inner voice. Trying to hold back a chuckle, she asked if he was alright.

Helping the man to his feet, Nathan asked, "What happened?"

"Electrostatic shock. Residual, but packs a punch." Natasha smirked as she pulled on her thick rubber gloves.

"Doctor Kournikova's correct." Michelle couldn't resist adding, "Anyone who understands anything about the cloud storms knows that."

Doctor Dull Thud scowled as he rubbed his hand, and Michelle wondered why she'd snapped. Did she wake up on the wrong side of that horrid cot? While insulting Brendon needed no apology, she offered one.

With gloved hands and proper care taken, the three scientists removed the panels from the crates and collected the drives from the devices. If their actions yielded nothing more, they'd discovered forcing electronics to run on batteries during the blackout was a death sentence for the equipment.

"Hooray for the scientific method," Natasha said with a wink.

***

Visits from Vice President Barnes were rare. Michelle raised an eyebrow when Nathan greeted the first in succession to the most powerful office in the world as "Ray."

As anxious as everyone was to check the camera footage, Michelle had to agree when the V.P. insisted they start the process of uploading data from the drives onto the supercomputer on loan from the NSA. Once the computer began its work of parsing, sorting, and processing the vital sensor results, the organic brains could evaluate the visual data.

Silence reigned over the conference table as Michelle loaded the video file and pressed play. At first, they saw what naked human eyes had seen many times. In an open sky void of even the slightest patch or band of cirrus cloud, an altostratus cloud layer suddenly appeared. Its gray sheen spread over the earth like a massive semi-translucent shell. In seconds, it turned into something that Michelle explained mimicked a stratus or nimbostratus cloud layer, thickening into a darker silvery gray and blotting out all celestial luminaries.

Next, what meteorologists agreed could only be likened to cumulonimbus—thunderstorm—clouds seemed to fold themselves out of the nimbostratus layer. Few had lived or averted the madness to report how the clouds had rolled and churned in the atmosphere as if created from the air itself, not carried in from airstreams or fronts and not forming from smaller moisture collections caused by evaporation. "Scientific guesswork" was how Michelle described it to Nathan.

What happened next, no one had seen—at least no one alive or of sound mind. Michelle recalled her vision darkening to black at this point, and she stood stiff, every muscle burning with anticipation to see what Nathan had not allowed her to look upon last night.

Black.

Dense black.

"Did it go out?" Doyle asked.

Natasha tapped her chin. "I think by this point the equipment died."

"No, I don't think so." Michelle limped toward the wall-filling display and pointed to the seconds advancing on the timeline.

She returned to the computer and adjusted every playback setting, quality correction, and filter she could think of to enhance the image. Nothing but black showed, with a hint of slightly less black occasionally folding along the underside of the churning clouds. The video played for fourteen more seconds before the screen filled with white fuzz and stopped abruptly.

"What was that?" Doctor Wilma Jones asked.

With a crinkled brow Michelle replied, "It cut off. We knew it wouldn't last long. But this is the longest video recording we've ever captured of the clouds."

"I meant, did anyone else see that?"

"See what?" Michelle turned from Wilma to Natasha. "Did you see something?"

"Just the cut to black."

Wilma stood and pointed at the screen. "At the end, just before it cut off… Did none of you see that?"

Hoisting himself to his feet, V.P. Barnes lifted his barrel chest over the table. "Go back, Michelle. To whatever Doctor Jones saw."

Without answering, she slid the scrubber back ten seconds and played it at half speed. Everyone rose to their feet and leaned in to examine the replay. They watched the endless black, the hard-to-spot folds, and…

"There," Wilma declared. "Go back a couple of seconds and play it as slow as you can."

Michelle did that.

"Stop. Right there. Do you see it?"

"What the hell is that?" Natasha exclaimed.

Doyle folded his arms and puffed his chest. "I thought I saw that the first time too. A speck of blue, like a spark of light."

Michelle doubted Doctor Dull Thud had seen anything the first time. It took all her willpower not to ask the V.P. why Doyle still needed to be on her team.

"Some form of electricity," Wilma suggested.

The I-want-to-believe guy of the group said, "Like from a ship. An alien vessel of some kind."

Doctor Jones, the highly respected astrophysicist and the leading candidate for smartest person in the room, had a long rebuttal for O'Malley. Like Michelle, Wilma had made clear from the start how utterly ridiculous she considered it to have an exobiologist on the team. Listening to the two of them verbally duke it out gave Michelle—and the others, by the look of it—an amusing break.

But when Wilma reached her conclusion, she shocked everyone.

"Although, once we've ruled out everything else, what remains..."

"Thank you," Patrick O'Malley said from his smug face.

"Blue electricity," Michelle blurted. Unable to refute the remote possibility of Pat's ideas, she decided to move on. "The man, the guy from Africa. Don't roll your eyes at me, Brendon. This is the second match to something he said, two keys to unlocking the mystery of the clouds. First the madness, with the same words my father keeps saying. Now the blue electricity. That man saw it too. But he saw it on the ground. We need to find this guy."

When her eyes met one pair in the room, Michelle knew she had the right person to help her find the man from Africa. "Mister Vice President, I need you to find Jonah Blankson."

Twenty-Three

A TOTAL MESS. THOSE poor kids had been paraded before the Twelve like gods in human form only to be left outside in the storm. Left to go out of their minds and suffer massive burns all over their bodies. Blame heated Ferguson's blood as she pierced Tartagni with Amy's steely stare. A stronger fire ignited within her, consuming the one for the elder who had brought this young couple before the counsel for the trials.

"It's all my fault," she muttered.

Tartagni's eyebrow inched up. "What was that?"

"Those poor kids. Look what we've put them through. And for what?"

Sato stood before Elder Ferguson and held her by the arms. His kind eyes offered sympathy, while his lowered brow warned her to watch her words.

"We?" Like a scolding parent, almost half her age, Tartagni assaulted her with a scowl. "*We* didn't put them through any-thing. They believe they're the Guide Couple. They willingly came before us for the trials, showing exemplary faith and courage.”

“We left them out in the storm, under the clouds... to... to go mad.” Amy inhaled deeply, but no calmness entered her body with her breath. “And we watched them lying there... the rain... What have we done?”

“We have done as we should have done.” Sato raced the words through his lips before Tartagni could utter a syllable, leaving the Italian elder with an open mouth. “We followed the most current interpretation of the Code and conducted the proving trials. Under your dedicated direction, Madam Chairperson.”

Nodding deliberately, Sato tightened his grip on her arms. Ferguson knew she had reached the precipice and was teetering over the edge. Of all the elders, Tartagni was the last one who needed to see any weakness in her, any lack of faith on the part of the chairperson—the role he’d expected to occupy when the Guide Couple from his clan was confirmed.

As soon as the cloud storm cleared, Tilda came. One of Tartagni’s young aides arrived shortly after. Ferguson’s attendant cared for Isis’s abused flesh while the young man tended to the burns peppering Nickos’s skin. They dared not change their clothes in their delicate condition. The two limp bodies glimmered in the glow of candlelight flickering over their ointment-saturated skin. Restored electricity brightened the room. Amy thought the two looked like plastic mannequins. Idols. Objects of veneration to take up the mantle of saviors.

"This isn't enough. They're badly burned." Considering the burn on her hand and the pain trapped beneath the ointment, Amy couldn't imagine the excruciating agony those two were suffering. "We need to call an ambulance and get them to the hospital."

Tartagni stood from his kneeling pose over the two he had touted as the Guide Couple. "And how do we explain this? You need to start acting like the chairperson and thinking clearly. They'd arrest us all for this."

"You do think us culpable, then."

"What? No. But *they* will." As if to puncture it, Tartagni jabbed his finger at the wall. "They'll blame us, call us religious fanatics, and try to charge us with abuse. Criminal negligence, at the very least."

"And you think covering this up and letting these poor children suffer is our way to... what...? To cover our own backsides? Is *that* what worries you?"

Sato stepped between the pair. "Wait—just wait."

"Stop defending her, Sato. Haven't you noticed you're the only one of the Twelve doing that? Our illustrious chairperson has been derelict in her duties, and she—"

"*Derelict*? How dare you." No matter the level of her conviction, Ferguson was not about to let a derogatory comment about how she handled her responsibilities slide. "I have done nothing but uphold the Code and bring balance to this group when blind zealots like you try to manipulate the text into whatever suits your purposes. You pushed that gullible couple into thinking they were the Guide because *you* wanted them to come from *your* clan." She hadn't noticed her finger stabbing his chest. If her fingernail hadn't been chewed to the nub, she'd have broken the skin.

"I have doubted your faith for some time. Leader of your clan, *Elder* Ferguson, sitting chairperson, I should call for an inquisition into your loyalty to the Code and to the Council of Twelve."

Flabbergasted, Ferguson had no rebuttal. She had given herself away and stood naked, exposed before the one person she considered an enemy.

"You will do no such thing," Sato bellowed. "And you know you will not have the support of the Twelve. Elder Ferguson is an excellent chairperson and has shown her loyalty to the Code and the Glorious Transition. If you dare challenge her, Tartagni, after you brought us a false Guide Couple, you may end up expelled from the Council and banished from the Order."

The hotheaded Italian elder stood there with no witty comeback. Sato's scathing dose of reality must have hit him where it hurt—his lofty position as clan elder. He was so close to ascending to the office of chairperson, and the thought of suffering the humiliation of a judiciary hearing appeared to have shaken him to the core. Amy's heart swelled with appreciation toward Sato for saving her from her own senselessness.

"So beautiful." Sitting up, Isis spoke again. "Can you see it? It's so beautiful."

The three elders pulled their stares from each other to look upon the young woman. Close to consciousness, Nickos only mumbled. Isis repeated the words she'd shouted when she pushed and fought to go back into the storm. What did they mean?

"Enlightenment," Tartagni said, reaffirming. "They have not gone mad. They have seen the beauty of the Celestial Maker. They are the Guide Couple."

As he fell to his knees and bowed before the couple, Isis rose to her feet. Repeating those words over and over, she walked in a circle around the room. Nickos didn't move or speak. The couple's caregivers looked on with blank faces of confusion. What must those young zealots have thought of all this?

Ferguson looked at Sato—her friend, who'd saved her from a fall from grace—and had no idea what to say or how to act. The Twelve would look to her for answers, for what to do next. Had enlightenment been bestowed upon this couple through their gaze into the darkened clouds? Would the last traces of Amy dissolve if the revelation of the foretold Guide Couple surfaced Elder Ferguson's lack of faith?

Only Isis spoke coherently. That intrigued Amy.

***

As a concession, the elders called in medical doctors and psychologists from among clan members. The closest were obviously from clan Ferguson, and Tartagni grumbled but accepted their assistance. Nickos and Isis were treated by a general practitioner and a burn specialist. With a dollop of the medicated balm for her hand, Ferguson felt immediate relief and shed a tiny bit of her concern for the physical welfare of the now sleeping young couple.

When they woke, Isis tried again to get outside. Nickos wandered around the room in circles. No discernable words formed from his nonsensical mumbling. Isis repeated her earlier words before slurring into incoherent gabbling. After being given a mild sedative to keep them awake but manageable, they settled and responded to physical directions while ignoring verbal communication.

The last of the middle-of-the-night arrivals—two psychologists—began their work. While Tartagni stayed close to Nickos, Sato and Ferguson took positions on either side of the youthful Isis, Amy wiping occasional drool from the girl's lip with the end of her sleeve.

After an hour that passed like a week, the two mental health professionals left the room to confer in private. Whatever conclusions they would draw, Amy saw no trace of sanity remaining in the teenage boy's mind. All Isis had produced over the last sixty minutes amounted to gibberish with a sporadic "It's so beautiful... You need to see it" breaking the pattern.

The air was always crisp and the skies clear directly after the clouds dispersed. Sato escorted Amy outside, leaving Isis in the care of Tilda and Nickos with Tartagni's aide. In the garden, Amy stared blankly at the flattened grass within the circle of ancient stones. The shape of those young frames pressed into the ground reminded her of a police outline of two dead bodies. In this homicide investigation, where would the guilt lie? Even if these children survived, to Amy, they were as good as dead. She and the elders had taken their lives, squandered them, and robbed them of all their years to come.

"You need to keep it together."

Amy looked upon Sato, her dear friend and only supporter, with focused eyes. "I know. I *am* trying. This is all just... too much. We ruined those kids' minds. Made them vegetables. And for what?"

"You did as you should have done. As the council would have done regardless."

"Telling me that, that if I hadn't done this someone else would have... That sounds too much like the excuses war criminals use to justify their actions. Were we only following orders, Sato? Orders written thousands of years ago and interpreted by us. We should have acted sooner, before subjecting those children to the storm."

The damn broke and Amy sobbed bitterly. Once again, her friend was there, and she was in his embrace.

"I can't do this anymore. Can't pretend any longer. Not after what this role, this faith, made me do. Made me become."

"You can't blame yourself. As chairperson—"

Cutting him off, Amy pushed herself from Sato's arms. "As chairperson, I was the one who could have stopped it. I can't blame the Order, the Code, or anyone's interpretation. I did this."

"*No.*" Sato grabbed her arms and squeezed. "They willingly came here and endured the trials. *They* lay under the storm and refused to get up. *They* looked upon the clouds."

"Because of the faith we postulated for them."

"It was their faith. Their choice."

"Did you think they were the One?"

Sato hesitated. Both cast their gazes upon the imprints in the grass.

"Yes. When they proved all the trials, I thought they would pass the final one. Thousands of years of our faith, our hope, would be upon us." Without turning to face her, he added, "On some level, so did you."

Twenty-Four

They wouldn't allow him to tour the White House. It had all happened so fast. No one had let him speak, to explain why he needed to talk to the man in the blue suit. As if Jonah had drawn a weapon, men in black suits rushed the distinguished older man out of sight. They must have considered Jonah a threat. Or perhaps a raging lunatic. Either way, this presented a major setback. He had been so close. It didn't seem likely he'd be able to ask anyone about Doctor Anderson now.

After an hour of waiting—or longer, as he'd found no clock in the tiny room—the door opened. A large man in a speckled green uniform entered, and Jonah wondered why soldiers wore camouflage in cities and buildings where it did the opposite of its intended purpose. A distinguished older woman entered behind the soldier. The woman in the black business suit and white blouse sat facing Jonah and thumbed through a tablet on her lap.

Considering it best not to speak first, Jonah raised an eyebrow and studied her. As he rehearsed his lines in his head, he sounded mad. A crazy old fool who'd entered the White House with a stamped paper from a foreign Embassy and caused a commotion. They thought he'd tried to attack that man. The word *terrorist* ricochetting around his skull like a pinball.

"Please state your name." The woman didn't look up from her tablet.

"Jonah Blankson."

"Age?"

"Fifty-six."

"You have no identification, no passport."

"No, ma'am. I was robbed on a bus and am waiting for a new passport from my embassy."

Still focused on her tablet, she nodded. It seemed she already had answers to those questions. For the first time, she looked Jonah in the eye. "Why did you attempt to assault Senator Jackson?"

Taking a deep breath, Jonah considered his words. "I merely wished to speak with him. I meant no harm. I traveled from—"

"From Ghana, we know. And you decided to join a White House tour group, yell at a United States senator, and attempt to force your way through a barrier of secret service personnel."

Silence stretched across the small room as the interrogator returned her eyes to the tablet. She hadn't asked him for a reply, and he didn't know how to give one.

"Were you after Jackson, specifically?" She raised a steely glare. "Or just trying to make some misguided political state-ment?"

"I didn't know the man in the blue suit. I came to Wash—I mean, to DC—to get help to save my wife."

"Is she a political refugee here in America?"

Jonah shook his head. "Juliana has never come to America."

"Then how is it, Mister Blankson, that coming here to tour the White House would save your wife in Ghana?"

When Jonah fidgeted, the soldier stepped beside him.

"My wife was lost in the cloud storm. Not the one from last night. I mean the one before that. A week ago."

"Your wife disappeared in that storm, a week ago, in Africa? It's common knowledge that no missing person has yet been recovered from a cloud storm. Yet you came all the way *here* to somehow save her? Explain that logic to me."

"I came to find Doctor Michelle Anderson. She is the meteorologist who—"

"I am well aware of Doctor Anderson, as is most of the world." Studying him again, she said, "To my knowledge, you're the first one to seek her out in hopes of finding a person lost to the clouds."

"My Juliana isn't lost, only missing. Doctor Anderson can help me find her. No one knows the storms better. She predicts their activity, studies them, and she can help me find my wife."

With a deep sigh, the woman shook her head. "I'm not convinced your intentions were honorable, Mister Blankson. For all I know, you may be telling us a story to mask your true purpose... Or you may just be nuts. We'll hold you here another day for a psych eval before pressing charges."

She reached into her jacket pocket to retrieve her mobile. What the woman saw on the small screen made her eyes widen. With the phone pressed to her ear, she said, "Mister Vice President, sir."

***

Tears welled in Jonah's eyes. Sitting across the table from Doctor Anderson renewed the hope every obstacle he encountered along his journey had depleted. Finally, he would get the help he needed from the one person in the world who could offer it.

The vice president of the United States of America looked Jonah in the eye and said, "Tell us why you're seeking an audience with Doctor Anderson."

"Thank you, sir." Jonah looked upon Doctor Anderson's blurry face. After running the back of his hand under his nose, Jonah said, "Hello, Doctor Anderson. I'm a simple farmer, but I know you are the famous scientist who understands the cloud storms better than anyone."

"Mister Blankson, I'm sorry to disappoint you... No one fully understands these storms. In fact, I have some questions for you that may help us better understand them."

"It is my wife, Juliana." When Jonah leaned forward, the guards at his sides pressed closer. "She is missing. I tried to tell these people. This is the reason for my journey here, why I sought you."

Doctor Anderson said, "Mister Blankson, we cannot help with a missing-person situation in Africa. You will need to—"

"Please, she isn't a missing person. The storm took her. I'm sure she's not dead. You're the only one who can help me find her, to get her back from those clouds that stole her from me."

As the words fell from his lips, the bitter taste of their desperation clung to his tongue. Even to himself, he sounded crazy. Jonah knew he hadn't gone cloud mad. But if he had, would he have known?

The doctor tilted her head. "Perhaps we can help each other."

Jonah's eyes widened, arching his eyebrows. "Please. I will do anything you ask if you help me find my Juliana. Anything at all."

Folding her hands together and resting them on the table, Doctor Anderson leaned forward. "I can't promise anything. You know, don't you, that no one who disappeared in a cloud storm has ever been found."

"I believe this is because no dark-cloud expert has looked."

"Fair point, Mister Blankson. Around the world, meteorologists and other scientists are devoting all their time and resources to studying these clouds and learning how to stop them. This is why I've been looking for you."

Confused, Jonah crinkled his brow.

"Since you contacted my brother, I've been emailing you."

"My phone was stolen. And my wallet and passport. Your country has not been very kind to me. Except for Christina.

She's an angel, and I'm grateful to her that I have found you at last."

Anderson paused before saying, "I've been eager to reach you since you mentioned the cloud madness of your friend."

"It drove her mad. This didn't happen to my Juliana. She was taken. I don't see how this helps you find her, but I will tell you anything you ask."

"We hoped as much. The madness is only part of it. I asked the vice president to find you at all costs because of the blue lightning you saw."

"Yes, the blue light. The madwoman, she ran right to that spot... where I saw them. Those lights, they... in the storm, after my cousins... the ground lightning saved me."

At the storm doctor's request, Jonah related the account. Doctor Anderson asked many questions about how the light moved, its size and brightness, when he first noticed it, and how the area looked when he woke. Most of the details he provided were "rudimentary"—a word the doctor used. If that meant what Jonah thought it did, what help would she offer him in exchange?

"There was something else in the dirt when the blue light no longer glowed. Markings."

All eyes fell upon him, and Doctor Anderson asked, "What markings? Did you take any pictures?"

"Yes. But my phone was stolen, as I have said. They were symbols, or some type of writing. I've never seen anything like them."

The doctor sent the soldier out of the room. When he returned, he placed a stack of papers and some pencils before Jonah. Not an artist or even a doodler, he tried his best to draw the symbols. As he finished each one, Doctor Anderson yanked it from the table and studied it carefully. From memory, Jonah drew seven symbols, but he told her he thought there were more.

When the door opened, a lanky man rushed into the room. A razor-sharp part on the side of his head split a puffy mound of hair. Without a word, he began flipping through the papers piled in front of the doctor.

Raising her tablet, Anderson pushed it into the newcomer huddling over her. She snarled at him and fastened a button on her blouse.

"Eyes on the tablet, Pat... It's not some *alien* language. It's probably Sumerian or Akkadian."

He took the device and studied it, raised one of the drawings, then looked back at the tablet. He did the same until he'd examined all seven symbols. "Even if you're right, Michelle, you don't find it strange that some random guy from Africa found markings in the oldest known written language in history at a place that happened to have the same blue lightning?"

"I'm sure there's a perfectly *reasonable* explanation that doesn't involve aliens who visited thousands of years ago coming back to say 'Hi' using the same language humans used back then."

"We're *all* waiting for yours, then. Tell us, self-professed dark-cloud expert, what are these markings, and how'd they get on the ground in Africa during a storm?"

After a scathing glare at the gloating man standing over her, Doctor Anderson leaned toward the V.P. and whispered something Jonah couldn't hear.

"Mister Blankson," she said. "Before we go to Ghana, I'd like you to meet someone."

Twenty-Five

No longer conflicted, Amy saw the couple's cloud madness as clear testimony of their failure to pass the final trial. In that poor girl's swirling, empty eyes, Amy saw no enlightenment. In the babbling of the young couple, she heard no revelation of truth. Tartagni's claim that Isis's repetition of "It's so beautiful" meant she'd seen the Celestial Maker sent a din of murmurs around the circle of elders before Ferguson called a recess. She needed to do research.

Reliable information on cloud madness proved less abundant than Amy had expected. After exhausting her brain with every conceivable search string, she saw a button to try the latest version of an AI-based assistant built into her web browser. Her first prompt about cloud madness yielded nothing new. Then, rushing in like a sudden stiff breeze, something she had *not* found before appeared as a notable result. She typed:

>*Have any cloud-madness sufferers said the words "It's so beautiful" or "Did you see" or "You must see"?*

The first result contained the words Isis had spoken, stating two cloud-madness sufferers were known to have said those words. The source was the US Climatological Society blog, posted by Dr. Michelle Anderson.

Having found what she needed, Amy clicked the source link to open the Climatological Society's blog site. Her fingers trembled with both fear and exhilaration as she filled in the contact form and entered a brief description of the young couple's experience under the clouds and the suddenly all-important phrase Isis had repeated. Until that moment, Amy had no idea where she would take the couple—only that she needed to help them any way she could.

Beyond submitting the form, using her personal email address and mobile number, she could do nothing. In seconds, her phone's screen came alive with a new alert—a text message received from a US number.

> *Thank you for submitting your experience with*
> *cloud madness. It is urgent that we speak with you.*
> *Please check your email for further information.*

In her excitement, Amy hurriedly opened the email app on her phone. The waiting tested her patience and the light hurt her eyes.

***

Alone in the darkness, Amy allowed Sato's words to loop in her mind. Sometimes, that man understood her more deeply than Alexandar ever did. What he pulled from the cavernous well that was her soul often surprised her. She had not considered it possible, but Amy felt more at a loss than ever as to how to think or feel. She knew what she wanted to do next but had no idea how or where to start.

When Amy didn't open her door to the loudening knocks reverberating through it, Sato sent her messages. Every few seconds, the faint glow of her mobile opened a crack in the blackness shrouding her in the silence of her chamber, disturbing the solace she wished to fall into. She turned her phone over and folded the end of the blanket over it.

Her one friend and confidant on the Council of Twelve, Sato, had been a lifesaver. The rare times she still petitioned the Celestial Maker, Amy thanked him—him/her/them/it, she had no idea—for Sato's companionship. More often, she thanked Sato for her sanity. Contemplating his friendship often resurrected memories of Alexandar. A new melancholy rushed into her—like nothing she had felt in decades, maybe ever, and a single tear joined itself to her loneliness. When that failed to soothe it, a flood of others followed, and she drowned herself in the quagmire of her reality, consumed by thoughts of escape.

And so Amy lived on and pondered the death of Elder Ferguson. Had that persona ever inhaled the breath of life or been more than a façade? Perhaps. Yet Amy felt no grief for her passing, only... relief.

Pulling herself through the shroud of darkness surrounding her bed, she sauntered toward her door without pausing to illuminate her way or don her elder cloak. When the hinges squeaked and light spilled onto her face, Amy walked out into the open, no longer concerned about the consequences of revealing herself from the shadows of her solemn heart. A cautious fright filled Sato's eyes as he watched her pass, and he followed her toward the Guide Couple's chamber.

In her flowing floor-length dressing gown, Amy passed Tartagni and Nickos without a glance or a care for the elder's reaction and laid her hand on Tilda's shoulder. The young servant stood and stepped away from the now-restful Isis lying on her bed. Amy knelt beside the young woman with burns healing under the cream and gently brushed her hair with her fingers. Placing her lips upon the girl's ear, she said, "Don't worry. I will get you out of here and get you proper help. Everything will be all right."

Amy didn't know how she would do those things, nor did she believe her own comforting words. It felt right to assure the misguided and abused young woman she had not thrown her life away in the naïve pursuit of induced fanaticism.

For some minutes, no one said a word or dared to move. As she stroked the semiconscious girl's head, Amy felt the eyes of Tartagni and Sato burning the back of her neck like cloud-storm rain. Such a beautiful creature. Her eyes held no hint of awareness. Searching her memories, the disillusioned elder recalled reading of many cases of cloud madness, but not even one of them had recovered their mental health. Many had died, and the remaining survivors were institutionalized. That didn't fit Amy's definition of survival.

Without addressing anyone in the room, Amy stood, cast a final glance at the peaceful and mentally unaware young woman, nodded for Tilda to resume her care for Isis, and exited. Sato and Tartagni followed, neither speaking until they stopped behind Amy. Standing in the center of those so-called holy stones, her feet sank into the flattened grass that had retained the shape of Nickos. As her eyes fell to the imprint of Isis, decades of tension fled her muscles. An unusual tranquility wrapped around her. Whatever happened next, Amy would be done with this, leave the cathedral, the Twelve, the Order, and never look back.

How to help Isis was a mystery Amy needed to solve. The answers were in an email that still hadn't come. Tartagni stepped before her, his heavy feet defiling the verdant memorial of a girl not yet dead but not fully alive. Until this moment, Amy would have used that description for herself.

"Elder Ferguson, your actions are highly irregular and not at all appreciated. As chairperson, you should be in your robe and leading us in the next stages of following the Guide Couple."

Staring at his feet, she replied, "You wish me to hold the ceremony now?"

"I wish you to fulfill your role... to follow the sacred Code."

Sato said, "Don't rush the process for your ambitions to replace Elder Ferguson as chairperson. She will follow the Code, as she always has."

Amy looked Tartagni in his trembling eyes.

"We have found the Guide. This is a glorious time," Tartagni said with a huff. "The Transition is upon us, and *she* mopes around as if something awful has occurred."

"They are *not* the awaited Guide Couple."

The color drained from Sato's face. He looked as shocked by Amy's words as she was.

"That's outrageous... And heresy." The red-faced Italian's raised finger nearly hit her nose. "How dare you profane the Guide Couple in this way. This is an—"

Wielding her authority as the still-seated chairperson, Amy raised a hand to silence the raging outburst Tartagni would likely have stretched into a long-winded and scathing denunciation.

"If you continue to insist the mumblings and rambling of those poor children signifies enlightenment and fulfills the foreshadowing of the Guide Couple, the council will vote."

Offering a welcome release, Tartagni stormed off into the inner sanctum, leaving Amy and Sato under the silvery glow of the after-storm moonlight.

With closed eyes, Amy raised her chin to the clear sky. "Sato, you know how I cherish your loyal support and friendship. All these years, you have kept me grounded, sane. Now I'm going to need your help... one last time."

Twenty-Six

Michelle couldn't be sure where this road would take her. The thought of O'Malley accompanying them, of being on a plane for hours with that pseudoscientist with a staring problem, almost brought her to nausea. As the V.P. made the travel arrangements, Nathan escorted Michelle and the man from Africa to the hotel across the street and up to her father's room.

After a brief update from the nurse regarding his preexisting heart condition, Michelle asked if there had been any "change"—her code word for asking whether her father had shown any signs of lucidity. Every time she asked, the answer was the same.

Blankson approached her father and rested his hand on his shoulder. "What is his name?"

"Hank," Michelle squeaked. "Hank Anderson."

"Hello, Mister Hank. I'm Jonah Blankson. It's a pleasure to meet you, sir."

After offering no response for a few seconds, her father twisted his neck to face the stranger.

"There you are."

"So beautiful." Her father lifted an open palm toward Blankson's face.

Without turning his gaze from her father, Blankson asked Michelle, "Had he stopped saying that since the storm passed, the one that took his mind?"

"Yes. How... how did you know that?"

"It was the same for Miss Ashanta, in my village. By the second day, she stopped speaking the words. Only mumbling after that. Then, after I saw the lightning on the ground, she ran to it and spoke those words again."

Nathan snapped his fingers loudly. "The blue lightning. It's connected."

"But my father had said nothing until now, with... *him*."

Michelle turned to the peculiar man peering deeply into her dad's eyes. Her father was looking into this man's eyes with equal wonder. He'd not looked with any focus or comprehension upon her or anyone else since going mad.

"It's you. There's something about you, Blankson," she said.

"I'm a simple man, as I have told you."

Nathan stepped closer to Mister Blankson. "You said that woman in your village ran toward the spot where the lightning came from the ground—that exact spot. She said the words there, with you. But it was *the lightning*." Turning to Michelle, he continued, "It *is him*... but it isn't. It's that mysterious blue lightning. Blankson's connection to *it* linked him to the woman in his village and now to your father."

Michelle chewed on that for a minute. She had no better theory or explanation for the connection this man had to the clouds, but she couldn't deny he had one. "What about the woman in your village—once she started speaking the words again, what did she do?"

For the first time since stepping into the hotel room, Blankson pulled his eyes from her father's and focused intently on Michelle. "She died. At that spot in the dirt, where the lightning had been."

No words formed in her clouded head.

"He must come to Ghana with us," Blankson said.

Michelle's contemplative pause gave Nathan room to object. "You can't be considering this. He's getting the best care here and..." He pointed at Blankson. "What did he just say? That woman died at that spot. Michelle, you can't be considering taking him there."

"It was the Mawu-Lisa. You needn't worry for your father."

Thinking this man had started blathering like he had cloud madness, Michelle said, "Sorry? Who is this Lisa and what does she have to do with my father?"

"The Mawu is the creator, ruler of the night. He spares people caught in the storm, leaving some mad while taking others away, like my Juliana. The Lisa rules the day. She claimed the soul of the old woman spared by Mawu as punishment for being caught in the storm. This is how our village elder explained it."

Shaking her head, Michelle said, "That's superstitious nonsense. O'Malley's ideas are more sound."

"I don't expect you to believe our ancient voodoo traditions. I don't believe them all myself. I do believe the blue lightning called Miss Ashanta for a reason, but perhaps she was too old and weak to survive the encounter."

Nathan pointed his thick finger at the drooling man. "He's in no condition to survive an... an encounter."

"Nathan, he has a point. Not the voodoo stuff. But that's a common thread in many cultures, as far back as we can trace humanity. These... *gods* either save us or condemn us to destruction. If we've found some ancient text, the people who inscribed it likely believed the same. Whatever's going on, my dad's part of it, and we're taking him with us."

Turning to the nurse, Nathan asked, "Can he travel?"

"His heart condition is under control. With his medication, he should be fine. The only thing... He gets rambunctious at times, trying to wander off and go out. Someone needs to watch him. Closely."

Taking her dad's hand, Michelle peered into his lifeless stare. "I'm his daughter. I'll take care of him... Nathan, get us to that plane."

***

The huge black Suburban pulled into the hangar. Giddy at the prospect of having two cloud-madness sufferers for her next experiment, Michelle clicked send on an email and tucked her phone into her back pocket. The aircraft looked like a black arrow that could slice through a building. After following Nathan out of the vehicle, Blankson ran around it to help Michelle pull her bag from the truck. All she had was a backpack for herself and one for her father. With three bags slung over his shoulders, Blankson headed toward the gleaming plane's few stairs.

A clang boomed, and a rush of high pressure chased it into the hangar. The thin corrugated metal walls surrounding the large space breathed in and out like giant lungs, and howls of warping metal played over the abrupt chaos like an out-of-tune trumpet. The general dropped the silver cases from his hands to steady Michelle and her father.

"What's happened?" Michelle's muffled voice pushed through the ringing in her ears. "Nathan, what happened?"

Without a word, he raced over to a small communication room carved out of the space by a modular wall. Blankson rushed to help Michelle with her feeble father. When the roof rattled, the three stopped midstride toward the plane. The clatter sounded like a tornado clawing at the sheet metal. A soldier in a leafy-green uniform raced toward the massive hangar doors that hung from a track. As he pulled one side across the gaping opening, a gust of wind grabbed it like a giant's hand and ripped it off. The tempest sucked the young man into the sky, his camouflage not enough to fool the sudden storm.

"It can't be a cloud storm," Michelle yelled.

Blankson helped her haul her father to the plane. Pat O'Malley had jumped back into the vehicle. Exhausted from the struggle, Michelle and Blankson couldn't get her father up those few steps into the plane. The roof plates shook and roared, and the hangar's walls flexed as if gasping for air.

One of the massive metal shingles peeled back to uncover a cloudless sky. No darkness outside—only peaceful calm, like in the eye of a hurricane. The air surrounding them quieted, the metal walls and ceiling at rest after the violence. Nathan emerged from the office.

"They're reporting it as a flash hurricane."

Cocking her head, Michelle said, "There's no such thing as a flash hurricane."

"Your office says differently. They say it formed suddenly over the Potomac River and came here."

"That makes no sense—not before the clouds, and certainly not since."

"We saw no rain," Blankson interjected, "but we did feel a storm."

Stepping out of the safety of the government SUV, Pat joined the conversation. "This was targeted."

"Pat, please. What, are aliens trying to stop us because we're onto something?"

Through a scowl, Pat said, "I think so, yes."

"It isn't even hard to dream this stuff up. It was weather. *Wea... ther.*"

"Okay, Miss High-and-Mighty-Meteorologist... What's your brilliant explanation, then?"

While she said nothing with her tongue, her eyes could have burned through his skull.

A sound like a freight train smashing into the hangar jolted everyone's bones as a second wave hit. The missing shingle presented a sky as clear as the storm's eye had been. The metal roof banged again, and the general ushered everyone onto the plane. A flight attendant sat on the floor, curled into the crash position. Nathan pulled the door closed with a thud and turned the locking handle tight.

"Pilot, get ready," he commanded. "As soon as this settles, get us out of here."

Twenty-Seven

A NEW EMAIL HAD arrived from Dr. Michelle Anderson of the US Climatological Society.

Miss Amy,

I must be brief, as I'm headed to Africa to investigate the second known case of a cloud madness sufferer saying "It's so beautiful." You indicated having another. We need to see them as soon as possible but cannot come to Norway before investigating something of great importance in Ghana. I will phone you as soon as possible. I have attached my personal contact card to this email.

Best,
Dr. Michelle Anderson, PhD, MDA
United States Climatological Society

Amy saved the contact on her phone and immediately tried calling the number. The call failed to connect. She sent a reply email. As briefly as possible, she explained her position in the cathedral and the financial limitations she would face once she left. To heighten the urgency of her situation, she stretched the truth a little. She wrote that she needed to leave immediately, as she felt herself and the young couple were in danger. Assuming this Doctor Anderson had a government plane that could make the journey from Washington, DC, to Ghana without fear of being caught in a cloud storm, she made a request—a plea, as she considered it.

Now she needed to amend her plan of escape beyond getting past Tartagni and out of the building with Isis and Nickos—if she could handle him. The cash box for miscellaneous expenses didn't hold much. If no one saw her take those five thousand kroner, it had to be enough.

As arrogant and ambitious as the man was, Elder Tartagni followed the rules and upheld the Code. He had refused to leave the couple's room, and Amy needed him out of there. She asked Sato to remind Tartagni of the need for him to review the ascension procedure outlined in the sacred text with each Guide Couple candidate individually before bestowing the honored title upon them. With the Twelve set to vote on the Guide Couple, she hoped Tartagni would readily agree to do it early this morning.

While this solved an immediate problem, it caused two others for Amy. It meant a rushed goodbye when she sent Sato from her chamber, and she wouldn't see him again to properly thank him. As he leaned into that parting embrace, she thought their lips would meet. But he lifted his chin and kissed her forehead.

Amy's only friend in the world stepped out of her room.

Out of her life.

In the Guide Couple's chamber, she found Isis sleeping calmly, thanks to a mild sedative. Nickos had left the room with Sato and Tartagni—the second problem her diversion plan had created. Looking like she had just woken, Tilda sat beside Isis. Now Amy faced a task that would either free the stunted cathedral servant or devastate her faith and possibly ruin her life. It depended on how the young lady saw it.

"Tilda." Amy hesitated. "I know some of my conduct and comments these last couple of days had you... a little concerned."

"I am here to serve, Elder Ferguson."

"Yes, and you have done very well, dear. Now, I'm afraid, I must again trouble you with my words."

The girl stood then looked back at Isis before locking eyes with her elder.

After a breath, Amy continued, "You're an avid student of the Code, are you not?" The young lady nodded. "Tell me, honestly, when you look at these two, what happened to them in the storm, does it seem to you they passed the final trial?"

"Humbly, I look to my elders, the Council of Twelve, for guidance."

Taking Tilda by the hands, Amy searched the girl's eyes, trying to find the individual underneath the zealot. "Forget the Twelve and Tartagni's self-righteous zeal to push the couple through. Dear child, I am asking you, Tilda, what *you* think. Look at them."

Tilda looked at Isis for a moment. The young aide's head dipped with what looked to Amy like the shame she recognized from her own mirror.

"Do you see enlightenment? Or... do you see madness? Simple cloud madness." The girl didn't reply, but Amy saw a new radiance lighting her eyes. "I think I found someone who can help Isis, but I can't get her off the grounds alone. What I ask is *not* a duty you must fulfill. Do you understand?"

"Yes, Mistress. If someone can help Isis, I wish to assist you."

A sigh of relief expelled a fraction of Amy's anxiety. "Thank you, dear. A car is waiting to take us to the airport."

"*Oslo?*" The high pitch of Tilda's voice betrayed her trepidation.

"If my request is granted, an airplane will meet us there."

Tilda's alabaster cheeks paled further. "You will take Isis on an airplane?"

"Hopefully. If Doctor Anderson comes through. What's wrong?"

Looking faint now, the young lady didn't answer.

"Oh, child, don't worry. I just need you to help me get Isis out of the cathedral and to distract the night guards. You... You've never been on an airplane?"

"Apart from films and television, I have never seen an airport."

***

Had Tilda's eyes been opened, or was this more misguided do-whatever-your-elder-asks submission? Amy couldn't know but welcomed the support. If they were careful, no one would learn of Tilda's participation, and the young lady could return to cathedral service or to whatever life she wanted to live. Amy hoped she would choose the latter.

With one arm each, Tilda and Amy hoisted Isis to her feet and led her out of her room. A small tote filled with what she'd taken from her chamber dangled from Amy's shoulder. All the possessions she now had in the world amounted to a mobile phone and charger, a scarf, a spring jacket, a folded paper map, a few pens, tissues, and a small notebook. Assuming it could be useful, Amy had also grabbed the binder full of documents she'd compiled on the Guide Couple. Tilda had nothing but the servant's pale-green cotton dress she wore and the sandals on her feet.

The mindless young woman they escorted had only a thin dress draped over her frail body down to her bare toes. Amy pulled the jacket from her bag and had Tilda slip it over Isis's shoulders, as even the warmer-than-usual pre-dawn air could still hold a chill this far North.

The other elders would soon wake and emerge from their chambers. It wouldn't take long for Tartagni to read the procedure to Nickos in Sato's presence. To give her as much time as possible, Sato would stall. It had to be enough. At least Isis had been quiet. Leaving Nickos bothered Amy. She had hoped to save both—though she wasn't sure exactly what salvation she had to offer. Getting out was as far as she had planned before contacting Doctor Anderson. Now she could take Isis to someone who could help.

One door stood between her and freedom. Then a walk across the grounds, through a locked gate, across a public square, and into a waiting car. When Isis began to mumble, Amy cupped a hand over her mouth. In the outer sanctum, Tilda pulled the handle of the exterior door. The three-meter-high wooden door squeaked open on its iron hinges.

Pausing at the point of no return, Amy asked, "Are you sure about this, dear?"

After examining Isis, Tilda nodded.

"You only need to distract the guards for a few minutes. Then, please, return to your quarters. Remember, you may choose to live your life *any way* you wish. I trust you to make wiser choices than I have."

A blue hue blanketed the landscape of the courtyard, making the bushes and short trees look like cartoon drawings. Isis perked up at being outdoors. The two night watchmen escorted Tilda through the rear garden, allowing Amy her chance to cross the front walkway. After fishing the skeleton key from her pocket, she stabbed it into the keyhole of the green metal gate. A touch of anxiety fled her bones when she heard the click. Struggling to manage Isis on her own, she raced across the square. The site of the waiting taxi permitted her shoulders to sag in relief.

A hand on her shoulder made her freeze.

Her loyal aide helped Isis climb into the back seat of the taxi. When Amy pulled her door closed, she raised her eyebrows at Tilda buckling her seatbelt. "Dear child. If you stay, no one will suspect your involvement. I can manage Isis from here. Go—live your life."

As she pulled the door shut with a thud, the young woman wore the unfamiliar face of certainty. As if in a spy thriller film with an army of armed guards in pursuit, Tilda slapped the back of the driver's seat and said, "Go, go, go."

No one had come out of the cathedral after them.

In poorly enunciated Norwegian buried under a thick Ukrainian accent, the driver said, "Where to?"

"Airport, Oslo."

"Lady, that's three hours. Expensive."

"How expensive? I have cash."

After a little haggling, they headed to Oslo. Soon Amy would learn if the freedom awaiting them lay within the secrets of the clouds. For the first time, she pondered what cloud storms could mean if not a foreshadowing of the Glorious Transition. Would she find a truth worse than what she read in the Code?

Twenty-Eight

The howling winds pummeled the metal building and shook the little aircraft within. Fierce gusts rocked Michelle worse than any bumpy country road her father had ever driven over in his old Suburban. Thoughts of what was causing that roaring tempest outside her pseudo-safety cage left no room for fear. Since the first cloud storm more than two years ago, no other types of storms had occurred on the planet. No hurricanes. Whatever they were in the middle of made no sense to Michelle.

After barking his order to the pilot, Nathan said nothing, his face glued to the window over the front-row seat. His leg twitched with ardor. Blankson's eyes stayed open and round as the flight attendant offered him reassurances she didn't seem to believe. O'Malley buckled himself into the other front seat and covered his ears.

With no plausible explanation of the freakish storm raging outside, a singular thought circled Michelle's brain in search of an answer. It came to rest on a coincidence. Never believing in coincidences, Michelle would have almost accepted aliens at this point.

"It's... *somehow*... attracted to us."

"I told you," O'Malley blurted.

Nathan turned his gaze from the window. "Michelle, what Doctor O'Malley is saying—"

"I have no idea. Something's pulling this weather phenomenon to us... like a magnet. We have two people connected to the storms in one place. And that blue lightning..."

Turning to Michelle, Pat said, "Lights from alien ships hidden in the clouds."

The rocking of the plane persisted. While Michelle ignored O'Malley, she couldn't ignore the possibility. And Nathan's straight brow suggested he was considering it as well.

"Blankson, you said you went into the lightning, right?" Michelle asked.

"Not exactly. It was more like a bubble of blue electricity around me."

After pulling her lips back from forming a word, Michelle took a breath. The bobbing lessened in intensity. "You said the blue light saved you from the rain and funnels. My father sat under the clouds and gazed into them for several minutes." She paused, examining the ceiling. "What if whatever people see in the clouds that's so beautiful *is* the blue lightning? This may be the first time two 'survivors'"—she used air quotes—"have been in the same place."

"I agree," O'Malley said.

Hearing Pat agree with her on something was refreshing—until he added, "These men have been contacted by the aliens."

Pulling back a half nod, Michelle showed no sign that she thought he could be even a little correct. If she accepted the possibility they were not alone in the universe, she couldn't accept that whatever was happening to her planet was beyond her understanding. Beyond her ability to fix.

The plane's thick rubber wheels squealed over the polished cement floor as they rolled toward the wide opening. Everyone buckled in, Michelle behind Nathan, her father across the aisle, and Blankson behind him. The flight attendant disappeared around the wall.

In a raised voice, Michelle said, "When the storms first came, they screwed up the weather cycles of the entire planet. And in recent months, it's only gotten worse. These storm phenomena have propelled global warming ahead by thirty years. We mostly have clear days and cloud storms."

All passengers swayed and resettled as the airplane banked onto the runway.

Blankson asked, "What was this storm? We saw no clouds, no poison rain."

"And we didn't see a hurricane or anything like any known storm. What we just experienced must be related to the cloud storms, or... a byproduct, a side effect."

"We were targeted," Pat insisted. "They don't want us making progress or discovering their existence."

"Patrick," Nathan said. "The V.P. put you on the task force to consider all possible—and impossible—options. But the president needs a scientific explanation."

"The evidence points to my conclusions. Besides, your pet scientist doesn't have any better explanation. Michelle's guessing, not... *sciencing*."

"My scientific guesses are credible. As I was saying..." Michelle paused as the acceleration of the takeoff pushed her into the soft beige leather. "I've studied the clouds for two years, as well as their effect on natural weather cycles. That storm back there was unlike anything produced by earth's climate or elemental weather patterns."

Nathan twisted in his seat to face her. "And you believe having your father and Mister Blankson in close proximity acted like... a storm magnet."

"It's the first known case of such an isolated weather incident in over two years. Cloud storms are global. *That*"—she pointed to the rear of the plane—"whatever it was, was localized, somehow, around these two men."

"Are you saying the clouds are intelligent?" Blankson asked.

"See? Even *he* gets it," O'Malley said. "Targeted storms, mysterious blue lightning, clouds *you* haven't been able to explain... No matter what you may personally think about my theories, when the *evidence* is clear and *you* have no other explanation, the thing left, no matter how improbable, must be true."

"You'd make a terrible Sherlock Holmes, Pat." She chuckled wryly.

Three thumps, a pause, and three more thumps turned everyone's attention to Michelle's father. He had his face pressed into the oval window. Blankson leaned forward and grabbed his arm. When the two men's eyes met, the obstreperous man instantly calmed.

"Miss Ashanta was the same," Blankson said. "The madness drives them outside."

"They want to see whatever beauty only they can see in the clouds. Somehow, without going mad, you have a connection with my father. Let's hope the answer's in your patch of ground in Ghana."

***

Morning light twinkled through the windows, and the smell of coffee filled the cabin. The flight attendant brought everyone a cup and a plate of eggs with "near-meat" sausages and toast. When Pat woke and returned from the restroom, his tray table was still stowed. Michelle's scrambled eggs had congealed. O'Malley snatched the fake sausage from her plate, jiggled it in her face with a juvenile grin, and ate it greedily. The pilot stood with the flight attendant, chatting through the steam swirling up from their cups. After draining his last drop of coffee, the pilot announced they would be landing shortly. When the flight attendant stepped from behind the wall with Pat's breakfast, her colleague returned to the cockpit.

"I'll phone the church lady when we land," Michelle said to Nathan. "Can I tell her the plane will be there?"

The general set his coffee cup on the tray table and turned to face her. "We'll send the plane to Oslo to get them."

With a mouthful of sausage substitute, O'Malley asked, "How long after touchdown will it take us to get to that encounter point?"

"A few hours," Nathan replied.

Theories she didn't want to admit were plausible aside, Michelle didn't care for Pat. Yet a fleeting thought crossed her mind that she tried to squash. At some level, Pat was right. Her indignation came from not finding the answers she sought. After two years, she had nothing more than this wild goose chase to bring her father and this farmer to a mysterious circle in the African dirt.

To break her train of thought, Michelle asked, "What time is it in Oslo?"

"Same as here," Nathan replied.

Seeing that she had a signal, Michelle dialed the number for Amy Ferguson. No one answered. If this was another "man from Africa" situation, it would take days to find her. A few seconds later, her phone rang.

"I just called you," Michelle said.

"Sorry. We're in a taxi to Oslo. The phone was in my bag."

After some back and forth about the plane going to get them and the expected time of arrival, Michelle cut to her main point.

"Did you get the girl out of the convent?"

"Cathedral, yes. We have Isis with us."

When the plane came to a stop, Nathan announced that their escort had arrived. Blankson sprang to his feet and began helping Michelle's father toward the door.

"This Isis is the one who saw the clouds and said 'It's so beautiful' and that we must look at them, right?"

"Yes."

The muggy air felt like the bathroom after a long hot shower. As Michelle placed her black-and-white Converse All Stars on the first step, she examined the unexpectedly modern and large airport.

Speculation ran rampant in her mind about the village this man came from. Mental projections of tiny mud huts with men in grass skirts and topless women with babies at their breast painted the scene. It had been a long time since she'd glanced at a National Geographic magazine, and she had to recognize that the image was skewed by ignorance and an unjustifiable stereotype.

"Doctor Anderson, can you help her?" the woman on the phone asked.

Studying Blankson dutifully assist her father, Michelle had no idea why all these people thought she, a meteorologist, could do anything to help them.

"I hope so."

Twenty-Nine

In the waiting area of the private terminal, Amy sat under the weight of her actions. Did Tilda have any clue what she was getting herself into? In many ways, the girl's childish innocence left her ill-prepared for the world. Yet Amy wondered the same about herself. What had *she* been thinking? Her former life had ended when she left the cathedral, left the Order, left all she had ever known.

"Be careful, and stay safe," Sato had told her.

Amy didn't think she had been careful or safe. Tartagni and the elders must have learned what she had done by now. Perhaps they were already pursuing them to rescue Isis from "the crazy old lady" who took her. Amy couldn't think of what would happen to Tilda if they caught up with them. It had been about six hours since Doctor Anderson said she would send the plane. A five-hour flight, if her estimation was correct.

The only "protection" for the fugitives and their kidnap victim was an overweight middle-aged man slouched against the doorframe. Amy had to hope no one suspected she had taken

Isis to Oslo airport. Isis had become fidgety, so Tilda walked her around the waiting room. The security guard with buttons straining to contain his beer belly reached into his pocket and handed something to Isis. With the girl calm, Tilda escorted her back to her seat.

In amazement, Amy watched as Isis fondled the fidget spinner. Her face looked more alert than it had since she'd lain under the clouds. Amy assumed her zeal and calmness during the trials might have been a mask, like the one Amy had worn for decades.

"How much longer?" Now Tilda fidgeted like nervous chihuahua.

"The plane should arrive soon."

"I have never even seen an airplane. Will we be safe... up there?"

With surprising strength, the frail young woman gripped Amy's hand.

"Air travel is quite safe. Tilda, dear... Are you *sure* about coming with us? I truly appreciate your help—you've been invaluable. But once we get Isis on the plane, I think I can take it from there."

"I think so, yes."

"You think I can handle it? Would you like to go back? Because I'm sure—"

"No. Not after what I have seen them do to this poor woman." Tilda examined Isis again. "Look what they have done to her."

Peering into those grey-blue eyes, Amy said, "No one knows you helped me. Everyone will assume you left the cathedral before I kidnapped Isis."

"*Kidnapped*? Is that... is that what we have done?"

"From their perspective, I should think so. And Tartagni is still convinced he has found the Guide Couple meant to lead us through the Transition."

"Elder Ferguson, do you—"

"Please, child, call me Amy."

Those words reddened Tilda's cheeks, and she looked away.

"I'm sorry for revealing my name, but you must realize, I am no longer anyone's elder. I have betrayed the Order. I have—"

"I understand. It will... take time to adjust."

Amy forced a consoling smile as Tilda continued, "What I was going to ask, if you do not mind..."

Amy nodded.

"Do you still believe in the Code?"

Although she expected such a question, it took Amy aback. "Do you?"

Studying the laminate floor, Tilda nodded. "I am not saying what Elder Tartagni, what we all did to the couple was right... I think *that* was against the Code. Do you believe the cloud storms herald the coming Transition?"

"I believe *something* is coming and these cloud storms are a harbinger. Of what, I don't know. The Code calls it the Glorious Transition. As with much of the foreshadowing, we will best understand it after it happens."

While Amy was unsure whether that answer proved satisfactory, at least Tilda lifted her head to make eye contact. Amy saw a softness in her eyes replace the worry they held for the last few hours.

"I like the hat," Tilda said.

While it covered her bald head as she hoped, Amy didn't care for the only hat the duty-free shop carried.

"Tilda, dear. You can return to your family and await the Transition. Maybe see the true Guide Couple—if they are ever found."

"All my life, I have done as people told me. My parents volunteered me for cathedral service, knowing what the elders sometimes... *require*. I was happy to serve—truly. Especially to serve you. You always treated me kindly and with respect."

"But child, this is a huge step, and there is no going back."

"All I have ever seen or experienced is our little town of Otta, its temple, and the cathedral. This is my first time in Oslo. The most exciting thing I have ever done was to go skiing. When I turned thirteen, all my time was devoted to my training. I *want* to go to Africa."

"I think your plane is here," the security guard announced.

***

Amy stood beside Isis and grabbed her arm. Sitting as though made of marble, Tilda didn't move. She didn't blink. She wasn't breathing. Shouts of her name couldn't rouse her from her comatose state. The pop of Amy's slap induced a blink. A sign of life. When Tilda's lungs drew an overdue breath, she began hyperventilating. Overcome by panic, Amy screamed.

Summoned by the commotion, the security guard rushed to their aid. His thick hand clasped Tilda's shoulder, and he said, "You're okay, dear girl. You're safe. Slow your breathing and inhale deeply."

Using his fingers, he formed Tilda's lips into a pucker and told her to keep them like that. He pressed one nostril closed. Alternating with each breath, the guard had her breathe through one nostril then the other until her breathing regulated. Sweating profusely, she turned as pale as a ghost.

Once she'd calmed, the guard told Amy to place a hand on the back of Tilda's neck and keep assuring her she was safe. "It's not uncommon with such intense fear of flying," he said. The gentle man went off to meet the plane taxiing up to the small terminal.

"Shh... Shh... You're safe, child. I'm here."

If not for the fidget spinner, Amy didn't know how she would have kept Isis still while she tended Tilda back to a coherent state. The guard returned and escorted Isis to the plane so Amy could assist her aide. Up from the chair and on shaky legs, Tilda's feet shuffled toward the door. When she saw the sleek black aircraft, she yelped.

Trembling, Tilda said, "I do not think I can do this. I am sorry, Mistress."

"Nonsense, child. You have done so much. That taxi driver said he would wait by the main terminal for the morning flight. I will offer him what money I have left to take you home."

The girl's eyes filled with tears. "I wish to accompany you. To help with Isis."

When Tilda tried a step forward, she collapsed in Amy's arms. The elderly woman struggled to keep her upright. Despite the help she would need with Isis and her wish for Tilda to be free, Amy realized what she must do. As she prodded Tilda back toward the waiting area, two black SUVs raced toward them. Sirens wailed, and blue lights strobed through their windscreens.

Exiting the plane, the helpful guard said, "Now or never."

***

Looking out the window at the pure azure sky, Amy tasted freedom for the first time in her life. The horizon stretched over the Sahara's golden-brown waves of sand with reddish sparkles of sunlight fondling the creased lines defining the dune ridges.

She could only imagine what the crisp-suited flight attendant must have thought of them. Their race down the runway pursued by the police. Isis in her sleeping gown with the remains of healing boils on her face and arms. The old woman whisking her off to Africa. And the naïve young lady following along like a loyal puppy. An anxious concern blended into an unusual cocktail of emotions as Amy felt excitement, anticipation, and worry flooding her like divergent rivers funneled into one.

Once Isis tired of her new toy, she settled and fell into a deep slumber. Tilda had finally fallen asleep too. Given a sick bag to control her breathing, Tilda wouldn't release her white-knuckle grip on the armrests to use it. Amy had held it to her face until her breathing had calmed. Closing the window shade beside her had helped. Now Amy studied the peaceful faces of her young companions. Dozing on and off herself, her mind didn't allow more than short breaks from its frantic conceptualizing of every conceivable what-if scenario of her new adventure.

These girls were children, born into a confusing and complicated world and with a demanding faith thrust upon them by nothing more than the family line from which they sprouted. All they knew, Amy had ripped from them like a bandage. She had to hope it would lead to healing—emotional, spiritual, psychological—and all other forms of inner growth it was possible to achieve in their abrupt liberation.

Amy had no guarantees to offer Tilda in exchange for her assistance. Taken without consent from her world, did the gentle pleading for help Amy inferred in Isis's eyes justify sneaking her out of the cathedral, onto this plane, and off to Africa?

Time, Amy hoped, would provide the answers she needed. Not part of the Guide Couple, could this young woman hold a special role in understanding the clouds? Perhaps she would aid in some—dare Amy call it—*transition* to a healed world. In this, Amy found more purpose than in the seven decades of her prior life.

This became her new faith.

Part Three
Ground Zero

Thirty

As THEY RODE THROUGH the Ghanaian countryside, Jonah explained how it had been much greener before the clouds. Doctor Anderson said the ride was another obstacle delaying her from finding the answers she needed. About halfway to the village, the general received a call from the V.P. and handed the phone to Anderson. After some back-and-forth, she switched to hands-free mode.

"You're on speaker, sir."

"I'm betting the farm on you, Michelle. Your friend Kournikova says the recent storms, the most severe we've seen thus far, are advancing the timetable. She wants to sound a worldwide shelter-in-place advisory and says we have little time, given the rapid rate of increase she's measured since the last storms. If we get more storms like that, she says max, three months."

"I know, Natasha sent me her data. Listen to her, Barnes—she's brilliant. You should have sent her with us instead of O'Malley. Now let me get on with trying to figure out how to stop these cloud storms and save the planet."

***

The Humvee rocked with a steady rhythm. Jonah had managed a couple of hours of shut-eye. Looking at Doctor Anderson clicking away on her laptop, he wondered if she had slept at all. He could hardly believe he had found her, she'd agreed to help, and now was here with him in Ghana. Seeing her focused determination, he knew she would help him get Juliana back.

Leaning over the large hump between seats, Jonah indulged his curiosity with a stolen glance at O'Malley's tablet. The article about UFO sightings in the dark clouds held the doctor's undivided attention until Jonah pressed his finger into the smooth glass to point to a photo.

"Is that what is in the clouds?"

As if Doctor O'Malley had just become aware of Jonah's existence, he twisted his head and stared at him, open-mouthed. Turning back to the tablet and wiping the screen with his shirt, he said, "Despite what *some people* say, alien activity is the most plausible explanation for all this."

"Can it, Mulder." Anderson didn't free her eyes from her laptop.

"I'll take that as a compliment. Even if you're no Scully. Although... the red hair would look sexy on you." He snickered, and Doctor Anderson waved off his comment.

Jonah's blank expression broadcast his confusion.

"It's from The X-Files. You know, the TV show. She just compared me to a brilliant FBI agent whose belief in aliens was *proved true*."

"Then I'm glad to see you two are getting along better now."

A puff of air passed through Anderson's pursed lips.

Enlarging the photo on his tablet, O'Malley's eyes twinkled with excitement. "No one's gotten a decent photo of the clouds. They're too dark and interfere with all kinds of equipment. I had hoped the million-dollar camera we used at the Pentagon would capture a better image."

"This image is not clear."

"Not clear enough to capture a craft. However, we did see a trace of blue lightning for the first time. That's what's got Michelle's panties in a wad."

"Doctor Anderson said we would help each other. If she needs new undergarments, I will be happy to purchase some for her."

After a chuckle, O'Malley whispered, "Watch your back with that one. You didn't meet the team. Brendon, Doctor Doyle, is a more experienced meteorologist, much better than Anderson'll ever be. She pushed her way into that cush job she has."

Jonah's face withdrew. "Doctor Anderson is the leading expert on cloud storms."

"Because she stole Doyle's job. Of the entire storm task force, the only field we have doubled up is *two* meteorologists. Yep. One of everyone else." He cast a hard gaze at Anderson and pulled his eyes back to Jonah. "She's nothing more than the pretty face they put on the storms, the so-called expert. I'm sure you can guess how she got her job."

"She is a brilliant scientist."

O'Malley's head bobbled. "*Right*. Let's just say, she knows how a woman gets *on top* in DC, if you get my meaning."

Jonah did not but decided not to pursue the topic. Doctor Anderson said she would help him find Juliana, and she had the full confidence of General Nathan Tucker and the vice president.

"I don't know if the answer will be found in alien spaceships or scientific discovery, but I am confident it will come. And we will find my Juliana. Of that, I am sure."

After laying a slap on Jonah's shoulder, O'Malley smiled. "Well, Farmer Brown, I admire that optimism. Looking on the bright side, if we don't find our answers in time, we won't have to live with the failure for long, will we?"

***

The convoy rolled to a smooth stop about a mile from Jonah's village. When they stepped out, he saw what looked like a refugee camp. Not long ago, not far from here, a field had been full of white tents labeled with UNHCR in thick blue letters. The refugees had mostly come from Côte d'Ivoire, with displaced Nigerians filling similar camps on the eastern border. The storms had only amplified the worldwide migration crisis.

A soldier named Commander Rodriguez greeted them. Doctor Anderson protested the general's direction to be shown their quarters first, insisting she be taken to the science lab. Only when Rodriguez told them the lab tent had not been set up did she comply. Most of the equipment was being unloaded. On the way to the habitat tents, Rodriguez pointed out the shower and restroom facilities and something called a "mess hall." Its description answered Jonah's unasked question.

A team of scientists was on their way from around the world. When Doctor Anderson questioned why they left most of their task force in DC to bring in other experts, General Tucker told her the V.P. wanted his team to stay on task, working with any data she would send them with full cooperation of the DOD and every resource of the US government.

"Alright," Doctor Anderson said. "While the G.I. Joes finish setting up my lab equipment, let's go to ground zero."

***

The ride in the Humvee jostled them as they drove through fields, crested small hills, and advanced over bumpy terrain. As they entered a clearing of endless grass under an endless blue sky, Anderson asked the general if he had any update on the plane sent for Miss Ferguson. It had collected its passengers and was headed back to Accra.

Anderson explained her theory of putting people connected to each other by the dark clouds together. With no scientific or logical explanation of why or how she thought that would work, she expressed certainty that it would do something. On that, O'Malley agreed.

They were all jerked forward by the abrupt stop. Anderson flung her door open and climbed down from the vehicle. Jonah and Nathan helped her dad down. As the "expert" for this part, Jonah led this team of a meteorologist, a US general, and an exobiologist to the tree line. Rodriguez stayed behind with Mister Anderson. When O'Malley pulled a tin hat from his bag and placed it on his head, Anderson exhaled a mock chuckle.

"'I want to believe,' eh?" She pointed to the hat and grimaced. "I want to believe... you look like an idiot."

"You may end up begging me for one of these mind-scan protection helmets."

"Everyone," General Tucker said in a commanding voice. "Let's get those scanners or whatever doohickies you brought and get started. This is why we came all this way."

With a hand gesture from Doctor Anderson, Jonah crept forward and entered the tiny forest, tiptoeing between the trees. Moisture pooled under his arms.

"Don't be nervous," Anderson said. "There's no storm. Nothing to worry about."

"Whether this is from science, aliens, or the Mawu-Lisa, Doctor Anderson, we cannot know it is safe."

When Jonah halted, Anderson bumped into his back. They all stopped. As if on the precipice of a towering cliff, Jonah stepped aside. Anderson pressed forward. Laying eyes on it for the first time, she gasped and studied the perfect circle of packed dirt. On her knees, she leaned forward, flattened hand extended, and examined the phenomenon. The ground within the circle had the appearance of old metal. Anderson's silver camera case resisted her efforts to open it. After finally freeing the camera and cursing her first shot of solid black, she removed the lens cap and snapped dozens of photos.

"Blankson, hand me the Geiger counter... That thing by your foot."

Crackles and pops emitted from the device as Doctor Anderson waved it over the circle. Back on her feet, she continued scanning the surrounding trees. The general asked if it was safe.

"More or less, yes." Anderson looked up from the device. "It's tipping two hundred just above ground zero, but less in the surroundings."

"I thought one fifty was the high side of safe. Two hundred could be dangerous."

"I wouldn't pitch a tent and camp for the night, but it should be safe enough."

O'Malley chuckled mockingly. "You're supposed to be a scientist. Aren't numbers sort of your thing?"

"What are you worried about? You have that hat to protect your tiny brain."

Commander Rodriguez called the general to say he was having difficulty keeping the older man contained. Instructing him to keep Mister Anderson there, the general left to help him do that.

Anderson and O'Malley set up scanning devices. Doctor Anderson explained they would measure radiation, thermometry, seismic activity, air density, moisture, pressure, and electrostatic activity. Dutifully, the machines logged their findings. Initial readings would give them a baseline, and the data collection would continue 24/7, with a live webcam feed being recorded. Hoping what they were doing would lead to finding his wife, Jonah understood little of that.

Addressing Anderson, O'Malley asked if the two "storm-connected" people should step inside the circle. "Blankson and your father have been in proximity the entire time on the plane and the journey from Accra. Nothing's happened. If you believe in their connection to the clouds, it's the next logical step."

After initial hesitation, she said, "We need to test it first."

"Blankson's already been in it, during a storm, and he's fine."

Without a word of rebuttal, Doctor Anderson stretched her leg over the circle and took a long step. Yanking her other leg in, she stood in the center of the mysterious ring. Nothing happened.

"Geiger counter me," she demanded.

O'Malley obliged and made rapid "blip" noises with his mouth when he passed the wand over her rearend and chest. She balled her fists at her hips but said nothing. "No change. You're just as hot—I mean, *radioactive*—as before."

As if playing "the floor is lava," she hopped out and said her father and Blankson should go in the circle. Jonah set off to collect the others.

Thirty-One

After waking and using the restroom, Tilda devoured the sandwich and water the courteous flight attendant provided. The plane's almost imperceptible steady motion seemed to put her at ease enough to resist hyperventilating again. After brushing back a lock of white-golden hair from Isis's forehead, Tilda clasped the armrests. In those youthful blue eyes, Amy envisioned how a daughter or, more realistically at her age, a granddaughter might have looked upon her. One of many things she had forfeited for her people's faith.

"I guess you answered my previous question about your arranged marriage."

Dropping her eyes to the aisle between them, Tilda nodded sheepishly. Everything she did, she did sheepishly. Amy hoped that would soon change.

"Tilda, dear. I'm still unsure why you chose to come. I'm afraid I have no guarantee to offer you of what we'll find in Ghana. While I hope this Doctor Anderson can help Isis, I have some doubts anyone can recover from cloud madness."

As the flight attendant came to collect the plates and cups, she announced their approach to Accra. After checking that their seat belts were fastened, she disappeared again behind the wall.

"I truly hope to be of assistance to you," Tilda said.

"Child, I am no longer your elder. And you are no longer obligated to serve anyone."

"Not that." Hands clamping the armrests, the girl turned her cautious gaze out the window for the first time. "I never thought I'd see the world like this. From an airplane, I mean. The sky is full of such extraordinary beauty. Looking up from the ground, I never imagined it."

Giving Tilda the moment of contemplation, Amy didn't press further. "It's beautiful."

"Mistress, what beauty do you believe Isis saw in the clouds?"

Leaning over, Amy took Tilda's hand. "You may call me Amy, or Miss Amy, if you prefer. As for Isis, I don't know. She may not be part of the Guide Couple, but I believe she is special."

"I believe so as well." With a nod, Tilda added, "She is one of very few who have seen something beautiful in the dark clouds. I believe that may be the Celestial Maker. If it is, and the people we will meet in Africa have also seen it, we need to take her there. I believe we can help Isis. And, perhaps, you will find what you are searching for."

"This is my wish, and why I am doing this. And it's my hope, dear Tilda, that you, too, will find what you need to move forward and live your life."

Thirty-Two

A TINGLE CLIMBED JONAH's body from his feet like the needle pricks of stepping into icy water. The man in his arms mumbled on, unaffected by the enigmatic ring in which they stood. Jonah looked up to the sky, unsure what he expected to see beyond the treetop canopy. The patchwork of pure azure fighting through the brownish-green leaves gave him the sudden realization that he felt nothing beyond his own anticipation.

He hadn't stood this long in the circle during that storm and didn't know how long he had been lying there before he woke and ran home. The Mawu-Lisa god and whatever otherworldly powers he expected—feared, if he were honest—to encounter when he stepped into the circle did not greet him. He could have been standing on any patch of dirt in Ghana, anywhere on the African continent, or anywhere in the world.

Unsure whether he should be relieved or disappointed, Jonah looked to Doctor Anderson with a thousand questions written on his face. The foremost of those had put him there. Standing in this unholy place, Jonah didn't know how this would help him find Juliana. He had to hope the African proverb would prove true with the American scientist—hands wash each other.

"Anything?" The scientist had only questions of her own.

"I feel nothing. Do you see anything on us, any blue light?"

"Nothing. Dad, what do you see? Anything... *beautiful*?"

Mister Anderson paused his babble to look at her for a second then turned back toward Jonah and resumed his incoherent mumbling. Unconcerned about the future of the storms, the damage the clouds had done and would do to the environment, Jonah's mind shifted to one horrific thought. If he had brought Doctor Anderson and her team all this way for nothing, if he couldn't help her in her research, would she still be willing to help him recover Juliana? How did a person with one hand wash it?

"I don't understand. In DC, the two being together brought that storm. I was sure of it. Why's nothing happening now? This spot's clearly connected to the storm. The two of *them* are. Nothing's happening. Where's my blue lightning?"

Jonah hadn't heard such desperation in the woman's voice thus far. It had exuded confidence and certainty—and occasional annoyance at Doctor O'Malley—but never such perplexity. True, he'd known her for mere hours. Until this point, Doctor Anderson had measured up to his conjectures of the person he needed to help him find his wife. Now he watched her sink into a mire of doubt. On seeing this, Jonah tried his best to submerge what was mounting within him. It felt like mourning.

Squinting at the tree canopy above, Doctor O'Malley said, "It doesn't seem like they're ready for us."

"Who's not ready?" the General asked.

"He means our alien invaders," Anderson snapped. "Blankson, come out of there. If nothing else, my *esteemed* colleague is correct about the timing not being right."

Shaking his head, O'Malley said, "Michelle. When are you gonna admit this whole thing is beyond your—I mean, beyond *our* scientific knowledge."

"Clearly, we're dealing with weather phenomena, and your expertise is invaluable." General Tucker hunched down to look Doctor Anderson in the eye. "But you're one part of a team, all experts in various fields. Doctor O'Malley is on this expedition, or whatever it is, because the science behind this threat is beyond our understanding."

After a lengthy back-and-forth, Anderson agreed to return to the camp to set up the lab. At the very least, she postulated, they had accomplished something. With a final check of the sensors they'd placed around what she called "ground zero," they returned to the Humvee.

Silence accompanied them on the bumpy ride back until General Tucker asked Doctor Anderson what their next steps entailed. One point she and O'Malley agreed upon was that they needed to visit the ring again with the other cloud-madness victim.

"Where is the nun with my other cloud-madness subject?" Anderson asked.

The general said, "From what I know about the Order, she was much more than a nun. Amy Ferguson served on the Council of Twelve, the ones running the whole thing. They have millions of adherents around the world."

"And she abandoned *that* to bring a victim of their... *zeal* to us?"

"Didn't she tell you that she hopes you can help the girl? Michelle, please tell me you didn't promise that. We've made no progress with your father."

"*We*, Nathan? You mean me. *I* have made no progress. I hoped him and Blankson being here"—she pointed out the rear window—"at ground zero would have done... something. I'm sure there's an answer here. Maybe with three of them, with this other cloud-madness victim who saw beauty in the clouds, we can find it."

Nodding adamantly, O'Malley said, "I agree. We try again when she gets here."

"I hope you do find a way to cure your father," General Tucker said. "And this young lady coming here. I really do. But we have the future of our environment to think of first. Doctor Kournikova says we have less time than we thought."

After a long sigh, Anderson said, "I'm well aware of Natasha's updated projections. We have a few months, at best. And you never answered me... Where are they?"

"They landed in Accra a few hours ago. They should be halfway here by now."

Thirty-Three

THEIR LONG, ARDUOUS JOURNEY reached its end in an open field littered with white tents. Isis had stared out the window with an open mouth for the duration of the ride in the massive vehicle that felt cramped inside. Now Amy had to hope everything she had sacrificed, all she had stolen from Isis and Tilda, would be worthwhile.

With little more than the clothes on their backs, the three exited the vehicle to be greeted by a tall man in green camouflage. He introduced himself as Commander Rodriguez and offered to have someone fetch their bags.

Amy handed him her tote. As he examined it, a barely audible chuckle escaped through Amy's sigh. "We left in a hurry."

The man dressed as a tree looked Isis up and down with greater confusion than he had shown for their lack of luggage. Amy examined the poor girl dotted with burn marks and wearing only her night dress. Their trio must have been quite a sight for anyone unfortunate enough to look upon them—from the taxi driver to the guard at the airport, the flight attendant, and now Commander Rodriguez. What would Doctor Anderson think of this motley bunch?

"Accommodations are basic. You'll bunk with Doctor Anderson in a habitat tent." Looking them over again, Rodriguez added, "I'm afraid we don't have much in the way of clothes or supplies to offer."

"I'm sure it will be fine. Maybe we could... freshen up a bit before we meet Doctor Anderson?"

"She's anxious to meet the young lady... but of course. You've had a long journey. Let me escort you to the facilities tent."

Once again, Tilda proved a loyal and invaluable companion as she tended to Isis. Amy knew she would have struggled to manage without her help. When she caught sight of herself in the mirror over the sink, that thought solidified into reality. Although her newfound freedom imbued her with the pseudo-vigor of youth, she looked older now. Even her once smooth-as-an-egg-shell shaved scalp had wrinkles. She tossed on the French-style, curled-brim hat she'd bought at the Oslo airport to hide the unladylike sight.

Tears rolled over the bags drooping from her exhausted eyes—eyes holding deeply ingrained doubts she tried to convince herself she didn't have. Now that they had arrived here, in this wondrous landscape of Africa, would these children with her be free?

Outside the facilities tent, Tilda and Isis were nowhere to be found. An unknown but recognizable woman stood there, arms crossed, under the late afternoon sun. Doctor Anderson extended her hand and introduced herself by her formal title. After the initial *pleasantries* concluded, Amy asked about Isis. She assumed Doctor Anderson had already taken her for observation and whatever tests she might conduct on the poor girl. Neither expected the other not to know the young lady's whereabouts. Doctor Anderson ran off without another word. Not knowing what else to do, Amy hurried along at a slower stride and followed her into a tent.

"…has no idea where the girl went." Doctor Anderson spoke abruptly with a distinguished man in a crisp military uniform. "They went to wash up, and by the time Miss Ferguson came out, Isis had run off with the other girl."

The man stood and tugged the end of his double-breasted jacket. Without knowing its significance, Amy assumed the mosaic of tiny colored squares covering the upper-left side of his chest meant he held a rank of some import in the United States military. He extended his hand and introduced himself as General Nathan Tucker with exponentially more grace and politeness than Doctor Anderson had shown.

Turning from the general to Amy, the doctor, who was clearly all business said, "Do you have any idea which way they went?"

"No, I'm sorry. As you said, they were gone when I came out. They couldn't have exited more than a few seconds, at most a minute, before me."

"They must be headed for the ring. Nathan, we need to go find her. And someone's got to get my father."

"We will."

"The ring?" Amy asked.

Ignoring the question, Anderson marched out of the tent, leaving Amy with the general. Several machines hummed, and computer screens lit the tent with graphs and charts. The tall and thick general apologized on Doctor Anderson's behalf and escorted Amy outside. In the distance, Anderson had shrunk into the brownish-green waist-high growth. With a wave of an arm, General Tucker summoned the commander who had first welcomed them to the camp.

The three climbed into a small open vehicle and sped off after the tiny doctor. They caught up to her in seconds, and she climbed in, her chest heaving with heavy breaths. As the four-wheeler drove on, they spotted Tilda. Ahead of her, the waves of a silken gown wafted like a wake behind Isis as she ran toward the approaching tree line.

They passed Tilda and caught up to Isis. Anderson jumped out first and grabbed the young lady by the arm. Isis pulled against the grip, flailing, about to break free. As Amy reached for her, Isis tripped over her own feet and fell onto her backside. Tilda ran up and knelt beside the mumbling, frantic girl and adjusted her gown. With shushing noises, she stroked her head as if to calm an upset child.

A deep voice from behind said, "How'd she know where to go?"

Amy turned squinted eyes to Rodriguez, who looked intently at Doctor Anderson.

"Something must be pulling people with cloud madness. Maybe it's an audio frequency we can't detect, or a pheromone of some kind. Or it could be a form of biomagnetism." After a pause to look at the trees, she added, "Strange—my father didn't run off there."

"That villager did," the general replied. "But we brought your father straight to the ring. If we'd delayed, he might have run off for it too."

"Where is this inflicted villager now? Is he at the ring?" Confused by this entire scene, Amy added, "Oh, and what is the ring?"

Piercing Amy with her steely gaze, Doctor Anderson said, "She's dead. Ran to the ring, said 'It's so beautiful,' and dropped dead."

"You brought us to this ring, knowing it could kill Isis?"

"We know little about anything going on here," the doctor confessed.

The general hunched to set his steady eyes upon Amy. "We don't believe that elderly woman's death was caused by the ring. That's a place on the ground where this young lady was headed. We believe it's related to the dark clouds. Doctor Anderson's own father is also a cloud-madness sufferer, and we had him in the ring earlier today. Nothing happened to him."

"Thank you for clarifying that, General."

"Ma'am, you may call me Nathan."

"Again, thank you." Turning to Doctor Anderson, Amy said, "If I understand correctly, you needed to have Isis here with the other... um, with your father. In your email, you mentioned three. If that villager died, you only have two."

Nodding, the doctor said, "We also have Jonah Blankson. He discovered the ring, and it protected him from the madness. And from the rain and the funnels. He may be the only one in the world who has survived outdoors during a storm without going missing, succumbing to cloud madness, or ending up dead."

"I see. And you said Isis could somehow help you in your research to find a way to stop the storms. I do hope so. But, Doctor, I brought her here to get her the help I believed you could provide. Can you help her? Is there a cure for cloud madness?"

Doctor Anderson stared at the grass below her feet. "No. But I believe the answer is here, in the ring." Lifting her eyes to the general, she said, "We need my father here—now."

Thirty-Four

Since Jonah's mother-in-law offered, O'Malley graciously accepted a plate of jollof rice. He also insisted Jonah call him Patrick. The aroma of roasted tomatoes and spices filled the home. Jonah recounted his trek to America and the ordeal he had endured trying to find Docter Anderson. While the aged woman didn't quickly relinquish hope, her voice had lost its optimistic timbre in the week since Jonah had said goodbye and hopped aboard that bus to Accra.

Clean clothes awaited him along with the hot meal. Between his wife and mother-in-law, Jonah had always been well cared for and comfortable. His role in this family had him working the field while Maame looked after the house and Juliana sold her wares at the market. Evenings together filled this modest home with warmth and love, a mundane existence he longed to restore once he found his lost wife. He couldn't imagine going on without her.

With all the care of feeding one of the village preschoolers, Maame helped Mister Anderson eat, all the while trying to coax a dictionary word from his mouth. Jonah added a spoonful of *shito* to his rice, and his mother-in-law smiled. "It's Juliana's," she said. "She made it—oh dear, I mean *makes* it—almost as good as me." Her eyes filled with tears.

Jonah rested a hand over hers. "You taught her very well, Maame."

When Patrick's mobile phone played a melodic song, he said, "X-Files theme."

After several "Ah-ha" replies into his phone, Doctor O'Malley hung up and reported that the religious women had arrived and that the girl with cloud madness had taken off running toward the markings in the woods. He stood and said they needed to go.

Jonah struggled to pull Mister Anderson from the table, but with O'Malley's help, he managed. A Humvee pulled up as they stepped out, and Maame wished them luck.

***

As soon as they reached the tree line by the ring, Doctor Anderson ran up to them. "Is my father okay?"

"Well fed and content. See for yourself," Patrick replied.

Turning to the general, Anderson said, "How could you let Pat take my dad?"

The burly yet gentle general hunched to look her in the eyes. "You know how he gets. He needs to walk. When Jonah went to see his mother-in-law, O'Malley took your father along."

Anderson's shoulders relaxed. "Well, Blankson's been good with my dad."

"As was O'Malley."

Replacing the red-cheeked aggravation, the usual fierce determination returned to Anderson's face. "I need my dad, Blankson, and the girl with me."

"Isis. She is called Isis," the elderly lady said.

Calling the young lady by name, Jonah introduced himself. Isis said nothing in return. Another young woman named Tilda spoke politely and with the utmost respect in her tone.

"I need everyone else to stay here," Anderson ordered.

"No," the older woman protested. "Isis needs help, and it looks like your father does as well. I'm responsible for her, so I'll escort her to this ring of yours."

The lady reached out and struggled to hold Isis. Young Tilda quickly assisted her.

Anderson grimaced. "If you insist on helping, help."

"I've got her. Let's go see this magic ring."

Jonah led, holding tightly onto Mister Anderson as the man's daughter held his hand and walked beside him. Once they started walking, the barefoot teenager in the nightgown needed no assistance. Her elderly escort struggled to keep the girl's excitement and energy at bay.

At the small clearing between the massive trees, they studied the two-meter perfect circle with its twelve engraved symbols no computer or human had yet deciphered. The closest comparison they had found was to ancient Akkadian, but some authorities Doctor Anderson had consulted told her they more closely resembled those of its "mother" civilization of Sumer. When Jonah had asked her who they were, she told him the Sumer were the oldest recorded people on earth, from earliest Mesopotamia, which was modern-day Iraq. Jonah had heard of Iraq and settled on not needing to know the rest.

Oddly, Patrick O'Malley's explanations were easier for Jonah to follow when he and Doctor Anderson had argued on the airplane. His theory was that aliens must have visited earth even before the Sumer civilization and left markings. Perhaps they were the ones who taught early man to read and write. Not understanding science and doubting his village traditions of voodoo and ancient gods and goddesses ruling the night and day, Jonah figured, why not aliens? Even the vice president of the United States of America kept that option on the table, as the American saying went.

"Let's do this." Again, Doctor Anderson took the first step into the ring.

Assisting Mister Anderson into the circle didn't require much effort from Jonah. The older gentleman eagerly stepped onto the hard, metal-like surface. When the girl called Isis also willingly entered the space, her caretaker followed. What had seemed large for an unusual circle of flat empty space in the otherwise lush detritus, now felt cramped with five people standing in it.

"Nothing's happening." Anderson looked up into the forest's crown with little left of the dwindling sunlight diffusing through. "What do you want from me?" she yelled to the sky.

"It's you and the older woman," Patrick said. When Anderson looked at him with a stern, cold face, he explained, "We agree these three, specifically, are linked to this artifact. You two aren't."

"That's decent scientific reasoning... *Mulder*."

Once the lady in the funny hat released the thin girl with scars on her face and Doctor Anderson let go of her father's hand, the two madness sufferers raised their arms and embraced the sky. With bright eyes and mouths open as if to catch the drops of twilight trickling through the treetops, the two with Jonah looked up. When Jonah did the same, salty sweat leaking from his brow stung his eyes.

Once again, the pinpricks wrapped around the thin skin over his shin bones and up his thighs. No visible signs manifested. No blue light. If the women were hindering it, Jonah thought he could have been as well. But as the doctor insisted, Jonah had a connection, so he remained in the circle.

Looking at the wonder-filled faces of the two beside him, he noticed their chanting of nonsense had changed. In unison they said, "It's so beautiful." Jonah squinted upward to match their gaze but saw only the purple haze breaking through the thickness of leaves crowding the canopy above. First Mister Anderson then Isis asked him, "Can you see it?" He saw nothing beautiful besides the evening sky. What did they see that he did not?

"So... beautiful," they repeated.

Doctor Anderson became almost giddy—a side of her Jonah hadn't yet seen. "They're saying it! Something's happening. Blankson, do you see or feel anything?"

"No, nothing."

As the words escaped his lips he felt it—felt something. The familiar crackle that haunted his ears like a nightmare that day he got caught in the storm surrounded him.

"Blankson," someone yelled.

Pulling his eyes from the sky, he looked at the earth below his feet and saw what these people had all come to Ghana to see. It was... indescribably beautiful.

Thirty-Five

"There it is. There it is. Putting them in the circle brought the blue lightning." Anderson rocked on her feet. "Blankson, what do you feel in there? Can you feel the lightning?"

No reply came from the spectacle of swirling electric blue. Doctor Anderson's subjects were trapped inside their own personal laser light show. Daring the closeness, the spectators all leaned forward. Isis's eyes shone as they had when the storm had taken her mind, with that same glimmer of awe and wonder. What those eyes saw beyond the dome of a crystal-like webbing of electricity, Amy couldn't guess.

When she extended her hand toward Isis, the force of the phenomenon pushed back. It didn't hurt. Amy felt as if something had warned her to stay away. It almost had the sensation of... communication.

The general said something about the scanners and monitors being inundated with data. Beaming with excitement, Anderson said the lab computers would take days to process it all. One device emitted bright yellow sparks that turned white-hot as they fell to the ground. Another and another followed suit. One of the units sparked so intensely, the dry brush on the forest floor smoldered into a flame. Stomping it with his massive boots, General Tucker put it out in seconds.

As if a hundred trees were split down the middle by a booming lightning strike, the glowing blue dome crackled to life. The air outside the electric area began to swirl. It carried the hot metallic odor of the sparklers children lit to welcome the new year. A misty column of light obscured the three standing like statues in the ring.

Solidifying into an intense beam, the blue light climbed into the heavens, leaving a gaping hole in what had been a dense canopy. Howling winds stirred behind them and grew into a deafening roar. It rattled Amy's brittle old bones and assaulted her eardrums more than anything she had ever experienced. The others crowded in behind until they pressed into each other.

Patrick O'Malley shouted something about a hangar, and said, "Tell me this is *not* an alien encounter."

"Science be damned," Anderson yelled over the din. "Somehow this storm formed around us."

A crashing clatter of heavy metal being thrashed sounded behind them. Amy couldn't imagine the force at play in the raging tempest surrounding them—their proximity to the ring seemed to be their only salvation.

No rain fell, and no clouds formed.

A piercing, high-pitched shrill rang out from the blue lightning. Bombarded by an intense noise diffusion, Amy squinted from the brightening display. Something was happening inside the column of light.

Isis, Jonah Blankson, and Mister Anderson began to glow. They looked like the gods or saints of so many faiths. The skyward beam of overpowering light intensified, turning white. As if staring at the sun, Amy pinched her eyes shut.

A whooping clamor rushed in and drove away the roaring noise of the storm. Dense silence fell over the forest. A second later, the only sound in Amy's ear was the ringing. Through slivered eyelids, she dared a peek. As if someone had flicked a switch, the blue lightning went out.

"*Isis*!" Amy screamed. "Where did they go?"

The ones Doctor Anderson had used for her experiment disappeared. In her desperation to help that young lady, Amy had allowed it. Guilt washed over her trepidation. In the hope of saving Isis, she had justified kidnapping the girl and dragging Tilda to another continent. She had come to set them on a new and liberated life, the details of which she couldn't guess. Now her mind focused upon a single plaguing thought. Had she made a rash decision based upon her own faltered faith and longing? Had she ruined these young lives?

The scene turned into chaos. Everyone scampered about as if to find the missing behind a tree or under a rock. Shouts of their names bounced off thick-barked trees and rustled through the foliage to dissipate without finding those lost ears.

"Did the cloud-storm funnels take them?" Amy asked no one in particular.

While the others searched in vain for Isis and the two men, Doctor Anderson checked her damaged equipment. She turned a scrunched face toward Amy. "There were no funnels with the localized storm we experienced." Letting out a sigh, her face softened. "I have no meteorological explanation for what happened to them."

"I must find Isis. Where is she?"

"Yelling at me won't help me find them. *My father* was in there." Anderson jabbed a finger toward the circle. "I want to get them back as much as you do. But we need answers that we just don't have and I..." With a forced exhale, her shoulders dropped. "I don't know how to find them."

O'Malley said, "They were abducted. It's the only plausible explanation left."

The tall man had been kicking at a thick mound of dried leaves and twigs as if one of the missing could have been under it.

Amy had never believed in such things. She wondered if she had ever believed in anything. Anderson cast a dumbfounded look at the man. The others gathered around, evidently conceding the futility of the search.

"Do you really think we're dealing with an alien invasion?" Amy asked.

"*Yes.*" Enthusiasm shone from his face. "For two years, not a single scientific explanation for the dark cloud storms has been found. People go missing without a trace, bodies never found.

Others look up into the dark clouds and lose their minds. And that acid rain, don't even—"

Catching the words in O'Malley's mouth, Doctor Anderson said, "It's *not* acid rain. It's something else entirely. Acid rain only affects metals, paint, and stone. It doesn't burn through human skin. And cloud-storm rain only targets a few animal species, including *us*."

"What's your explanation for it, then, Michelle? You know what it does, but you have *no idea* why or where it comes from. Alien technology is the only remaining plausible cause."

The burly general stepped forward. "Barnes and the president are interested in Doctor O'Malley's conclusions. And the White House is very much keeping an alien possibility on the table."

"I know, Nathan. I know. At this point, I guess anything's possible." Doctor Anderson returned to examining the burned equipment.

Timidly, Tilda raised her hand.

Looking at her with a satisfied grin, O'Malley said, "Yes, young lady."

"Excuse me, sir. I know little about these matters." A surprising calm filled Tilda's voice. "Do I understand correctly that you are saying the cloud storms, from the beginning, have been the work of extraterrestrials? And... that they have been here for at least two years?"

He nodded eagerly.

"And now they have taken Isis and the others. For what purpose do they do these things?"

All traces of smugness fled the man's face. "We don't know that yet. In causing the dark clouds and their effects, they must have an agenda or an underlying plan. I believe they can't live in our atmosphere as it is—well, *was*—and may be trying to... terraform this planet."

While Tilda nodded to the theory as if it made total sense to her, Amy gasped aloud. Doctor Anderson continued her dissection of one of the tree-mounted boxes of charred electronics. Rodriguez and General Tucker looked at each other intently.

Rodriguez said, "Sir, if there's any chance he's correct, we need to consider military action."

"Action against whom, or what? All we ever see are those clouds." Anderson pointed up. "How do we fight clouds? Launch nukes into the sky?"

No answer came. When General Tucker pulled Anderson away from her inspection of the dead equipment, the group plodded back toward the vehicles. As suspected, they had been tossed about by the storm, the smaller cart-like one mangled beyond recognition. Even the massive "tank" they'd arrived in had been lifted and thrown several meters and lay on its side, smashed as if slammed on all sides by a massive sledgehammer.

Rodriguez's whistle pierced the cool evening air. "Looks like we're walking."

Thirty-Six

Blackness filled Jonah's vision as if he had gone blind from the blue light intensifying into pure white. Thick darkness surrounded him. No clouds had formed, but Jonah's body had tingled with the same sensations as when he had been caught in the cloud storm. Now he was caught in nothingness.

Hoping to reach his companions, he lifted his hand. His hand hit nothing. He reached farther. When only air brushed under his palm, he stepped once, then again. "Mister Anderson," he called. "Young lady...? Is anyone there?" His voice reverberated, surrounding him in an echo.

When no one replied, the emptiness reminded Jonah of being lost and alone as a child. Something under his feet felt... *wrong*. The dirt in the circle was as hard as steel, but he must have stepped out of it by now. Yet the ground absorbed the pressure from his footfalls like metal. His feet pushed through no leaves, nor did his ears receive the crackle of dried foliage and twigs. Two more steps confirmed this oddity. Had the circle grown?

"Doctor Anderson, what has happened?" His raised voice cracked.

No reply. In fact, he heard no sounds beyond those he made. When Jonah stood still and quiet, his ears detected only the subtle whir of his own breaths. The drumming of his heart escalated into pounding beats. Every pulsation in his neck felt like a raging river surging through his veins. The evening temperature had dropped, and the air laid a forgotten cool caress on his skin.

Another step, followed by another and another. If he didn't bump into another human, he surely would have hit a tree. His steps became strides, and his stride accelerated—but not to a run. All the while, he saw and felt nothing. Everything had gone. Everything but the ground. He bent over to lay a palm on what should have been dirt and moss and leaves and twigs. A smoothness like a polished glass surface held nothing but him. No matter where he slid his hand or how wide he swooped his circles, not a crack or seam met his fingertips.

If this were a manufactured ground cover, where did it come from? And how had it suddenly covered the earth beneath him while leaving him standing upon it? Jonah had now stepped several meters through the hollow enclosing him in this vast openness, hitting nothing.

Beyond the vanishing of the two in the circle with him and the absence of Doctor Anderson and the others, a profound sense of loss overpowered him, collapsing him to his knees. Thoughts of Juliana hammered in his skull. In that hopeless moment, Jonah's face sank. His heart imploded in his chest, leaving a hollow more expansive than the void that now consumed him.

The dark silence swallowed the minutes like a time-eating monster or—his now frantic mind conjured up a childhood image—the Mawu-Lisa. Had the gods of his ancestors come to claim his soul?

Thirty-Seven

A NEARLY FULL MOON floating in an otherwise empty sky turned the field silvery-blue as they trudged back to the camp. Michelle had tuned out Patrick O'Malley and the constant repetition of his otherworldly theories. Surprisingly, the feeling those theories were nonsense had lost the bitter obstinance she'd held on to for so long. While she had no hypothesis to offer, she believed the answer could be found in science—good, old-fashioned, *terrestrial* science.

Passing ghostly silhouettes of distant trees, they marched onward in welcome silence. All the while, Michelle's brain churned with ideas, wild speculation, and recollection of vital bits of what she had learned about cloud storms. An idea settled in Michelle's mind, screaming about the scientific method and its process of discovery. Perhaps they were on the verge of an understanding beyond their experience or realm of knowledge.

Fighting its way in, her heart pried a wedge into her mental focus to consider the loss of her father. Whatever the eventual, logical answer was for what had happened to him, he was gone.

What would she tell Bobby and her mother? Saving the world, as grandiose a goal as it was, slid into equivalent importance with finding her father. Saving him. Holding to her original hypothesis, she believed saving him would guide her on her quest to save everyone.

Rodriguez led the way with O'Malley close behind and Miss Ferguson in the tight grip of the teenage girl's hand. Lingering in the back, Nathan strode beside Michelle. When they reached the camp, it looked like a battlefield. What had been a miniature town of white-topped tents and temporary structures had been reduced to a torn and tattered mess. It appeared as if it had been dumped onto the field from a massive toybox and scattered like Lego pieces. Standing tall in his general's uniform, Nathan Tucker stepped forward and pointed out the lack of humans. None moved about or lay dead on the ground.

Like floating through a horrible dreamscape, roaming through the rubble felt illusory, yet its reality needed no pinch test. Michelle and the others followed General Tucker's orders and spread out to search the debris field, lifting sections of tent cloth, pushing mangled... *whatevers* aside in hopes of uncovering survivors. Some relief came in not finding dead bodies. That faded into the acceptance that not a single member of the camp remained. Like those taken by storm funnels, they had simply vanished.

After trying the radio and satellite phone and searching the surrounding area, Nathan and Rodriguez had everyone pause for a moment of silence for the lost soldiers of the camp.

With greater gusto than Michelle had given the rescue attempt, she rifled through the damaged components of the equipment that should have been processing the sensor data from the ring. The most intact thing she found was a closed laptop, which she eagerly pried open. When she sunk her finger into the power button, flickering light filled the cracked screen. Distorted text flew by too fast to note. The display filled with the unwelcome blue of a fatal error message garbled beyond legibility.

"There may be data on the hard drive." Pointing to the bottom of the computer, Nathan said, "Military models all have removable drives. We should take them from any laptops we find."

She and Nathan found three more notebook computers and salvaged the drives from each before reuniting with the others. They had searched what was left of the habitat tents and the surrounding area for their bags and personal items. Rodriguez suggested they find a place to camp for the night, perhaps sleeping on salvaged bed mats and using tent clothes for cover.

"The village isn't far. A couple of miles that way." O'Malley pointed... east? "I know where the Blankson house is. His mother-in-law is there."

"We're six. That may be too many," Nathan replied.

Patrick shook his head emphatically. "The people are extremely hospitable. We can ask Blankson's mother-in-law if the women can stay with her. I'm sure the men can be put up somewhere too."

"Do they have a computer there?" Michelle asked.

"Jonah's old laptop's barely good for email."

Michelle turned to Nathan and patted the sack she had made with scraps of tent fabric. "We need to analyze whatever's on these drives."

Hunching as he did, Nathan looked into her eyes. "We do need answers. And I—I can't imagine how this is for you... I'm truly sorry about your father. But we're all way past exhaustion and need some rest. We'll head to the village."

"*Fine*. But we need to get some new equipment here ASAP."

***

Finding the soldiers from the camp at the village surprised and delighted them. After retreating from the storm, they were geared up and ready to search for the team at the ring. No longer needing to do that, they headed to the camp to start rebuilding and to sleep under the stars. What was left of Michelle's team headed for the Blankson home. His mother-in-law—who said her name was Grace but asked them to call her Auntie—eagerly welcomed the women and directed the men to the next house over. In no time, their hostess had set dinner on the table.

Michelle didn't recognize most of the food but ate something called *Waakye*, which turned out to be spicy rice and beans. Studying the young lady eating silently beside her, she said, "Are you enjoying your first taste of freedom as much as you are that banana?"

"It is fried plantain," Grace said.

After a sheepish nod to Michelle, the girl looked at her mentor.

Miss Ferguson said, "She has always had freewill, even before she realized it. Now I hope this new sense of individuality, of self-worth, will grow roots and sprout." Laying a hand over the girl's, Ferguson smiled warmly.

When Grace stood, the teenage girl hopped up to help her clear the table. As the girl washed the dishes, Grace returned to the table and asked about her daughter and son-in-law. With nothing hopeful to say, Michelle shook her head. Clearly misreading the gesture, the woman's eyes flooded.

"Are you saying my children are dead?"

"My father's with Blankson, so I hope not."

Ferguson said, "As was a young woman in my care. We mustn't give up hope."

"It may have been their glorious transition," the girl said over the rambunctious water splashing in the sink. "Unless the other doctor's theory is correct."

"You are of my daughter's faith? She, too, believed in this transition. My Jonah did not, but he is certain Juliana is alive. I pray they both will be found."

Folding her arms, Michelle evaluated these varied beliefs against her science. "First aliens, now you think your god is taking these people?"

"Is it not all faith, Doctor Anderson?" After closing the faucet, the girl turned and continued, "Your colleague has faith we are not alone in the universe. Miss Grace has faith in her tribal gods and, judging from the cross over the door, that of Christianity. The Order has its Celestial Maker. And you have science. In the end, we are all seeking answers, are we not? We all look for something more than us, something greater than our present understanding."

Astounded by the young lady's reasoning, Michelle was at a loss for words.

"Doctor Anderson," Miss Ferguson said, "Faith may seem a ridiculous notion to someone of science like yourself. But is it not faith you show that you will find your father and cure his madness? That you will solve the problem of the storms?"

"No. That's, that's a belief in science."

Miss Ferguson replied, "Science you have yet to prove yet still believe. It is no less outrageous than the system of faith I had devoted my life to—no, that my life had been devoted to by my parents all those years ago. It is no different from Doctor O'Malley's beliefs."

As she took her seat, the teenager's eyes shined vibrantly. "If I may—the Order teaches that things we believe, or hope for, are best understood after they are realized. We must patiently wait to see the truths we desperately seek."

Grace took the teenager to prepare a bed. As much as Michelle hoped Ferguson wouldn't continue the conversation, the silence between them was unnerving. It reminded Michelle of being taken to church for Sunday school and having to sit through the youth pastor's lectures about the dangers of this immoral world.

"I wasn't always an elder."

"I assumed you were a kid once. I wasn't always a scientist."

"No. I mean, I was married. To a wonderful man."

Perking her posture, Michelle said, "Oh. I thought elders had to be celibate."

"Single, yes. I had to end my marriage with Alexandar to accept the nomination. He was a good man, faithful to the Order."

"And he just accepted it, like that?" Michelle snapped her fingers.

"He had no choice." Ferguson sighed. "Of course, I realize now that he did. We both did. I blamed my parents—and the Order. In the end, I went along with it. I'm here because of my decisions. Not just my decision to leave the cathedral, but the culmination of my life choices."

Lowering her brow, Michelle said, "And now you're trying to give your servant the choices you forfeited?"

"Something like that. Tilda is stronger than I ever was. But I think you have more in common with us than you'd care to admit, Doctor Anderson."

Rounding her face in curiosity, Michelle said, "How so?"

"Putting your career over your family, over relationships, over the people in your life. Our obligation was a religious one. Yours is your career and position, your obsession with proving yourself right and fixing this storm issue." Taking Michelle's hand, she asked, "What will be the culmination of your life choices, Doctor Anderson?"

Thirty-Eight

Not a sliver of light or even the faintest glow came to lift Jonah from his despair. He had walked in the same direction for what felt like an hour, or perhaps much longer. Realization that nothing lay before him summoned a dread so deep his bones winced. A blend of confusing ideas filled Jonah's mind, none of which he had accepted before. Perhaps he had died unworthy of a heavenly reward he'd never believed anyone would receive.

Long ago, Europeans had brought Christianity to Ghana. Everyone in his village, everyone he knew, had been raised with it. Every Sunday, mindless drones following a tradition they knew little about filled the little white church in the center of town. Songs and repetitive prayers passed the time when he was a child. As an adult, he couldn't bear the routine and had not stepped inside that wooden chapel with its phallic steeple in years.

The best thing about Juliana's newfound faith in that cult was that she had stopped pressuring him to go to church. The nearest chapel for her new religion was, to Jonah's delight, not in the country. Memories of her ramblings about the clouds flooded into his thoughts now as he continued traversing the dense darkness of this most unnerving place.

"The cloud storms are a fulfillment of the foreshadowing," she had often warned him. How that made any difference, he'd never understood. Right or wrong, in her view, the outcome wouldn't change. If some ancient writing had predicted those dark clouds, he couldn't see how it mattered. His darling wife had repeatedly told him only the chosen would experience the Glorious Transition, as she called it. If Jonah knew one thing about the Order, he was not among those selected to be saved.

Perhaps she was. Inside her chest, his beloved carried the biggest heart Jonah had ever known. Her selflessness was part of the reason she couldn't help but go to aid her sister every day. Sometimes twice. Despite all the conflicting faiths he pushed down into the darkest recesses of his soul, Jonah knew Juliana was worthy of salvation. If he couldn't achieve it, even if this place became his eternal damnation, he could find comfort knowing she had been saved. If the clouds heralded a glorious transition, his darling wife had made it to the other side.

Chasing these thoughts away, memories of all those articles he'd read by Doctor Anderson rushed in on him. All those interviews he had watched on YouTube. While she presented scientific explanations for the storms and their effects, she never could answer the question as to their cause. She believed *he* was the key. Well, he and her father and that poor young lady who had been burned by the rain.

Now, wandering through this purgatory, a disturbing sense of relief fell over him. If the inevitable result of the clouds was that they would soon make the world unlivable, perhaps his Juliana had been spared a worse fate. A Bible character called Enoch came to his mind. Apparently, the world of his time had become so bad, God "took him" to avoid him having to experience a worse death. Would that have made Enoch a chosen one? Juliana?

What did that say about Jonah?

The Biblical Jonah had run away from his God-given assignment and had been swallowed by a huge fish. That analogy was a better fit to this present circumstance. The ancient scaredy-cat who shirked his responsibility had been in the dark belly of his personal hell until he prayed. Once he repented, that massive sea creature had vomited him out.

What sin had he committed running into the storm to find his Juliana? Jonah couldn't bring himself to pray to the god of the European's holy book.

In a memory, his wife smiled as she spoke of the Glorious Transition. A couple was supposed to be found to guide them. A revelation overwhelmed him, and he placed his palms over his blind eyes. That child with cloud madness. She was supposedly one half of that couple. The one Juliana expected to come and lead them. And he had entered this place with her. If that was his transition, it failed his wife's faith. Perhaps something greater lay beyond this transitory place. Considering death, eternal darkness, or being puked back to that dying world without his Juliana, he latched on to his wife's faith for a spark of hope in this wretched abyss.

Hoping someone would hear, anyone would hear, he spoke the words he thought came from the clouds. "So beautiful," he shouted. In a muttered undertone, he added, "Now take me or let me die."

Thirty-Nine

SHE'D HEARD HIM—MICHELLE WAS sure of it. Her father's voice called her. The same words he had said after gazing into the clouds—the only words he had been able to string together since. Instinctively, she looked up into the clear lavender sky as it readied itself to welcome the rising sun. Michelle had been trying to find Nathan for an update on a replacement computer to analyze the data on the recovered hard drives.

The general had no update beyond "A supply vehicle is coming," but he did have a thermos of coffee. Michelle joined him at the little picnic table. Her upper lip pulled in the rippling black liquid with an unapologetic slurp. Through the bitter steam she found Nathan's face uncharacteristically downcast.

"I heard him, Nathan. My dad. He spoke to me."

"You found him?" Nathan pursed his lips under a raised eyebrow.

"I didn't *see* him. I heard his voice. All he said was, 'It's so beautiful. You must see.' Like before. It was him—he's alive."

"Could you tell which direction the voice came from?"

Until Nathan asked, Michelle hadn't considered that. Running her eyes around the village, she said, "It... it was all around me. Like it came from above me." Both looked up at the endless azure stretching across the cloudless sky. "He isn't... here. But he is... *somewhere*. I'm sure he's alive, trying to contact me."

Nathan looked deeply into her eyes. Before he could speak, she assumed his next words and forbade them.

"No. Don't you dare."

"Yet your mind went there, Michelle. What's *your* explanation? We've found a mysterious artifact of hard-as-metal dirt in a perfect circle with ancient writing engraved on it. It's connected to the storms and the blue lightning. It took three people right from under our noses, vanished into thin air." The snap of his thick fingers rang in Michelle's ears. "New storms form around people connected to the clouds. You said that yourself, and we witnessed it—*twice*. Now you heard a voice from the sky."

Michelle rubbed her hands over her face and through her hair. Interlocking her fingers on the back of her head, she stared through the man across the table.

"I sent an update to the president," Nathan said. "She's very interested in Doctor O'Malley's conclusions."

The corner of Michelle's mouth drilled into her cheek.

He added, "Of course, she wants your report as well. President Carter is considering all opinions, and she wants answers. She has Barnes working with the rest of the task force and the military to strategize various action plans and will choose one based on the most probable scenario our team presents."

Freeing her hands to finish her coffee, Michelle puzzled over that idea. "She plans to what... attack the clouds?"

"She knows we're running out of time, with even less than we thought a week ago. Doctor Kournikova is convinced, and Jessica believes her."

"Jessica? You're on a first-name basis with the president?" She shook her head. "Anyway, as I said before, Natasha knows her stuff, and we're out of time. It's why the government is throwing money at us to solve this. Why we came here and put those people, my dad, in that stupid ring. I *cannot* have lost..." Words would no longer crawl out of the arid cave her mouth had become. She wiped a tear from the corner of her eye.

Nathan squeezed her hand. "I know. And if he's alive, what about Jonah and the girl? We should find Miss Ferguson and the others."

As they rose to head toward the Blankson home, Miss Ferguson, the young lady, and Jonah's mother-in-law rushed up to meet them. The girl reported hearing her friend with cloud madness. When the woman said she'd heard her son-in-law, she lamented not hearing her daughter's voice. The drought of absolute loss deflated her full cheeks. With confirmation of hearing all three of the missing, Michelle decided to head back to the strange circle in the woods. If answers were to be found, terrestrial or otherwise, she believed they would be there.

***

The journey slowed to allow the older woman to keep up. Not Miss Ferguson, but the plump aged mother of the long-disappeared woman Blankson had been desperate to find. O'Malley wouldn't stop his yapping about an alien abduction and how this was a good thing because it got them closer to discovering their extraterrestrial visitors—to finding their much-needed answers. Exceeding a weather phenomenon's reach, that idea at least held an ounce of hope. With all her willpower fully engaged, Michelle said nothing.

Thick-trunked trees towered from the ground like majestic columns supporting the blue ceiling above. Leaves, twigs, and other forest debris littered the ground all around them, except for the "artifact," as O'Malley called it. Not the smallest bit of dried foliage had landed upon it, and not so much as an ant dared step inside it.

"Michelle." O'Malley pointed to the ominous ring. "You said those three were connected to the clouds. I agree. I also believe *we* have become... connected. We were at the center of the localized storm in DC, *and* the one here. We may not have cloud madness, but neither did Jonah Blankson."

Crossing her arms, Michelle asked, "Do you have some sort of a point?"

"We should step inside. Whatever took them may take us too. If we're as connected as Blankson, it should work."

Strangely, the man's words made sense—as much as anything could in this nonsensical situation.

Nathan gave her a nod.

Miss Ferguson, still dressed in the unbecoming hat and gown with buttons from neck to knees, cleared her throat.

"I will enter the ring with you."

The teenage girl's eyebrows climbed her forehead.

Putting himself between them and the ring, Rodriguez said, "I don't think it's safe for anyone to step onto that platform until we understand what it is."

The tall soldier's protest was hushed as Jonah's mother-in-law pointed to Michelle and said, "You heard your father. Tilda heard the young lady. And I heard my Jonah. I believe we were called here. To them."

"Then why Tilda? I'm responsible for Isis. I should go."

"Go where, Miss Amy?" Tilda asked. "We do not know what will happen, if anything."

"She has a point," Michelle said.

The older woman grimaced.

"It should be those of us who heard the voices," Michelle confirmed.

"I agree. They must have chosen the ones who heard them." O'Malley poked his chest. "And since *I'm* the only one who believes, and I've been in both storms, I'll go too."

Nathan motioned Rodriguez to step aside. "Settled. Doctors Anderson and O'Malley, along with Miss Grace and Tilda, will step into the circle. Who knows if anything will even happen?"

Unable to find a scientific basis to agree or launch into a counter argument, Michelle shrugged and stepped into the circle. Following O'Malley, the ladies stepped in last.

Forty

Under great protest, Amy stood one meter from the mysterious circle. The morning sun falling on her neck brought greater warmth than Amy had ever felt. For people in Norway, the rise in global temperatures had brought discomforting climate change, but nothing to the level of what accosted her flesh and sucked the sweat from her pores in Africa. Many lands had become unlivable from the dark clouds and lack of natural rainfall. Heatstroke and deaths of the elderly had steadily increased—and surged alarmingly in recent months.

Throughout the history of the Order, the elders had been sheltered from world events, politics, wars, famines, pandemics, and economic depressions. Their isolation had kept them safe from the effects of the clouds—well, except for the poor young couple. Now Tilda stood in that circle some hoped would whisk her away into another realm or whatever oblivion lay beyond. It felt like a sacrificial offering to an unknown deity. With no stone walls surrounding her, Amy felt unprotected.

Exposed.

Holding hands with Miss Grace, Tilda showed Amy a reassuring smile. In harmony, all four in the ring looked straight up into the unbroken indigo sky. Brilliant white engulfed them. Amy squinted, trying not to lose the definition of their shapes. As the towering column of bright light piercing the heavens intensified, her eyes lost them. In an instant, as if someone had yanked out the plug, the light went out. Through the spots in her eyes as they tried to adjust, Amy saw no one. Tilda and the others had been plucked from the earth without a trace.

The general and the tall soldier stood with gaping mouths, the sheen of bewilderment in their eyes. This is what the group had hoped for—to step into the unknown and find the elusive answers in the clouds. Or perhaps the four had died, just as Isis and the others had yesterday.

Not giving the moment the thoughts it requested, Amy jumped into the circle with more energy than her legs had mustered in a decade. The general called out to her with words her mind couldn't decipher over its own raging storm of memories, excerpts of the Code, the foreshadowing, the Guide Couple, that darn Tartagni, and the potential culmination of millennia of faith and zealotry.

"Miss Ferguson, please step out of there," one of the men said.

The intensity in the words forced them into her consciousness. Unwilling to comply, Amy wiggled her toes, though she didn't know why. Perhaps an attempt to feel something. Anything. Before the others disappeared, they looked up. So Amy hoisted her chin as far as her neck allowed and stared into the empty sky. The leaves of the treetops swayed, expanding and contracting the hole in the canopy as if the forest itself were taking deep breaths.

"Take me!" she yelled to no one. Or she might have called out to the Celestial Maker. Could a vague deity have been responsible for the Code, the religion it spawned, and the events of these last years? For the first time in a long time, Amy questioned her faith from the opposing side. Were the storms and darkened clouds a prelude to... Had Isis and Tilda passed through the Glorious Transition? The Guide first, then the loyal believer.

"I'm here. I am Elder Ferguson of clan Ferguson, chairperson of the Council of Twelve and keeper of the Code. You have half of the Guide Couple, and she is under my care... Take me, damn you!"

"Miss Ferguson," someone shouted.

"Take me!"

A pressure squeezed her arm, and she thought it—he, she, they, or whatever had orchestrated all these peculiar events—had come to claim her next. A jolt brought her head level and spun her around to see the tall soldier, his cleft chin at eye level and his deep gaze peering into her eyes. He'd pulled her from the circle. The sting from an uncharacteristic slap reddened her palm, but the soldier didn't flinch.

"This is what they wanted," he said. "Doctor Anderson hoped to join the others and learn what's going on here. There's nothing wrong."

"Nothing wrong? How many people must we lose before this becomes... wrong?"

The general moved the other man away from Amy's rage. "Miss Ferguson, of course, you are correct. My colleague didn't mean nothing was wrong, in that sense. Only that this is what Doctors Anderson and O'Malley came here to do. He was convinced—Doctor O'Malley—that the ones who disappeared yesterday had not been killed but... taken."

"And Doctor Anderson insulted him and his mother when he said it. She insisted this was a climatological issue, not aliens abducting people."

"True, but she also believed, especially after hearing her father and the others hearing Mister Blankson and Isis, that they were not dead but had been transported somewhere. What just happened seems to have proven that hypothesis."

"Unless, like the ones yesterday, they were vaporized by that light beam."

Despite whatever resurgence of faith or mock epiphany she thought she had experienced a moment ago, Amy now stood an empty shell. She had arrogantly stolen those precious young lives and destroyed them.

Forty-One

Jonah heard a whisper. He walked toward the only noise he had heard in hours not made by him. It sounded feminine. Hoping to find Juliana, he quickened his pace.

"Dad?" he thought he heard it say. Not "Jonah." Clangs of something pattering on the glass-like ground loudened, blending with his footfalls to create the rhythmic pattern of a galloping horse. Its reverberation was almost deafening in the hollow devoid of light.

"Dad?" The voice neared, clearer now.

"Doctor Anderson?"

All footsteps halted and a still silence filled the enormous space.

"*Blankson?*"

"Yes, I'm here."

"Where? I can't see you. I can't see anything."

"I have been in darkness since arriving in this place. Follow my voice."

Softened calls of "Here" and "This way" shortened the gap between them until Jonah's outstretched hand touched Anderson's. Unexpectedly, the previously cold and distant woman embraced him.

"My father?" she whimpered.

"Until you arrived, I have been alone."

"What is this place?"

Although it didn't matter in the dense darkness, Jonah hoped he was looking at her face. "I wish you could tell me. How did you get here?"

"We stepped onto the ring. Me, O'Malley, the young girl, and your mother-in-law."

"Maame? Why did you take her to that cursed place?"

"She insisted. Actually, *you* called her."

"Me? I have been trapped in this… this purgatory—the whole time."

"She heard your voice. I heard my father. And the girl heard the young woman with cloud madness."

"Isis. Where is she? Where is Maame?"

"No idea. And what kind of name is Maame, anyway? She introduced herself as Grace."

"Maame means mother, or more like mommy. But she is not here. Juliana is not here. Until you, no one has been here. And you say you were called to this place."

"We heard the ones closest to us say those damned words. So we went to the ring."

"Wait, Doctor Anderson. Is that what Maame heard me say? She heard me say 'So beautiful' some minutes ago?"

"Yes—No, it was at least an hour ago. But she heard you say it. And I heard my dad, and the girl heard her friend too. I assumed you must've gone mad like them. Where's my father?"

Desperation dripped from her voice, and Jonah reached for Anderson's arm. When he touched her, she slapped his hand away.

"Watch it!"

"I'm sorry, Doctor Anderson. I reached for your arm. Forgive my disrespect."

"Let's just keep our hands down, okay? And enough with the Doctor Anderson. Since you just got so"—she cleared her throat—"*familiar*. It's Michelle."

"Very well, Miss Michelle. I appreciate the respect you reciprocate. I also prefer my first name." Considering what he'd observed about her, he added, "Jonah."

"If you're not mad, why'd you say that? I thought you lost your mind too."

"I called out a few times to anyone. No one replied. I couldn't think, didn't know what else to do. For some reason, I thought to say, 'So beautiful' to whoever brought me here."

"That's the question—who brought us here? I can't guess why or where *here* is."

A blinding white light consumed every speck of black from the surrounding space. Jonah pinched his eyes tight and raised his forearm over them. The tight grip of slender fingers clutched his arm, and he felt Anderson pressing herself into his side.

"It is all right." The booming voice roared with the sound of thunder. "The light has diminished to a comfortable level. You may open your eyes."

That voice shook them to the bone.

"Hello?" Anderson called softly.

Increasing her volume on each repeat, she called out three more times.

When she looked at Jonah, he must have shown her the same confusion that drenched her face. Releasing his arm, she stepped forward and paused. Again, she took a step closer to the voice. Or farther away—Jonah had no idea.

"Miss Michelle, wait. Stay with me, where it is safe."

"Safe? From what? And how's here—how is anything here—*safe*?"

"Do not worry," the voice bellowed. "You are safe here, Michelle."

She halted her steps under the booming reverberation bombarding them from all directions. The reassuring words from the menacing voice brought Jonah no comfort. He hurried to her and held her by the arms as they stared into each other's empty eyes, looking for courage neither could supply.

Raising her eyebrows, Anderson turned to face... well, neither of them knew what. "You know who I am?"

"We have been watching you, Doctor Anderson... And you, Mister Blankson, since you found us in the storm."

"Found you?" The steadiness of his own voice surprised him.

"In looking for your lost mate, you found the one place on the planet that could have saved you from the dark clouds. We became very interested in you then."

"We?" Michelle demanded. She raised her arms and spun once in a circle while looking into the endless white above her head. "Who are you and what's your connection to the cloud storms?"

"We should think the answers are obvious but understand it may take time for you to accept."

"Again with the *we*." Michelle put her hands on her hips and looked straight ahead as if facing this unknown being. "Who are you? And where are we?"

"Your colleague, Doctor O'Malley, deduced correctly... You could not accept it. We have watched your futile attempts to understand the darkened clouds and their effects for two of your years. Your solution for predicting their arrival was admirable. We believe it is the first time anyone has accomplished that."

With each new sentence, the virile voice lessened its intensity. Perhaps they had realized the impact of high decibels on human eardrums. Without realizing it, Jonah had slipped into thinking in terms of human and nonhuman.

"Exactly what do you mean by 'the first time anyone accomplished that'?"

"You are an intelligent one, Michelle. In fact, we have noted an increase in overall human intelligence in this cycle. We have been fascinated by this, though we are not yet sure what it may mean for future cycles."

Jonah looked up and said, "Stop speaking in riddles and tell us what this is. Is my Juliana in a place like this one?"

"No, Jonah. Your mate, as all who went missing in the storms, is no more."

"No more?" he shouted. "What do you mean? Is she... Have *you* killed her?"

"We are not killers. And we do not abduct and experiment on humans. Your associate, Doctor O'Malley, was incorrect on that point, Michelle. We know all we need to know about your species. When what you call funnels carry someone into the clouds, they are absorbed by the storm's energy."

"You know all you need—"

"Ahh!" Jonah's heart had been grabbed by the Voice's words and squeezed like a vise. "Ahh... She is dead!" His shoulders sagged and tears soaked his face before he doubled over, arms folded over his stomach. "Ahh!" A guttural moan saturated the space. He bellowed, "My Juliana is *gone*."

Forty-Two

As unbelievable as Michelle found the whole thing, the answers the Voice provided amazed her. While not ready to concede to it in the foreground, her subconscious had succumbed. What she had assiduously studied for two years under the precepts of meteorological science had been a blind and arrogant pursuit. More than hubris, common sense had forbidden the slightest consideration of an alien encounter.

An invasion, she concluded. This was a conquest of the planet.

Then there was Jonah. She struggled to see his connection. A shadow of the man who had been so optimistic and determined, now broken, stooped over in agony. Reflexively, she knelt and embraced him. He buried his face in her shoulder and groaned.

"I'm—I'm so sorry, Jonah."

"You said you would help me." He gasped for air. "You were supposed to find her."

"I never—" As the words caught in her throat, she wondered if she *had* promised. Nathan had warned her about that. "I wish I could have."

"No. I can't... I can't lose her. What about her faith? The transition?"

Rubbing his back, Michelle said, "I don't know. But faith is what we hope for beyond this life, right?" In the silence of Jonah's agony, she questioned her place to speak on this topic. "Your wife had faith in something more than this life. Something after."

Somewhat composed but still a mess of tears, Jonah peered into her eyes. "You don't believe that."

"She did, Jonah. She did."

Broken and on his knees, the white-haired farmer rubbed his eyes. When Michelle pulled back, he said nothing more. She didn't know whether she'd given him any comfort, but at least his wailing had been reduced to steady and somber sobbing. The Voice remained silent, and Michelle wondered if it was giving them the moment. If it knew humans so well, as it claimed, did it understand their grief? Amid a mountain of questions, one crested the peak.

Getting to her feet, she asked, "Where's my father?"

"He is safe and will be returned to the ring."

That assurance, which she uncharacteristically accepted, allowed curiosity to consume her. She fired question after question. The accommodating Voice patiently answered, keeping some replies frustratingly ambiguous. Within minutes,

Michelle had grasped the core of the situation and the purpose of the peculiar cloud storms she had tried and failed to understand. As much as she had tried to suppress O'Malley's alien terraforming ideas, even when she started to accept their plausibility, the thought of admitting he was right churned her stomach.

An obvious question came to her, and she shook her head for not asking it sooner. It was the one question that had fueled her drive and put her on that task force. Not caused by earth's natural weather patterns, the clouds instantaneously formed from "nothing" by forces unlike anything seen in the native climate.

"How are these clouds formed?"

A lengthy and technical explanation followed. A quasi-physical atmospheric shield lay between the exosphere and magnetosphere. The Voice described microscopically thin tendrils—which it explained they were not, but the imagery would help her understand. Reaching down into the thermosphere and ionosphere, they pumped base elements of chlorofluorocarbons and hydrochlorofluorocarbons into the clouds.

"Forcing," Michelle replied. "Your clouds have been acting upon Earth's climate, changing how energy flows through it. The gases you've been pumping into our atmosphere are reducing outgoing heat and causing the planet to warm at an accelerated rate. You told Jonah you weren't killers, but you *are* killing us."

"The storms are merely the final stage of a terraforming project to make the planet hospitable to our kind. Largely, the damage has been done by humanity without the aid of extraterrestrial influences. Our clouds merely quicken the process that happens on human worlds."

The idea of a species willing to exterminate over eight billion sentient beings to steal their home twisted Michelle's brow into a scowl. Her moral compass found no ethical balance with which any species claiming to be "superior," as the Voice asserted its beings to be, could align.

"You can't use that excuse to justify yourselves. We were making good progress countering climate change before the clouds came. This is your doing, your people, or... or whatever you are. How can you call yourselves advanced, *superior*, while killing us to get us out of your way?"

"Michelle." The Voice spoke more softly than before yet carried an arrogance in its tone. "You speak from an elevated position your species always fails to reach. We credit your people for aspiring to such, but your history is littered with much worse atrocities. Shall we recount some of them?"

Conceding this battle, Michelle folded her arms over her chest and tried to work out how to win the war.

"As we thought. It is understandable, given all you have now learned, for you to be judgmental. When you see yourself as the victim, it is easy to claim the moral high ground."

"This is… well, I guess the word is xenocide," she protested. "You're killing billions, sentencing the human race to extinction, so *you* can live here."

An enormous display encircled them, like a 360-degree glass screen. It immersed them in a city—Michelle didn't recognize which—surrounded by people rioting, looting, and fighting riot police.

Rising from his knees, Jonah asked, "What is this? When did this happen?"

"This is what your people do, Jonah. Michelle, behold your species' true morality, their… humanity, if you will. This is happening right now and being repeated the world over."

The screen shuffled through similar images of city after city across the globe. Fires raged, cars exploded, storefront windows shattered, people trampled each other, fights broke out among crowds gathered in the chaos, and people killed each other.

"Whu… Why?" Hoping it was speculative, Michelle asked, "Is this real?"

"News of your colleague's calculations has leaked. The world knows it is out of time, and how do they react? You would expect an elevated species with a sense of morality to rally together, to aid the less fortunate, to unite for the common good. Is this what you see, Michelle?"

"That's not fair. People must be panicking. If they… Well, they just learned they'll die in a few months. How do you expect people to take that?"

"We expect humans to do exactly this. In every cycle, they always do."

Forty-Three

As she watched men unloading small crates from the back of a camouflaged vehicle, Amy's eyes drifted to a tall slender woman climbing down from the Humvee. In a pencil skirt and heels, she wasn't dressed for jungle work. While her straight black hair caught glimmers of light in a silky sheen, she looked sleep-deprived and worse for wear from the travel. Eastern European, Amy surmised, and hiding her symmetrical beauty behind thick-rimmed black glasses.

When the general greeted this woman, it became apparent they knew each other. It was remarkable to Amy that this decorated general, who was on a first name-basis with the president of the United States, had such a calm and unassuming demeanor. He introduced Doctor Kournikova to Commander Rodriguez and then to Amy.

"Nice to meet you," she said. "Love the look—low maintenance."

Amy scrunched her face, considered the odd compliment, then chuckled. She didn't recall taking off her hat or where she had left it. "Oh, right. A weekly shave is all I need, and Tilda—" The girl's name tightened in her throat as she forced it out.

"I like this one, General. Now... May I see it?"

The general led the woman he called Natasha to the ring. As she examined it with eyes of glowing curiosity, her face brightened with childish wonder. The general stood directly beside Amy, about a meter from the circle, as the newest team member bent on one knee and tapped, rubbed, and clawed at the metal-hard surface.

"And the African man, Michelle's dad, and that girl just... poofed away?"

General Tucker confirmed with a nod as the woman studied the markings around the ring's perimeter encircling her. "And then Michelle and Pat had the bright idea to step onto it, with some elderly lady from the village and another young girl?" Standing straight as a board, she turned a blank face toward the general. "And they vanished as well?"

As Tucker replied in the affirmative, Doctor Kournikova hopped out of the ring with a pale face full of terror. "And you let me stand in there?"

The general raised a palm to her. "Relax, Natasha. Doctors O'Malley and Anderson concurred. The connection to the clouds is why people were taken."

"I read the reports in the Humvee. Michelle, the girl, and the woman from the local village had all heard the voices of the ones who had been taken first, so they thought they were being...

called, Michelle's note said. Then what about Pat? Was he taken as collateral damage, caught up by being next to them?"

"We don't know much. We only have O'Malley's speculation."

"And Michelle went along... with *him?* Incredible. She must have been desperate to find her father."

"No," Amy interjected. "She was desperate to find *answers*. I don't think she cared one bit about anyone, not even her own father. She was supposed to help Isis, not get her abducted—then Tilda, and the others." Blinking kept the tears bathing her eyes from falling.

Doctor Kournikova smiled. "The High Priestess has spunk—I like that. And you may not be wrong, my shiny-scalped friend. I'm not saying Michelle is heartless. I saw her concern for her father. But she's driven by a solitary goal—to understand the clouds and the storms and find a way to reverse their damage. We're all trying to save our environment."

"And are you here to do that now that she is... well, gone?"

"Not exactly. My field is slightly different, but I can process the data she collected and liaise with our colleagues in DC. Michelle concluded the blue electricity, or lightning, influences the clouds, or it could be part of how they're formed. As a climatologist, I'm here at her request to study that."

Extending an arm to the new doctor, the general said, "Come, let's get you set up. I told the men to prepare a desk and some computers first thing, before they get the tents finished."

Having stationed himself between her and the ring, Amy eyed Commander Rodriguez waiting for her to turn and follow before he moved. Her momentary loss of mental faculty had passed, so she joined the march away from the forest brim.

A thought stopped Amy's feet—a point everyone had masterfully avoided.

Rodriguez pressed behind her. "What is it, ma'am?" he asked.

Addressing no one in particular, Amy said, "None of you are willing to say it, but I must ask... Do we believe they are all dead?"

***

As Doctor Kournikova worked feverishly on three laptops with satellite connectivity, Amy made herself useful setting up what would be the habitat tent. With no idea how long they would wait or what they hoped to discover by waiting, she realized she had nowhere to go.

Two young men in uniforms had erected the tent in minutes and carted in the frames that became bunks. Amy unrolled the thin mattresses and unpacked a crate full of bedding and pillows. Making the beds kept her occupied, so she fought to keep her mental focus on the task as she performed it. The faces of those two innocent young ladies appeared under every blink. This trip had promised them liberation.

The cost of Amy's "freedom" was two young lives.

A commotion stirring outside drifted into the tent as shouts of joyous surprise. Through the canvas walls, Amy heard voices blending into something that sounded like a cocktail party. One word fought its way through the din into her diminished hearing, and she ran outside.

Full of disbelief, Amy confirmed what her aged ears had heard—the voice of Tilda calling Isis. The girls had appeared in the ring along with Doctor O'Malley, Mister Anderson, and that sweet older woman called Grace. Tears of joy washed away the guilt as Amy ran to the young ladies and pulled them into a tight embrace. Repeatedly saying, "I'm sorry," she squeezed as tightly as her tired arms could.

The general, Rodriguez, and a dozen others had run to see the bewildered faces of those who had been lost, still appearing so as they took in their surroundings. Silencing the crowd, the general supported Mister Anderson and asked the most obvious question: "Where were you?"

"It's hard to say," Doctor O'Malley replied. "It was total darkness for a few seconds, then we were here. I don't think we *went* anywhere."

Tilda and Grace confirmed, while Mister Anderson and Isis looked as detached from reality as ever.

"You were gone for hours," the general said.

Latching onto Tilda's hand, Amy added, "We thought we'd lost you."

"I was alone," Tilda said. "I saw nothing for a few seconds. Then I found Isis beside me when the darkness ended."

"General," O'Malley said. "Exactly how long have we been gone?"

"Over nine hours. It's almost dark, and you stepped into the ring this morning."

Squinting, O'Malley's eyes scanned the area. "Michelle? Blankson?"

The general shook his head.

"They must be alive too," Amy said.

Doctor Kournikova asked, "You said you didn't see each other. Did anyone see or hear Doctor Anderson or Mister Blankson?"

O'Malley and Tilda confirmed their isolation.

***

Once Isis had fallen into sound sleep, Amy and Tilda conversed in whispers on the senior's bunk. With little curiosity left in her aged bones, Amy wanted to leave. She had no idea where they would go and had little reserve money from the "appropriated" cathedral funds.

"I would like to take you home," she said to her youthful companion.

"I do not wish to go home."

"You're no longer anyone's servant, least of all mine. I will take the blame for all I've done, and you can return to your parents, to your home, to your life."

Folding her hands into a ball, Tilda laid them in her lap. "My parents gave up my life when they brought me to the cathedral." When Amy tried to interrupt to apologize, Tilda continued, "No, I am grateful I met you, that *you* were the one I was assigned to serve. You helped open my eyes, and I never wish to go back."

"They say there's little time left for any of us. Do you understand what that means?"

The girl pursed her lips. "I am not a child. Whatever time we have left, I wish to spend it as I decide."

Pulling Tilda into an embrace over their folded legs, Amy whispered, "I'm proud of you. I wish I'd had your bravery when I was your age."

When the rustling of sheets fractured the moment, the two looked at Isis in her bunk. As if she could see through it into the heavens, she focused on the ceiling. A siren sounding through the camp penetrated the tent cloth and drained into their ears.

"It's so beautiful," Isis exclaimed.

Forty-Four

The Voice offered to relate the story of its *people*. Although she couldn't be sure the word adequately described them, Michelle mentally accepted it. When it said she needed to see the human condition through their eyes, she asked if they had eyes.

"We are not of the same essence as you," the Voice replied.

Anticipation of what mind-altering truth it would reveal heightened inside her under the Voice's pause. Pacing in a tight circle, Michelle rubbed her temples. To steady her, Jonah placed his hands on her shoulders. As if seeing him for the first time, she studied his swollen red eyes.

"Your vital signs have settled." The Voice spoke evenly. "We believe you are ready to hear the truth about your world and its reality."

Freeing herself from his grip, Michelle turned from Jonah to speak to the Voice that came from every direction. "You're monitoring our vitals?"

"Yes, Michelle. We mean you no harm."

"No harm? You killed my Juliana," Jonah blurted.

Michelle added, "And you're destroying our planet."

"*Your* planet? We will get to that. Now, please hold your outbursts until we have explained all."

"Why are you even doing this?" Michelle asked. "You've been here for two years, and we have a few months left before we're wiped out. *Now* you decide to tell us what's going on?"

"We have been here since the beginning. As we said, your answers will come if you listen to what I have decided to tell you."

Repeating Michelle's question, Jonah asked, "Why have you decided to tell *us*?"

"You are the first to discover our presence. The first to find us."

"What do—"

A quickly raised finger stifled Jonah's tongue. Michelle's mind raced with a new set of questions.

"Wait a minute. We're the first. Earlier—yes, how did I miss that? —you said the clouds were the final stage of what happened on human *worlds*—as in multiple human worlds. There are other worlds with humans on them? And you've exterminated them all in what you called... *cycles*?"

"Michelle, we are being patient and have granted you what you seek most—answers. We have repeated such cycles on many worlds inhabited by humans."

Jonah's eyes filled with tears. "And on each one, you killed them all?"

As the glimmering droplets trailed down his cheeks, Michelle assumed not all were for Juliana. Billions were about to die. Billions more had already perished on other worlds.

"As we have told you, we are not killers."

Frustration raised Michelle's fisted hands and slammed them into her thighs. "Semantics. You say you're not directly killing anyone, yet the clouds you cause *do kill* people—his wife, for example. And worse, they've irreversibly destroyed our ecosystem. Our environment will no longer support life. You're killing everyone on Earth. And you've done this repeatedly on other worlds. Your people are savage murderers. For what sadistic purpose?"

"Survival. When humans spray insecticide on crops to safeguard their food supply, are they murderers? When you use bug spray, do you consider yourself a killer?"

"That's—*what*? We're sentient beings. Intelligent. No matter how supposedly advanced you are, you cannot make that comparison."

"We shall hold off the discussion of intelligence for the time being. Consider, when you use disinfectant or sterilizers, you kill trillions of microbes. You believe life on earth evolved from such basic lifeforms. Are you slaughtering your ancestors by such means?"

"Microbes are everywhere on Earth. The ones today are *not* our ancestors."

"Thank you, Michelle. You have made our point for us."

"I don't follow." Michelle set her hands on her hips, elbows flapping like chicken wings. "You're making a comparison of microbes we evolved from, and saying this is somehow like you coming here and invading our planet?"

"Who said this was *your* planet?"

Not our planet. Michelle couldn't place those words into any concept of the world she knew. The planet earth and humanity were perfectly suited for each other, existing in a harmonious symbiosis for millennia. True, human exploitation of its natural resources caused the environment's ruination. After decades of work, science had made great progress reversing that damage.

Until *they* came.

Their darkened clouds, storms, rains, and vanquishing of Earth's natural weather patterns had pushed the environmental crisis to the brink and beyond—to an extinction-level catastrophic state. The Voice said they had been here since the beginning. Could they have manipulated history to bring the environment to this point of ruination? Had they been leading humanity to this demise all along? Michelle needed some clarification.

"You said you were here since the beginning, and that this is not our planet. What *exactly* do you mean?"

"We have completed fifty-seven cycles on planets very much like Earth. Here, we have reached the final stages of the terraforming cycle. Currently, we have twenty-three other planets at various stages of preparation."

"You have or are destroying all life, human life, on over eighty planets? And you claim to be civilized? Superior?"

"You are worse than anything we've done to each other," Jonah added.

"Again, we must use comparisons your minds can understand. We are like farmers, and your kind are nothing more than seeds planted in the soil. The seed must die for the plant to grow. You have a history of slaughtering one another, your equals, in the most brutal ways. We are not the same."

The Voice paused as images again flashed over the projection encircling them. Haunting videos played a history lesson most people tried to forget. From muggings to gang rapes to murders to racial riots to mass shootings to global war to the holocaust. The sight of it caused Michelle to wince and shield her eyes, shouting, "Enough!"

"No human civilization has overcome nationalism, greed, and corruption to form one united world government, which is the only path to surviving and reaching its next adaptation. You have amassed an arsenal of nuclear warheads that can destroy all life on this planet multiple times over. Given the time, you *will* accomplish this. We have seen the same each time we intervened too late in our earliest cycles."

Under white knuckles, Michell's fingernails dug into her palms. "You can't say with such certainty that we would do that just because some other world full of humans did. We have our own story, *our* humanity, our hopes and dreams for a peaceful future. We make our own choices."

"Come now, Michelle. Surely you do not believe your words. Regardless, we have seen it every time. On every human-inhabited planet, history is repeated almost identically. Similar cultures develop, nationalistic pride thrives, and pervasive racism grows despite the voices calling for its end. Every planet has its industrial revolution and develops weapons of heinously destructive capability."

"But we were moving in the right direction. *We have a future.*" Desperation dripped from her words.

"No, you do not."

Shaking a finger above his head, Jonah shouted, "Because you're stealing it from us."

"If you will not see this any other way, then consider we are merely taking back what we have given you. You possess nothing we could steal."

"It's not our planet," Michelle recalled. "That's what you implied earlier."

"Correct. Your theories of how life formed on this planet are amusing, and not unique to this cycle. Humans were placed here by us, thousands of years ago, to seed the planet."

"Seed? No, don't tell me this is one of O'Malley's crazier scenarios... That you've grown *us* as food?"

"Nothing so barbaric, we assure you. As we have said, we are not of the same essence, and we therefore do not require the same carnal sustenance as humans."

That piqued Michelle's already monumental curiosity. "Do you have physical form?"

"In a sense you can understand, yes. As such, we require a physical atmosphere to live and reproduce. Our terraforming cycles ensure the preservation of our species, which grows at what you might consider an astronomical rate. If we do not continue to expand to new worlds, we will die."

"So you kill world after world for your own survival?" Jonah challenged.

"We plant seeds."

Michelle asked, "Why don't you show yourselves? Can we see you?"

"In a way, you have seen us."

Pausing, Michelle compiled the results of her studies, her findings on the task force, of the cloud madness. "The blue lightning."

"Correct. That is not our essence but is the visible representation of us, which some of this cycle's humans can perceive."

"Can you show yourself to us, in this place?"

"Those who have seen us have gone mad. We do not wish this for you."

Jonah said, "I saw the blue light... in the storm."

Michelle began to put the pieces into a picture. "He did. And several of us saw it—*you*—on the video we took of the clouds over DC."

"We protected you, Jonah, on our conduit. The light you saw could be compared to seeing a shadow of a person while not seeing the one casting it."

"And in the video? My whole team saw it, a spec of it anyway, in the dark clouds."

"Tell us, Michelle, what resulted from you seeing that glimpse?"

In the mental silence of a pause to ponder the question, she considered her actions since viewing that video. "We came here, with Jonah, to study the ring—the conduit, you called it. What is it?"

"One thing at a time—that is all your brains can process. After seeing that glimpse of light in the clouds, you became determined to see it again. That is why you journeyed to Ghana. That is why you risked Jonah, that young woman, even your own father on a theory you knew had no scientific basis. Although unadmitted, you even considered Doctor O'Malley's conclusions."

"Are you saying I started to go mad?"

"We are saying you can evaluate the results yourself."

Rolling her eyes up as if to see inside her own mind, Michelle added the new information to her dataset. "So you have a physical form we can't see without going mad. It's something so extraordinary that the few people who can see it become desperate to see it again. They describe it, you, as... beautiful. You exist in the clouds and are changing our climate to support your people and inhabit our world—which you say is not our world."

As if it knew she was still processing the data, the Voice did not reply.

"Wait... You said you seeded this world, and eighty others, with humans. Where did the first humans come from?"

Forty-Five

As he listened to the volley of questions, answers, scathing condemnations, and justifications, Jonah couldn't help but think none of it mattered. The most important piece of information, the one Doctor Anderson sought but didn't wish to hear, had been shared. There was no way to stop or reverse the damage caused by cloud storms. Soon, their world would end, replaced by an alternate version of a planet inhabited by these peculiar creatures of blue light.

The last question Michelle asked pulled Jonah's focus back to the conversation like a magnet. While the answer wouldn't change anything for the future of humanity—humanity had no future—he figured they might as well learn all they could about why they were going to die before that inevitable event.

"You listen well, Michelle, but with an occupied mind that does not, at first, process what you hear." As if sharing a secret with a friend, the Voice sounded more intimate now. "Do you recall my earlier analogy about the microbes?"

"Yes," Michelle replied. "Hold on... You just spoke in the singular."

"Eons before the current form of our essence, our origins trace back to fully corporal beings. In your language, you would call them humans. In your native Twi, Jonah, *nnipa*."

As Jonah processed that, Michelle said, "No... Are you... You evolved from humans?"

"You people and your theories. Never has anyone on sixty-one developed worlds uncovered your true origin, yet each eventually invent this concept of evolution. In time, the others will also. As a scientist, Doctor Anderson, you must realize how incredibly implausible such a process is."

"It's accepted by the greatest scientific minds on Earth."

"Again, you make our point for us."

Although Michelle didn't point it out, Jonah noticed the shift back to plurality. Never having accepted the concepts of evolution, he held no opinion about life's origin. He doubted even the outlandish teachings of the Order speculated alien insemination as the answer.

"Assuming I believe you about seeding Earth with humans..." Michelle pointed at nothing. "That doesn't explain where the original humans came from nor how they became... you."

"What you call humanity originated millions of your years ago in a distant galaxy you have yet to discover. While the origins of that life are debated to this day in small circles of our kind, our scientific community abandoned its study long ago."

"You mean to tell me you *don't care* how life began, where you came from?"

"We simply deemed it unknowable and a waste of time and resources needed to preserve and propagate our species. We know all we need to know about adaptation and the process of our transition from corporal form to our essence. Natural and artificial influences have made us what we are today."

Something Jonah could grasp—he had always considered certain pursuits of knowledge a waste of time. He never could understand how any field of science could focus on such useless things as the sexual habits of mice or why a tiny spider dances to impress a prospective mate who might eat it while things like cancer and climate change existed.

"We have the same potential. And you'll wipe us all away like... *germs*."

"No, Michelle. You will never reach even the next level of adaptation. We had what no human cycle has had since—one world culture unitedly working toward our survival. We developed the clouds on our planet to slowly adapt its atmosphere to our changing needs. Every planet we have seeded has begun this process for us via environmental ruination long before an adaptation they would never live to reach."

"We were reversing it. Finally, after decades of warning, it was working."

"To use Doctor Kournikova's expression, 'too little too late.' Even more extreme measures would not have been enough. As I said earlier, the clouds represent the final phase. Your people have done all the work for us. This is why we seed planets with humans."

"But, you said—"

Jonah paused when Michelle glared at him.

"Sorry, I have a question for him, um, them... You said you needed these planets, our planet, because your people reproduce in abundance. It seems to me this process takes many thousands of years."

Michelle said, "He has a point. And if you're so advanced, can't your people just keep it in their pants and control your population explosion?"

"I believe I understand your colloquialism. We do not reproduce in any way you would comprehend. If we do not expand as we do, we will lose our collective essence, become stagnant, and cease to exist. This process is gradual, and time does not pass for us as it does for you."

"If you won't reason, if we can't do anything but wait for you to exterminate us, why are we even talking?"

"Finally, Michelle, you asked the right question."

"So... are you going to answer it? Are you talking to O'Malley and the others?"

"Your associates and your father have been returned unharmed."

"You mean to tell us that, of the billions of people on earth, you decided to take me and this man up to—what, your spaceship—for a chat?"

"You were selected for your insatiable drive for answers and for being the only one on fifty-seven worlds reaching this stage who learned how to predict cloud storms and find a connection in the cloud madness victims."

"Then why me?" Jonah asked.

"I observed your efforts to find your mate. And that search united you with Doctor Anderson. We sent the localized storm to Washington to cement the idea of people being connected to the clouds. It had its desired result, to fortify your resolve to get to the conduit and to get the other madness sufferer here as well."

"Isis," Jonah clarified.

Michelle added, "You said, 'here,' as if we were still on the conduit."

"In a sense, you are in that conduit. As I said, we do not possess a physical form you would understand, therefore we have no spaceships that can hold our substance. You are in a construct of my essence made into a physical form by the conduit."

"You mean, we're... *inside* you?" Michelle turned a scrunched face to Jonah, who looked equally disgusted.

"You think in such limited dimensions. It is why your species will never adapt, never comprehend the true nature of physics, of time, of relativity, or of existence."

"Yet *you* did. You said you were like us, and you adapted. What right do you have to keep us from that eventuality?"

"We have every right, Michelle. I told you—you will never adapt as we have. No cycle ever has. But you strayed from your excellent question."

"Why are we talking? And while we're at it, why do you keep switching... referring to yourself in the plural and then the singular?"

"We are one essence and are many. It is most unusual for any of us to refer to our individuality. However, we are not intrinsically linked in a permanent state of oneness. You are speaking to a single entity now."

"And you, single, isolated you, decided to speak to us. To what end?"

"Although I have studied each one, this is my first time observing a cycle. While my superiors hold staunchly to the idea no human culture could adapt and survive their climate change—or, if they did, are certain to end their species by nuclear obliteration—you gave me pause."

"*You* think we can. That we should be viewed as more than microbes."

"There is where my problem lies, as I speak from my individuality. *We* do not."

"Will *you* help us?"

For the first time since the hollow space turned pure white, the Voice remained eerily silent when asked a direct question.

Forty-Six

Heavy shadows crept around the shivering huddle as Amy held her knees to her chest with one arm, Isis in the other. Pressed in on the other side, Tilda wrapped two arms around the girl and angled her bent legs toward her torso to keep her still. With unexpected vigor, Isis struggled to get up, again focused solely on getting outside, under the clouds.

This storm had come out of nowhere. General Tucker shouted over the commotion's din to Doctor Kournikova. For the first time since Doctor Anderson's alert system went online, the clouds came without warning. Kournikova had everyone check their mobile signals while Tucker used a satellite phone to contact the White House. Even as the storm raged, the official Climatological Society's Storm Tracker website showed nothing.

Under the thick steel table in the new lab tent, Doctor Kournikova sat with unnerving calm, pecking at a laptop, while Amy expected the tent to fly away and the table's false sense of safety to be ripped from the earth at any moment. The girls had not died when the light took them. This would be a more horrible death.

As if they had slipped into the tent and swirled directly around the table, the intense howling of the funnels rattled her bones. Amy tried unsuccessfully to bury her ears in her raised shoulders. Pressing in and expanding, the tent walls moaned with a constant warping roar. The explosive boom of something brutally ripping thick fabric dominated Amy's fear. Their white canvas shelter had succumbed to the storm, exposing the violence of the surrounding darkness.

Despite the anchors bracing the table to the ground, the wind's arm tried to shake it loose. Frightful confusion slackened the women's grip, allowing Isis to pull herself free. She fled into the storm, shouting those infernal words into the clouds. Before Amy could react, Tilda scurried from under the table, sprang to her feet, and disappeared.

Knowing the girls had no chance once the menacing clouds released their payload, Amy pulled herself up to pursue them. With no regard to how she hoped to catch up, Amy took her first hurried steps. Running up beside her, Doctor Kournikova held a hefty black object in her hand.

A white beam clawed out of the torchlight only to dissolve into the thick blackness laid over the land by the darkened clouds. Their voices shouted for Tilda and Isis. When something clasped her arm, Amy stopped. Doctor Kournikova shouted over the gale, "We should check the ring."

Huffing and giving her all to the run, Amy followed the doctor's bouncing light through the darkness for several minutes. Hours passed for Amy. Through a patch of barely discernable trees, they needed no torchlight to spot the young ladies.

A spectacle as ethereal as a transfiguration of angels stood in the center of the alien ring. Their gowns glowed brilliantly as threads of blue lightning danced around them. Both wore the same look, equally empty and full of wonder. Isis gazed into the black clouds filling the gap in the waving canopy. "Can you see? It's so beautiful," she cried.

The rain fell.

When Amy lunged for the girls, something pushed back. Doctor Kournikova shouted, "Remember Blankson... They're safe inside the ring. We're not."

Hoping the pattern held true and the girls would be safe, Amy relented. Pulled by the hand, she hurried behind the younger, fitter woman with longer legs. The darkness consumed her vision. She lost the hand that led the way. Rain pelted her hairless scalp, face, and hands—each drop an incendiary scorching her flesh. As she ran, splashes lifted off the saturated ground to prick like needles into her ankles and legs. Disoriented, seeing nothing, and in agonizing pain, her body gave out.

Amy collapsed.

The sound of her name penetrated the downpour and the excruciating pain to tease her ears with hope. Again, closer this time, the voice of that decorated general shouted her name.

Before he reached her, Amy lay on her back, opened her eyes, and gazed into the darkened clouds.

Words didn't escape her blistered lips but crowded her mind with one solitary thought. A drop slammed into her eye like a hammer. She felt her cornea burn. Beseeching a Celestial Maker she suddenly became desperate to believe in, Amy cried, "Watch over them through their Transition."

"Amy!" the general shouted.

A shiny black wave spilled over her, robbing her eye of the beauty hidden in the darkened clouds.

Forty-Seven

"WILL YOU HELP US?" Michelle demanded. When no answers came, she shouted, "You, I'm talking to *you*, the one being, not the whole... Will *you* help us?"

"That is why I brought you here. However, I am afraid there is no way to dissuade the whole from our course of action. We sail across the stars, exploring and ever growing in our knowledge. If we cease seeding and preparing planets to populate, we will lose more than our present way of life. We will become extinct."

Michelle said, "You say you brought us here to help us, but it sounds like you can't do a damn thing about it."

"I assure you of my sincerity. My observations of your discoveries, most especially your tenacity in pursuing answers to solve your accelerated climate issues, drew me to you. And Jonah, your devotion to your mate and determination to find her at all costs has shown me a side of ourselves lost to our adaptation and singularity."

"What about the others, like my dad, O'Malley, the girl, and her priestess? Did you lure them here too?"

"Your father and the youth, Isis, were drawn here through you. I wished to better understand what they saw in the clouds and how it affected their minds."

"With clouds on so many worlds, you still don't know that?"

"Michelle, I remind you how we view your people. Do you examine the cracked seed's shell, or care how it dissolves back into the soil once the plant begins to grow?"

"Wait," Jonah said. "If you think so little of humans, why help us?"

Addressing Jonah, Michelle said, "He, *it*, spoke again in plurality. We need to understand if the singular one... whatever it is, can help us."

"I believe I am the first of my kind to consider the morality of human seeding. We place five thousand adult humans on a new planet and monitor their progress for what you consider to be thousands of years. This is solely to ensure they progress as expected and work their way to an industrial revolution. On each world, they always do. Consistently, they engage in horrific wars, destroy their environment, and develop weapons that threaten their existence."

Wearing a fierce scowl, Michelle said, "You've already recounted how unworthy of life we are. Now, speaking to you as a single entity, what are you going to do to prevent the obliteration of eight billion sentient beings on Earth?"

"I will rejoin the consciousness, and it will absorb my request for consideration of your people. I will attempt to convince us of the potential you possess. One day, perhaps eons from now, you may rise out of your spiral of self-destruction to progress naturally toward joining our essence."

"You said that would never work, that your people will never accept that."

"Indeed." The Voice paused, bringing an unnerving silence to the hollow space. "That is why I have what you might call a 'Plan B.'"

As the Voice elaborated on its secondary plan, Michelle became enraged, grateful, hopeful, doubtful, and despondent in a wave of emotions foreign to her. Singularity of consciousness aside, this being was responsible for the destruction of Earth's environment, for all the deaths, the cloud madness, and eventually, the end of all life on earth. How could she trust it now? With no other means of salvation, how could she not?

"I have the means to stop the storms."

With the damage to the ecosphere already beyond recoverability, Michelle knew this alone might not be enough. Something would have to bring healthy rain and allow a proper heat transference from the ground and atmosphere to initiate a slow and steady reversal of global warming. Humanity was resilient. They'd find a way.

Seeing a flaw in Plan B, Michelle asked, "If you act independently of your collective, won't they stop you? If they refuse to accept our merit as a species, they'll carry on the terraforming of Earth after, what, arresting or killing you?"

"My existence cannot be terminated by such means. I would be fully absorbed into the collective essence and stripped of the ability to isolate my thoughts as I am now."

Jonah asked, "What would that be like for you?"

"I would become a passive observer of the universe. For your minds to comprehend, it would be like sitting in a glass box where you can see and hear everything but cannot interact with the world or the people around you."

"That sounds like purgatory," Jonah said. "Like what we experienced before you switched the lights on in here."

"Not at all, Jonah. You saw and heard nothing. I assure you, for my kind that would be preferable to what awaits me if I fail."

The idea of the Voice being so noble twisted Michelle's face into a grimace. "Why would you risk everything to help us?"

"I believe the humans of this cycle have the potential to become the first to reach adaptation. Bringing what we ourselves shed so long ago would, once refined by our guidance, enhance our essence. Assimilation into our collective will uplift our kind to a higher adaptation, one we did not consider possible or desirable."

"Your collective thinks it's already at the peak, ever expanding but never growing."

"Correct, Michelle."

"And of what, trillions in your collective, only you think we could do this."

"Three reasons led me to this conclusion. The first was you, Doctor Anderson, and your scientific breakthroughs. In all cycles, humans have brought their planet to the brink of ruination without intervention. Yours is the first to make meaningful advancement in recovery. Earth is, thus far, the only human planet to reach the potential to survive beyond the cycle's final stage—if we had not implemented it, of course."

Lifting his arms in a Y, Jonah asked, "And that makes us worthy? Scientific advancement? What of our culture and heritage, the arts, our humanity?"

"None of those would enable a human planet to survive. Industrial revolutions, weapons of mass destruction, greed, commercialism, corrupt governments, and mismanagement of natural resources have led every human world in every cycle to self-implosion. If we had seeded those worlds and left them to their human inhabitants, we would return to find barren wastelands on each."

"You never said where these... *seeds* come from."

Before addressing the Voice, Michelle looked at the farmer in astonishment. "You take some from a completed planet to seed the next. Will I, um, *we*, be among those chosen to seed a new world?"

"If I gave you an incorrect impression, I apologize. Our seed stock comes from a genetic repository of the original progenitors from our home world."

"That means you're seeding worlds with your own ancestors... then *slaughtering* them."

"While I understand how you drew that conclusion, Michelle, it is flawed. Firstly, your evolutionary theories are false, as I have explained. Second, what we seed is from such an early adaptation we hardly consider them sentient."

"Yet you're willing to help us?" Jonah rubbed his shaking head.

"It would be best if you allowed me to complete my explanations without interruption." After a pause, the Voice continued, "In reminding me of a forgotten aspect of our adaptation, Jonah, you provided my second reason. The last limitation we shed before transcending. By bonding with you, I experienced your... emotions."

Jonah asked, "Your people have no emotions?"

"Not in the way humans do. Not as we once did. Pride, greed, and jealousy were among the first we purged as we advanced from your state to the next. This took centuries. In so doing, we sacrificed part of our very nature as a species to reach the next adaptation."

"And of everyone on Earth, *Blankson* taught you about... love?"

"And much more. As I said, we observe human cycles only for their progress toward the final stage. When Jonah stepped into my conduit, I fully absorbed his consciousness. The experience was, as you might imagine, overpowering. Those raw emotions blending love, hope, despair, desperation, and immense grief, stirred within me for the first time since my people transcended."

After a few speechless seconds, Michelle said, "You said you have three reasons for helping us, not including cloud madness. So the third must have something to do with the religious lady."

"Indeed. I found Elder Ferguson, or Amy as she preferred, most curious. Not only did she facilitate bringing Isis here for me to examine another madnesses sufferer, her apprentice, Tilda, is a most fascinating case."

"I don't understand. Ferguson's the priest lady leading the cult that worships, well, *you*. They see the clouds as the work of the Celestial Maker, which, come to think of it, is your people."

"Yes, Michelle, this is true. However, Amy Ferguson never fully accepted the teachings of the Order or the sacred Code they follow. Her wavering faith blossomed into complete disbelief when she freed Isis from the cathedral after seeing how her religion's convictions left a young couple in the storm. In contrast, Tilda was deeply devoted to her faith and conditioned to give herself fully to it."

"There are millions like her, I'm sure. My wife even joined that religion. What is special about that innocent child?"

Someone appeared on what Michelle's brain deemed a floor in the white expanse, a few yards away, motionless and in the fetal position.

Forty-Eight

WHEN HER EYES OPENED, white illumination saturated them. It called to Tilda's mind the visions of heaven some faiths taught. She wondered if it could be the start of the Glorious Transition. The Guide Couple had been debunked. Isis became a blithering idiot and would have died if Miss Amy had not saved her. No, Tilda no longer believed in the Transition—at least not as the Order defined it.

Yet they had discovered otherworldly visitors, and she considered her new surroundings to be... alien. It brought a feeling of sterile tranquility until she heard... something. On her side, lying on a smooth, glass-like floor, she saw only infinite white stretching out to eternity. She thought she had died, passed on to whatever came next, that perhaps none of the world's religions had gotten it right.

"Are you alright?" someone asked.

The question was asked a second time, calling her by name. The Celestial Maker, God, or whatever called her to this place would surely know her name. A warm touch lay on her shoulder. Tilda lifted her head off the floor and turned to behold the face of...

"*Mister Blankson?*"

"Yes, dear girl. Are you alright?"

"I... I think so. Where am I?"

Doctor Anderson leaned over from behind Blankson. "That's a bit tricky to explain."

The two helped Tilda to her feet. She felt intact and unharmed.

"Where is Isis? Miss Amy?"

"Isis is safe," someone said in a voice deeper than Blankson's. Tilda looked for another person and saw no one else. "I am sorry to report Cynthia Ameilia Ahlquist Ferguson expired in the storm."

"*What?*" Tilda shouted. "She cannot..." Her legs failed her, and she fell to her knees, sobbing openly.

The same thick, warm hand reached her shoulder, and an arm wrapped around her back. The kind eyes Tilda saw looking into hers held their own immeasurable sorrow. Immersed in total silence, she took the time needed to purge her tears. When she was ready, or as much as she thought she could be, the gentle older man helped her to her feet and extracted a tear from her cheek with his fingertip.

"Young Tilda, servant to the Order and aide to Elder Ferguson, welcome."

"Who are you?" she asked the open space that somehow spoke.

"I am that upon which your faith was built."

"What does *that* mean?" Doctor Anderson asked.

"Tilda," the Voice said. "What is the significance of all you have recently learned added to all you have ever known?"

Folding her hands in front of her, she replied, "You are an alien from another world with great power and insight. For some reason, you sent us the Code thousands of years ago, foretelling cloud storms... For what purpose?"

With full attention, Tilda listened as the Voice updated her on details already shared with Doctor Anderson and Mister Blankson. One new piece of knowledge explained how the twelve symbols on the conduit represented what became the twelve clans of the Order. She could hardly believe these creatures had seeded the earth with humans only to wipe them out of existence and colonize the planet. And that they founded the Order!

"If I may," she said to the Voice. "I do not understand your reason for producing the Code and giving it to those original twelve to create a religion. Why would you have millions around the world, like me, devote themselves to such a falsehood? Why play with us with foreshadowing and beliefs in a Guide Couple to lead us through a Glorious Transition? To what cruel end?"

"Young Tilda, there was no malice. As you are living representations of our past selves, I wished to see how ideals similar to ones our people once held would grow and spread through time and how such would culminate in a foretold end period."

Pointing at Tilda, Doctor Anderson addressed the Voice. "You played with these people. You turned millions into zealots as... an experiment. Religious wars and atrocities could have been avoided."

"Your conclusions are again incorrect, Michelle. I guided one group of people to become a neutral and mostly peaceful religious order. They have not participated in your wars and the religions that have were not of my making. The Order shed genetic superiority beliefs that were adopted by others to foster the most heinous war crimes of any cycle. Yet every cycle has seen the divisiveness of nationalism, race, and religion. Other than in the depth of its malevolence, yours is no exception."

A light went on in Tilda's head. "The Order was an experiment to see if you could create a unified people prepared to face the end. Only, what we considered a gateway to a better life, to salvation, is to be a transition to... oblivion. If you will kill us all anyway, what was the point?"

"The point was illustrative. While you are far from the next stage of adaptation, I believe you are the first in fifty-seven cycles to have the potential to reach it. The Glorious Transition was meant to prepare you for that and lead you toward transcendence to our form millennia after. You were to be the foundation of a new humanity on Earth, and I would use your people to plead your case to mine."

"Hold on a minute." Doctor Anderson stepped in front of Tilda and held a finger up to nothing. "You said points one and two were based on me and Blankson, by recent observations.

Now you're saying your third reason for helping us was something you started a few thousand years ago?"

"Michelle, Jonah, Tilda, you must understand, we do not experience time in the linear way humans at your level of adaptation do. These three factors came to me at once, while in this present state of isolation from the oneness of our combined essence. And when I return you to your time and relative positions, I will merge with the collective and we will consider your case."

"And when that fails, as you seem sure it will?" Anderson asked.

"Perhaps Plan B was not the correct terminology. Before merging, I will grant you some additional time by disabling the clouds. It will not take my people long to reactivate them. In your terms, the months you have will become, at most, the same in years."

"You're saying the most we have, *if* you're successful, is two or three years?"

"Correct, Michelle. This is why I will attempt to reason with the collective."

"Take us with you," Tilda demanded. "If you will use us to plead our case, let them see us. Let them see what they wish to destroy."

"Young girl, you do not know my kind, cannot know my kind. My chances are far superior if I do not show them your people in your current state. They will know I am presenting hypotheticals. As I am able to withhold some of my thoughts from being absorbed into the collective consciousness, I will attempt to make them see, not what you are, but what you can become."

Forty-Nine

Jonah stood in a now familiar place with young Tilda on one side and Doctor Anderson on the other. The trees rose like towers, and soft sunlight broke through the gaps in the canopy above. Anderson ran from the circle first, shouting the name Nathan as she slalomed around thick tree trunks. The young lady beside him looked paler than her usual near-white. Jonah didn't think her skin could have lost any more color.

"Are you okay?" he asked.

The petite girl nodded unconvincingly.

Taking her by the hand, Jonah led her through the last steps of the forest floor to the clearing. The new camp had been destroyed by the storm the Voice mentioned. A tall woman in glasses Jonah didn't recognize nodded emphatically as Doctor Anderson unloaded everything from their still unbelievable conversation upon her. Unblinking and focused, the general and Doctor O'Malley also appeared mesmerized by the unbelievable story.

Tilda pulled away from Jonah and looked in every direction. From the cloud of confusion in the void to the shock of being suddenly back on solid earth, Jonah had forgotten the child had lost her mentor, her spiritual leader, perhaps her only friend. He didn't object when she darted off to the only tent left standing—or the first erected after the storm. Unsure what to do, Jonah lifted his chin and allowed the warmth of the morning sun to console him.

Concern for the girl pulled him toward the tent she had entered. As she emerged from its flapping canvas door, her glossy eyes were trembling.

"She is not there."

"Dear child. I'm sorry, but your friend is gone."

Unexpectedly, the girl fell into him, sobbing. Placing an arm around her in a grandfatherly embrace, Jonah let her tears and mucus drench his shirt. Anderson, Tucker, O'Malley, Rodriguez, and the tall lady were nowhere to be found. Desiring to check on his mother-in-law but not wishing to leave young Tilda, Jonah took her along. Although he suspected she knew, he decided not to inform Maame of Juliana's death. The world would soon end. He didn't want her last moments to be drenched in the same agony consuming his soul from the inside out.

After walking most of the way in silence, Tilda's feet stopped, halting Jonah's stride. "Your wife was a member of the Order."

He nodded.

"She believed in the Glorious Transition. Do you believe she is somewhere... better?"

"I didn't share her faith but tried to understand it. And I supported her. From my ancestry, to voodoo, to the Christianity brought to us by European colonists, to the Order, and now aliens, I don't know what to believe."

"I choose to believe Miss Amy is in a better place. Whatever that may be."

"But you heard the Voice. You know your faith was constructed by them."

"Yet, throughout human history, ours, on Earth, we have believed in and aspired to something greater than ourselves. I do not believe that was from the Voice or its collective."

"I hope you're correct, young Tilda."

"Perhaps Miss Amy is with your wife now. I am sure she would love her."

"What makes you say that?"

"Because of how much you love her. You have the kindest eyes I have ever known, and a pure heart. Miss Amy told me the same. I am sure your wife has just as beautiful a soul."

***

Back at the camp, Tilda asked if Miss Amy had been taken by the funnels or if her body was there. Not knowing, Jonah asked a soldier busily struggling to secure a tentpole where they had moved the dead lost to last night's storm. Before going to the makeshift morgue of body bags on a patch of brown grass, Tilda grabbed something from a crate beside the dilapidated food tent. When they found the tag with Amy Ferguson's name, Jonah paused to ask Tilda if she was sure she wanted to open it. Her courage and fortitude left him speechless.

The folded flap of the body bag revealed the almost unrecognizable face of the elder from the Order. Blisters and boils covered her scalp and dotted her forehead and cheeks. One eye puffed out in a swollen, red mess. With a face full of tears, Tilda dripped palm oil over the wounds and gently brushed her golden hair over them to spread the glistening liquid.

With gentle footsteps, Jonah crossed to the opposite side of the body and kneeled. Silent at first, his gaze met the youngster's eyes. Both froze in a moment of mourning for the most important women in each of their lives. Tilda returned to her task. She pulled the zipper to the bottom and folded the top of the bag to open it completely. Despite the burns and distorted flesh, the woman looked at peace.

"I must anoint her body," Tilda said, eyes glossy yet focused.

Jonah understood and swiveled around to sit with his knees raised to his chest. As the girl worked behind him, he puzzled over the ritual. If the elder and her young servant had both lost their faith, as the Voice asserted and the girl confirmed, he couldn't understand why she would carry out such a religious rite on the body.

As if knowing his thoughts, she said, "It is to honor my Elder, my instructor, my friend."

"I think I understand," Jonah replied, passing the back of his hand under his eyes. This fresh set of tears fell not for Juliana but for Tilda's loss and for the future she would never have—the end of everyone's future.

Fifty

It could buy them a little more time. They needed to destroy whatever invisible mechanism had made the clouds. The Voice had provided no detail beyond its placement in the upper layers of the atmosphere. As if the Earth were trapped inside an evil snow globe, it encased the entire planet. Michelle imagined the massive hand of the alien visitor shaking the globe. The clouds filled the glass orb and killed all the tiny people inside.

Hope floated through the despair that their life expectancy would increase from months to the few years the Voice offered—if it turned off the clouds. If they found a way to destroy it, they would have even more. While it wouldn't end this, Michele thought it might just buy them the time they needed to figure out how to reverse the damage, as they had begun doing with pre-storm climate change.

All those years studying the phenomenon that had monopolized her life, ruined her relationship with Brian, and distanced her from her family, and a twenty-minute conversation had supplied more answers than she could have gleaned in decades.

Now her research, her work on the task force, her aspirations to save the world from the darkened clouds, amounted to futility.

The solution would be a military one.

Rodriguez and Nathan had been strategizing for the better part of an hour and speaking with the White House and the Pentagon when Michelle and Patrick O'Malley entered the tent.

"Nathan? Rodriguez?" Neither replied or pulled back from ping-ponging their thoughts across the table. With fingers plunged into the corners of her mouth, Michelle's whistle could have hailed a taxi on a bustling DC street in rush hour. "How do we attack something we can't see, scan, or identify as even being there?"

"We're working that out," Nathan replied. "Commander Rodriguez and I are only providing insights from our findings here and your conversation with what even Washington is calling 'the Voice.' The Pentagon's drafting a strike plan."

"Strike plan?" O'Malley barked. "We need to expand our communications, speak to the alien collective."

"We have no time for that. And it seems they decide if, when, and to whom they'll speak." Nathan raised a finger to prevent Pat's pending rebuttal. "A team of scientists added to the DC thinktank, specialists who have theories on the composition and function of the cloud device, are working on an attack strategy."

Slipping into the pause, Pat said, "You don't even know what you're attacking."

"We don't need to know if the buildings of a city are made of wood or steel or stone to destroy it with a nuclear warhead," Rodriguez replied.

Michelle straightened and placed her hands on her hips. "That's your plan—launching nukes at it? Do you have any idea what that'll do to the atmosphere?"

"A hell of a lot less than those clouds will if we don't stop them," Rodriguez growled.

Turning to face her, Nathan hunched to look into her eyes as he often did. "You've done your job. Now you need to leave this to us. We have people, Natasha included, working on projections for the fallout we can expect from fifty 1.5 megaton thermonuclear warheads strategically placed around the globe between the exosphere and magnetosphere detonated at precisely the same time."

"Just don't destroy us before the clouds do." On a less global topic, Michelle said, "My father's still unconscious in the infirmary tent. Any news of the young girl?"

"Nothing. Isis is the only one who hasn't come back from... wherever."

Michelle said, "The Voice told us it wanted to understand the cloud madness. Those people came close to seeing the aliens in the clouds. They didn't think humans could register their... essence, he kept calling it."

"He?" O'Malley questioned. "*You've* chosen the pronoun for the alien?"

Snubbing him, she continued, "He or it spoke with a deep booming voice. It made Darth Vader sound like a prepubescent schoolboy."

That made O'Malley chuckle.

"You think it's studying Isis to learn what she saw?" Nathan asked.

"Definitely. I got the distinct impression it surprised them to learn some humans in this cycle could see any trace of them. They'd assumed no one could."

"Now *he* is a *they*?" O'Malley asked mockingly.

With the hint of a quickly withdrawn grin, Michelle was proud of herself for ignoring him. Her mind raced over her initial thoughts of the cloud madness being a key. Now it seemed confirmed, at least for the ones who said it was beautiful.

"I hope that girl comes back," Nathan said. "The other young lady, Tilda, is pretty broken up over Ferguson's death. I hate to have to tell her Isis was lost too."

"I assume she's safe-*ish* in the same void we were in."

O'Malley had to butt in. "She says, like, two words. They're probably dissecting her as we speak."

"Pat, just..." After a forced exhale, Michelle said, "Nathan, I think—" and stopped herself when a new thought rushed in on her. "I need to go check something."

Fifty-One

The twisting flames climbed into the sky higher than Tilda had anticipated. Fortunately for her, the midday sun diminished the spectacle. While she had no way to anticipate anyone's reaction to what she'd done, she assumed it would be negative. In truth, Tilda knew little of the world or what norms people followed outside of the Order.

Regardless of the current state of her faith, the death of a clan elder demanded honor, an honor Elder Ferguson deserved. One Miss Amy merited in greater measure.

No one had bothered her when she collected splintered wood ripped from trees during the last storm. Or as she lugged that metal jug of gasoline from the Jeep. In fact, other than that kind white-bearded Mister Blankson, no one bothered to check on her at all. Invited to the simple ceremony, he stood respectfully at her side as she recalled the words of passage memorized from the Code.

That was not the faith that had motivated Miss Amy's selfless action in saving Isis. It was not the faith that carried them to

Africa. Faith as the Order defined it no longer burned in Tilda's heart. So using her own words, she decided to speak from what ignited it now.

"May the Celestial Maker, God, or the Majestic Universe keep this strong and loving woman safe for all eternity. May we meet again, Miss Amy, beyond the Glorious Transition or into whatever lies beyond this life. Until then, I shall honor your memory with my life, following in your steadfast example." A lump in her throat interrupted the eulogy for a few seconds. "I will cherish the freedom you have provided. Until our reunion, you remain forever in my heart."

After a look to ask if it was okay, Mister Blankson gave her a comforting hug. This moment was to remember a life, not to mourn a death, so Tilda didn't cry. Time for grieving would come. This pain lay heavier in her heart than when her grandmother passed away last year. Not that she didn't love her Gran. The woman had aged poorly and often hadn't recognize her own family. When she had acknowledged her granddaughter, she called her Dagny, Tilda's mother's name.

Doctor Anderson came up from behind, unheard until she asked what they were doing. Pushing past Tilda and Mister Blankson, her eyes widened at the fire and the body it was consuming.

"Are you crazy? They may have needed to do an autopsy. I don't even think anyone's pronounced her dead. We have rules out here in the real world."

Saying nothing, Tilda tossed some white flower petals she had gathered earlier over the flames licking the body of her mentor.

"Miss Michelle, please leave the girl be. She's grieving, and this is the custom for their people. We must respect it."

"She isn't in her cult commune. We have... protocols. This is the United—"

Holding up his hand, Mister Blankson said, "This is Ghana. This woman lies here dead because she came to bring that other girl to you for help, as I did. My Juliana is gone, and Isis is missing, trapped in that strange place." Pointing to Tilda, he added, "Let this poor child mourn."

"Tina, is it? I *am* sorry... for your loss. I'd like to help your friend—the other one. That's why I was looking for you. I need to know if she had any medical condition, particularly something with her vision."

"Isis? I know little about her. Miss Amy would have known. As chairperson of the Twelve, she would have had her complete medical history."

"Did she bring it with her? Is it here? Where are her things?"

Mister Blankson raised a finger. "You wish to rummage through a dead woman's things while the embers of her fire still glow?"

"I asked permission. It's important. Please, I need to see that girl's medical history."

***

In what had been patched together as the new habitat tent, they found the remains of the personal items collected from the scatterings of the storm. Miss Amy's bag sat among the pile on the floor in the far corner of the tent. Tilda lifted the tote onto the closest bunk and slowly withdrew the zipper. Each click of the teeth was a prick to her conscience for the invasion. After respectfully removing items and setting them gently on the bunk, she raised the binder Miss Amy had grabbed on their escape from the cathedral. Holding it firmly, she extended her arm.

"I believe this is what you requested, Doctor Anderson."

"Thank you." After grabbing the binder, Anderson tapped her open hand on the cover. "This could give us the answers we need about our visitor's existence and their interest in your friend."

Tilting her head, Tilda asked, "What do you hope to find?"

"If I'm right, a connection."

"To whom or what?" Mister Blankson asked.

"To my father. To the alien blue lightning. To the mysteries of the universe in the form of dark clouds over our planet trying to kill us all."

With no idea what Doctor Anderson expected to find, they followed her to the infirmary tent where her father slept. Tilda stayed close to Mister Blankson. Although she found comfort and safety in his presence, it widened the hollow created by the loss of Miss Amy. A field medic attending to Mister Anderson and those injured by the storm sat in the corner.

"Hi, Dad. It's me, Michelle."

Roused to consciousness, he looked upon her with eyes as empty as the cloudless sky after a storm. The same blank stare Isis wore. Speaking softly, Anderson explained what she intended to do. A condition with a long and forgettable name allowed people to see a much wider color variation than most humans. She believed this enabled them to see the blue lightning.

"Dad, I'm going to show you some images. I want you to look closely at them."

He said nothing in reply. Sitting on the bed beside her father, Anderson held her tablet close to his face. Explaining each photo, she let him stare for a few seconds before swiping to the next, asking each time what he saw. Like Isis, his irises never stilled. But then those unsteady eyes locked onto the tablet and rounded. "It's so beautiful," he shouted. "Do you see?" When his daughter pulled the tablet, the older man reached for it, grunting. Anderson jolted to her feet to keep it from his grasp and studied the screen ghosting her face in its pale light.

"What is it? What did he see?" The question raced from Blankson's mouth.

"Nothing. I mean, *he* saw something. This proves it. I was right."

Stretching his arms toward her, her father twisted to the side. Doctor Anderson held the tablet behind her back and leaned into his arms. When he lunged for the device, he fell off the bed with a thud. The medic ran over to help him into the cot but couldn't control him. Blankson assisted the petite woman, wrestling the man onto the bed as he desperately tried to grab the tablet in his daughter's hand.

In tears, Anderson darted out of the tent as a sedative flowed into her father's vein. Blankson and Tilda waited until Mister Anderson had settled into a dormant state. When Blankson asked the medic if she was fine, she lifted a bruised elbow and nodded.

Tapping Mister Blankson's arm, Tilda asked, "What did that man see?"

"I don't know. Did you follow Doctor Anderson's theory?"

"Yes. And I assume she believes Isis has the same condition."

"Do you think your elder, Miss Amy, knew about it?"

"As chairperson and presider of the Guide trials, she would have been familiar with their complete medical histories. I doubt she saw any significance in this eye condition." Tilda paused, contemplating. "If anything, my people would have seen it as a blessing. Enhanced vision would have been considered a gift from the Celestial Maker for Isis to guide us."

"I wish I had learned more of what your people believed from my Juliana."

"I am sorry for your loss, Mister Blankson." When she took his hand, hers disappeared in his grip. "We have many beliefs that are largely unknown, except for some internet posts by disgruntled former members. The public would mock or even persecute us if they knew everything."

"I tried to dissuade my Juliana at first. When she was determined, I trusted her judgement. If nothing else, it kept me from having to go to our former church on Sundays."

After a warm smile, Tilda said, "Now I wonder if Elder Tartagni considered this gifted sight as evidence of her guideship when he submitted Isis and Nickos to the council."

Looking kindly into her eyes, Blankson said, "You no longer believe in that? And Miss Amy was the same?"

"She helped open my eyes to how the Council interpreted our faith."

"What do you plan to do, young child, with the rest of your life?"

"There is no rest of our lives, Mister Blankson. When the end comes, I wish to know I made my own choices in what time I had left."

Taking her other hand, he lowered his head to look deeply into her gray-blue eyes. "I admire you. Even if not by choice, you were privileged to serve a brave and wonderful woman. I saw your tender care for Miss Amy and know you loved her. Now that you have the freedom to do as you please, you choose to help people."

"Thank you, Mister Blankson." Looking at the ground, she said, "I did love her—first as my elder then... as my friend. One thing about the Order you should know, perhaps what attracted your wife, is that we care for one another. If nothing else, I believe that was a worthy value it instilled."

"Come, let us find Doctor Anderson. Perhaps her conclusions will lead to recovering your missing friend."

Fifty-Two

Winded and with her hands on her knees, Michelle couldn't hold back the excitement of her discovery. Nathan waited patiently as he reminded her to breathe. If she had caught her breath by then she would have had a snide comeback.

After spitting out half-sentences interrupted by gasps for air, Michelle explained how her test with her father and the medical records from the dead elder's bag proved her hypothesis. Even O'Malley listened without interrupting. She didn't ask why the exobiologist was still in the strategic meeting for the nuclear attack on the unseen enemy. At least having Natasha in Ghana divided his attention.

If Michelle's conclusions were correct, she might have found a way to pull the cloak of invisibility from humanity's conquerors.

O'Malley broke his unusual silence. "Let me get this straight... You're saying people with a fourth cone in their eyes, who can see far more colors and a wavelength of light most of us can't... They can *see the aliens*?"

"Yes—well, sort of. People who don't have tetrachromacy look up and just go mad. Those with the condition, well, they also go mad. But they see it. Blue lightning more intense than what we caught on video."

"We all saw it on full display at the artifact," O'Malley said.

"Not exactly. We saw a conduit the Voice wanted us to see." Turning to Nathan, she added, "You told me to leave the military strategy to the military. But... I don't think any weapons we've got will kill them."

Waving his hands like her dad exaggerating a fishing story, Commander Rodriguez said, "Then what's the point? We'll proceed with our strike at the altitude you gave us and set them back in their plans to completely destroy our environment."

"I'm sure Natasha's already told you what will be left of our environment. Even if your attack is successful, with that many nukes, we'll ruin the world without the alien's help." Getting a nod of confirmation from Natasha, Michelle continued, "That's beside the point. What I'm saying is, I think your plan to launch your bombs around the globe is flawed."

"How so?" Rodriguez asked. "You said this... thing, whatever they're using to make the clouds, is wrapped around our entire planet like an eggshell between... between those layers of atmosphere you told us about."

"It is, yes. But like any huge machine, I believe there are control centers. I think the aliens are at those controls and that's where we see the blue lightning."

"But *we* don't see it," O'Malley said. "Only those people do, the ones who've *lost their minds*. And so far, they haven't been very talkative."

Arching one eyebrow, Nathan asked, "Michelle, how does this help us?"

"People with tetrachromacy, who have that fourth cone, can see the aliens... Well, their shadows, so to speak. When the next storm clouds form, we'll have strategic targets to hit them at the heart of their operation."

Patrick O'Malley raised his hand in objection. "Seriously? Your brilliant plan is to what, place these people under the clouds... um, *alien spotting*? And we have exactly two, that we know of, and the aliens have one of them."

"I'll leave the alien spotting to you and your tinfoil hat." Michelle added, "And we have another. Wilma Jones. That's how she was able to spot it on the first viewing. I had to slow it down and pause it for the rest of us to see that little spec of blue light."

"Two still doesn't give us much, Michelle," Nathan said.

"Remember how we recorded the cloud storm in DC? With those high-powered, wide-spectrum cameras, we saw a trace of that blue lightning."

"You're proposing we place thousands of such cameras around the world and wait for the clouds?" Rodriguez asked. "Do that many cameras even exist?"

Nathan replied, "No. Those were specialized military-grade cameras. It's not likely we have more than a few dozen."

"But our military must not be the only one to have them," Rodriguez said. "General, if the proposal is to use these cameras across the globe, we could request the cooperation of allied nations to furnish them. We already have six countries collaborating on the nuclear strikes."

While the discussion moved in the right direction, the men failed to consider another option Michelle thought viable. "Gentlemen, I reconfigured and used similar cameras scattered over the globe for my storm warning system. Every government, media corporation, and aerospace agency already receives their data feeds."

"*Satellites*," Nathan exclaimed. "That could work."

"I think we're forgetting something," O'Malley said. "These are advanced and intelligent aliens who have observed humans on dozens of planets. I think they can figure out that our satellites have cameras that can see the lightning."

Shaking her head, Michelle replied, "I don't think so. I mean, you're right, Pat. But they were surprised any humans saw them. What if we're the first human planet with tetrachromats? There must be countless variations of genetic and environmental mutations. And we had to calibrate our camera just to get a glimpse."

"Let me get this straight," Rodriguez said. "We don't need the ones with the extra cornea. We just need to configure as many satellites as we can to look for the lightning in the next cloud storm?"

With a confident nod, Michelle said, "Exactly."

"*Brilliant,*" Nathan exclaimed. "And the satellites could send the exact coordinates of any sightings to our targeting computers in real time. If we get that before they go offline... Michelle, this could be the key to stopping them."

Fifty-Three

Hours went by—some flew while others dragged on forever. After failing to convince Tilda to go get something to eat, Mister Jonah got up and brought her some food. She smiled at his kindness. His grandfatherly nature warmed her heart and caressed away a little of the pain. The eternal blue stretching out in all directions above allowed her mind to drift away from reality. Wide-eyed to the heavens, she pondered what was truly up there. Beyond the sky, beyond the stars, beyond the limits of the physical universe, was there something more?

Texts from the Code scrolled over her thoughts. Some she now discounted as myths, others as principles of life worth remembering. As she had told Mister Jonah, some good had come from the Order. Now the time had come for her to move on, wherever that might take her and for however long or brief that might be. One thing she knew about her future—she wouldn't squander what Miss Amy had given her life to provide. The only problem was, she had no idea what she wanted to do before the world died.

The prospect of the world ending no longer frightened her. Her trepidation, what little she had, came in pondering what to do if or when Isis reappeared.

A sorry meal, the military rations emitted a tangy fragrance. Something called Salisbury steak tasted nothing like beef and had a toughness she didn't expect from a minced meat patty. The runny mashed potatoes dissolved in her mouth, and the peas were mushy and a bit too salty. They finished their meals in tranquil silence, and Tilda gulped down an entire bottle of water.

This gentle soul, the first dark-skinned African she had ever met—the elder from South Africa was as fair as she—stayed by her side, looking after her like a parent or grandfather. Hours washed over their discussions about their lives, losses, and hopes. In all those conversations in Elder Ferguson's chamber, Tilda hadn't known she was speaking to Miss Amy. While she had opened up more to her than anyone prior, Tilda had held back. A decision she now regretted. The elder-servant posture had been a wall between them. Reflecting on it now, Tilda saw how and why Miss Amy had worked to erode that wall. But even at the end, huge chunks of it had stayed intact. Nothing stood between her and Mister Jonah. Between her and anyone anymore.

Listening to Jonah speak of the beauties of Africa brightened her with wonder. Perhaps there was still a little room for aspirations and making plans. This world, dying as it might have been, held such sights to see. Things her life of servitude would have forbidden her. Now, more than anything, she longed to see more of this magnificent continent than the one field and that cursed artifact.

Conversation often took Mister Jonah back to his wife. While feeling wholly unqualified to be anyone's counselor or emotional support, Tilda offered reassurance that such a lovely soul as Miss Juliana could not be extinguished. In some way, she must have lived on. Although he wore the grief as a bleeding heart on his sleeve, she thought he took some comfort from her words. Or perhaps just her presence. As the words floated away on the warm breeze, she leaned her head on Mister Jonah's arm.

"It's alright, child. Do you know what you will do? You're welcome to stay with us. Maame and I would be delighted to host you."

"You are very kind, Mister Jonah."

"In my culture, it is appropriate for you to call me Uncle."

She smiled. "I would like that... I am not sure what I will do if Isis returns. I would love to see some of the beautiful places you described. If I can secure transportation with the limited funds Miss Amy had, I will head south to Namibia. Safari there sounds amazing."

"With the world awaiting its impending doom, I don't believe anyone is running safari now." After a long pause, he continued, "I will borrow my cousin's Land Rover. Good for travel and safari. It will be my pleasure to escort you along the coast. Isis as well—when she returns. We can drive through the Namibian jungle. Perhaps, if we have time, I will take you to see

Victoria Falls. It's my favorite place in all of Africa. One of the best moments in my life was spent there with Juliana."

Squeezing his arm, Tilda said, "I would like that very much, Uncle."

A crackling noise crept out of the forest behind them. Sharp cracks like splintering wood filled the air with the sterile scent of electricity. Mister Jonah rose to his feet, pulling the young lady up to hers to check the ring. Expecting Isis to appear, Tilda's lips flattened. Blue light danced over the images around the rim but didn't form a dome, nor did the column of white rise into the sky.

"This is different," Mister Jonah said.

Tilda squeezed his hand. "Do you think they wish to have another discussion?"

"That may be. The Voice said it would plead on our behalf to its collective. Perhaps it has and now wishes to report its conclusion."

"Then we should step into the circle and allow them to take us."

"No, dear child. If anyone, I believe they wish to speak with Doctor Anderson. Come, let us collect the others."

As they ran through the trees, Mister Jonah grasped Tilda's hand. When they cleared the forest, Doctors Anderson, Kournikova, O'Malley, the general, and Commander Rodriguez were running toward them.

"What did you see?" Anderson shouted before they reached each other. "Is there lightning on the ring?"

"Did the girl come back?" the general added.

Mister Jonah replied, "No. We believe they're calling us."

Together, the group raced into the forest toward the ring. They stopped a half meter from the glowing circle.

Rodriguez asked, "What do we do, sir?"

"Michelle?" General Tucker deferred.

"We go in," O'Malley replied.

Doctor Anderson said, "No, Pat. I'm truly sorry. Really. I wish you could go and meet our invaders. I know it's your life's work. But I think they want Jonah and me."

"She's correct, Patrick," Kournikova said. "The last time you stepped in, they returned you without engaging."

"The girl comes as well," Mister Jonah insisted. "She was brought into our conversation, and the Voice is interested in her."

Rodriguez objected, "I can't approve that. Sir, we don't yet know the potential dangers. She's a child, and we can't guarantee her safety in there."

"I am not a child, and I am going."

"I believe she should come," Mister Jonah affirmed.

"Michelle, what do you say?"

"I say she comes. Nathan, I think Jonah's correct. The Voice is calling us, and the last time we spoke to it, it was the three of us."

"Very well."

With Rodriguez holding Doctor O'Malley back, Uncle Jonah put one foot into the ring then slowly dragged the other. He pulled Tilda in beside him as Doctor Anderson stepped in as well. The blue light rose to enclose them in a dome of lightning, and everything Tilda saw became brilliant white.

Fifty-Four

AGAIN INSIDE THE ENDLESS pure white space that was somehow an extension of the Voice's essence, Michelle stood beside Jonah with him holding onto the girl. With both arms wrapped around one of his, the young lady didn't appear at all at ease.

"I do not like it here, Uncle," she said.

When did this man become her uncle? Holding her tongue, Michelle didn't point out that the girl had come at her own insistence. In honest appraisal, the apprehension and trepidation of the moment crawled up Michelle's back like a tarantula. No amount of wincing could shake it off. Despite all the Voice had shared, they knew little about this alien race or the place where it had brought them. They couldn't know whether it would crush them out of existence where they stood.

"Okay," she shouted. "You called, and we came. Do you have an update on our case? Has the collective reconsidered their immoral and barbaric ways?"

No reply came for a few seconds and Michelle began to pace. "*Hello*?"

"We did indeed summon you."

The thunderous Voice roiled in on them from all directions, causing a momentary glitch in Michelle's equilibrium. She needed to steady herself to stay on her feet. Jonah stood strong and helped lift the girl from her knees—her shaking an outward display of the same mess Michelle's nerves had become.

"Do you have an update for us?"

"What do you expect to learn from us?"

"Wait..." Michelle looked at the others, unsure if they'd noticed. "Are we speaking to the isolated entity we call the Voice, or do you speak as the singularity?"

"What do you expect to learn from us?"

In a whisper, Michelle told Jonah she didn't think this was the same Voice as the last time, or at least it wasn't detached from the collective. As soon as she finished, she realized how stupid it was to think the alien, which they were in some way—which she tried not to think about—inside of, didn't hear her.

"Where is the one we call the Voice?"

"We are one consciousness. What did you expect to learn from us?"

"You are persistent, I'll give you that. We know your... *people*, or whatever, can detach from the singularity for a time. We also know not every individual in your collective feels the same about your cycles and how you use humans as disposable slaves to prepare worlds for your habitation."

"Some of you know how wrong these actions are," Jonah added.

"The only wrong committed, Mister Blankson, was one of our whole using isolation to converse with lower lifeforms. In all our cycles, this has never been done and is unforgivable."

Before Michelle could, Jonah asked, "What happened to the Voice?"

"That is none of your concern, human."

Michelle couldn't endure the bullying tactic. "Then why'd you call us here? We thought it was the Voice. It seems he was the only voice of reason in your collective." Closing her eyes to think, she paused. "*Oh*, of course... the Voice is *not* the only one who challenges what you do to your own ancestors. To countless billions on eighty worlds. When your people are allowed independent thought, they question the morality of your ways."

"We are a singularity, one collective consciousness. Isolation is now forbidden. We are forever one."

What repercussions the Voice's actions might have had on this species Michelle couldn't begin to speculate. She assumed shedding the last vestiges of their individuality would fundamentally change them. How would previously conflicted minds handle that? How would they cope with the loss of self, forced to merge not only their thoughts, but also their values, their morality, their hopes and dreams, into a collective? A new understanding of her own quest for "independence"—and the life choices she'd made to get it—rushed in to consume her mind.

While she drifted in contemplation, Jonah again asked, "Then why are we here, speaking to the collective essence?"

"We wish to understand."

"Understand what?" Michelle demanded.

"How it is you value individuality so highly, yet your kind can become so attached to other isolated beings, going to great lengths to care for one another. Yet you are not one. For at the same time, you fight and kill each other. We find this paradox most peculiar."

"We call it humanity," Jonah replied. "It's what your people worked so hard to dismiss so long ago—you forgot what it means."

The young girl added, "All you care about is your own existence. In my experience, that will never lead to happiness. Never to fulfillment. What your species is now is not elevated but reduced to... academia."

In the long silence that followed, Michelle crossed her arms and rubbed her biceps. The void felt almost emptier, as if the alien presence had departed, leaving the three humans alone.

Looking at her, Jonah asked, "What happens now?"

"No idea. If they're done with us, hopefully they dump us back in the ring."

"And what about Isis?" the girl asked. "No one asked about her."

Walking in a tight circle, Michelle shook her head. "This collective isn't telling us anything. All we know for sure is that the Voice failed."

"I agree. We must hope your military is successful in stop—"

Launching a finger at Jonah's lips, Michelle said, "Don't say another word. Our world isn't lost. Not yet."

"I thought we established this was *not* your world."

Michelle became inexplicably hopeful. "Voice? Is that you?"

"Hello Doctor Anderson, Mister Blankson, Miss Ferguson."

Turning to Tilda, Jonah asked, "Your surname is also Ferguson?"

"It is the most common surname in Clan Ferguson."

"Were you related to Miss Amy Ferguson?"

"Not directly. If you go back far enough, I think all of Clan Ferguson are distant—"

"*People*," Michelle said. "Could we please get back to talking to the Voice about saving our planet?"

"Michelle, I am afraid that is not possible."

"But... the collective said you couldn't isolate. Not just you for your punishment, but all of you. And here you are."

"This is part of my punishment."

"They caught you trying to shut down the clouds," Michelle concluded.

"You could think of it that way. I could not stop cloud production, and they would not entertain my proposal. Unfortunately, the decision of the collective mind is to accelerate the final stage with one last extreme storm, more intense and longer than any prior."

"Excuse me," the girl said politely. "Mister Voice, why did your people make *you* tell us this? Does this... *sadden* you?"

An uncomfortably long pause left the three looking blankly at each other until the Voice replied in a somber, gentle tone. "I believe I have grown... fond of you. Of this cycle and what you have accomplished."

"I didn't think that was possible." Michelle's eyes glossed over.

"When we leave our momentary isolation, our consciousness, but not all our thoughts and memories, flood into the collective immediately. Before we could ponder my independent thoughts of you, we had judged your cycle no different than the others. My actions while in isolation were deemed traitorous to the whole, to our survival."

A tear rolled down the young lady's cheek. "You... felt emotion... for the first time in many millennia."

After another pause, the Voice said, "I believe so."

Looking straight up, Michelle rubbed a crick in her neck. "And because of that they're torturing you by making you tell us—just you, in isolation."

"Yes. And I have one more piece of information to share before I am rejoined, the last of my kind to ever experience the solitude of isolation."

"We're all going to die and there's nothing we can do about it."

"Correct again, Michelle. We know of your clever modification to target our blue light. This will fail. The residual fallout will not delay our occupation, nor will it stop our clouds or harm us. The metaphor is rather accurate. You are trying to kill a monster by shooting its shadow."

"Uncle, I am scared. I wish to leave this place. Ask it about Isis and if we can all go now, please."

"I am sorry, Miss Ferguson. Your friend will not be returned. Now that we know how she and others have detected our presence in the clouds, we must understand how to identify and prevent this in other cycles."

Jonah grumbled, "What have you done with her?"

"Isis has been transported to a world a thousand of your years behind this cycle for further analysis. I assure you she is being well cared for as we continue our studies."

"You cannot do that. *Please!*"

"I am sorry, Tilda. There is nothing I can do. Be comforted knowing she will be the sole survivor of this cycle. Of your world."

Tilda broke down into uncontrollable sobbing and buried her face into Jonah's chest.

"I have one final question. If your people—"

The sudden rise in illumination caught Michelle's question in her throat and blinded everyone behind quickly closed eyelids.

Part Four

Acceptance

Fifty-Five

The others had waited for them at the ring. It shocked Jonah to learn they had been gone only a few seconds from the perspective of Tucker, Rodriguez, and Doctors Kournikova and O'Malley. Miss Michelle raised her hand to check her wristwatch and compared it to the time the general had. There was a thirteen-minute discrepancy. That plastered a smug grin on O'Malley's face. To Jonah's surprise, Michelle smiled at him and nodded.

With Tilda still clasped to his arm, Jonah listened quietly as Michelle related the conversation with the collective and with the Voice. The main point Jonah took away was that all hope was lost. One final storm, likely without warning as the last one had come, would seal their fate and make Earth unlivable to the lower lifeforms humans evidently were.

"They know about our plan—details?"

"Yes, Nathan," Michelle confirmed. "We should have expected this. In our first conversation with the Voice, it knew everything about us, including things we discussed in private."

Shaking his head, Rodriguez asked, "What do we do now, sir?"

"Now, Commander, we launch as planned."

"Aye, sir." Rodriguez saluted and rushed off back toward the camp.

Jonah said, "General, sir. The Voice said we cannot harm them."

"Tell me, Jonah. If you knew an enemy *could* harm you and was planning an attack, wouldn't trying to convince them it was futile be an effective strategy? Wars have been lost because an army abandoned hope and gave up. If it *is* futile, at least we go down fighting."

"I think this is where I leave, then." Exchanging nods with Tilda, Jonah added, "And the young lady as well. We are of no further use to you."

"As you wish, Jonah. Godspeed... to both of you."

"Jonah, wait." Miss Michelle stepped before him with an extended hand, which he shook. "I'm truly sorry about your wife. I wish I could have helped you find her."

After a deep sigh, Jonah said, "When we met, you must have thought I was a simple farmer. A delusional man who couldn't let go of his wife. Couldn't accept the loss." When she tried to speak, he raised a finger. A softness he hadn't seen before filled her eyes. "I am a simple man. I married young and went from my mother's home to my wife's. I couldn't cope with the idea of being without my Juliana and put the burden of finding her on you. For that, I am sorry."

"Don't be sorry." After patting his arm, Michelle said, "If anything, I need to apologize to you. I treated you like a piece of equipment. A tool to help me"—twirling her finger, she rolled her eyes—"save the world."

"All my life, the women I loved took care of me." Looking at Tilda, he continued, "I think it's time for me to take care of someone."

"You cared for my father. And for me, when I needed a lit-tle..." She bobbled her head. "Grounding. And in the end, you helped me find the answers I sought. Thank you, Jonah."

With a somber nod, he replied, "You are welcome, Michelle."

"If nothing else, I hope you at least have closure."

"I hope you find closure as well."

Fifty-Six

By their sixth day of this marvelous adventure, Tilda had fully absorbed the sights of their drive along the Atlantic coast. The stunning sunrises and sunsets had brought her to tears. Elephants, giraffes, rhinos, hyenas, and lions had come so close to the vehicle she could almost touch them.

In this man's affection, she found something she'd never felt with her parents, who had been more attentive to grooming her for cathedral service than to nurturing a relationship with their daughter. During the long hours in the truck, they talked about their lives. Tilda came to love Juliana through his memories of her. She learned of the pain Jonah—old enough now to be a grandparent—carried in his heart for his inability to have children.

The vista that now filled the windscreen blew her away. Never had she seen so great a volume of water churning and burbling with such ferocity. The thunderous rapids plummeted into the glorious chaos of the rocky pools below. Victoria Falls was every bit as breathtaking as Uncle Jonah had promised.

Pointing out her window, he said, "I know a place we can enter the water."

From her flung-open door, Tilda ran barefoot toward the rapids. As he pulled off his shirt, Uncle Jonah asked if she had a swimsuit.

Shaking her head, Tilda said, "I will go in like this."

Having borrowed clothes from Jonah's niece, she stood on the bank in shorts and a T-shirt. Hand in hand, they stepped into the frigid water. He repeated his caution for her not to let go of him. Standing on her tiptoes in so much water both exhilarated and frightened her, as she'd never learned to swim. With her hand tight in Uncle Jonah's grip, she trusted his assurance they would not enter water above her waist. Giddy and laughing, Tilda followed his steps, climbing over slippery rocks.

"Come, let's venture a little farther." Jonah tugged her arm to nudge her closer and closer to the fall's unimaginable drop. "The current here isn't too strong."

Less than a meter from the edge, the falling water roared, and Tilda's first look out over the falls shivered her bones more than the frigid water had. With further reassurance—and the idea she would soon die anyway—Tilda mustered the courage to sit beside him at the very edge of the cliff. The spectacular sight left her mouth agape under rounded, unblinking eyes. All of Africa spread out beyond the rising mist. The falls had yet another treat to share.

"Look, Uncle... A rainbow!"

After enjoying the new sight for a few minutes, Uncle Jonah said, "One more thing makes a trip to Victoria Falls complete."

"What could top this? Thank you so much for bringing me here."

"It is truly my pleasure. Now, are you ready?"

With a gentle hand, Jonah aided Tilda to her feet to face the emptiness beyond the falls. Unfathomable amounts of water rushed around her to plunge over the cliff. As she bent her elbows, cautiously lowering herself to lie at the water's edge, the churning bubbles tickled her goosebump-riddled skin.

Looking down terrified her, yet she couldn't turn her eyes from the majestic awe. The beauty of the scene replaced Tilda's fear with laughter. As the sky darkened, she couldn't imagine a more perfect moment.

Fifty-Seven

As the end approached with voracious speed and certainty, Michelle had one last goal before saying goodbye to humanity—at least in this cycle. Greater than her drive to climb to the top of her career in meteorology, overshadowing her determination to understand the clouds and defeat the storms, Michelle had the burning desire to go… *home.*

Her last interaction with the kind yet assertive General Nathan Tucker had been an argument that turned into an emotional goodbye. After failing to convince her that traveling—even in their supersonic jet—was too dangerous if the aliens could bring a storm without warning, he consented. Next came a round of apologies. Michelle had begun with Pat, who was going to stay at the ring in hopes of making contact. She wished him luck before moving on to Natasha, and then to everyone she had snapped at, cut off to assert her opinion, or just been plain rude to. It was a long list.

Jonah had borrowed a Land Rover and gone on a bucket list excursion with young Tilda. He had wished Michelle closure. She boarded that jet to take her dad home to find it.

***

As soon as she had landed in DC, her first call was to Brian. Knowing he had lost his parents in a cloud-storm-induced plane crash two years ago, Michelle assumed he didn't want to spend his last days alone. But that wasn't why she rushed to his apartment to invite him to join her at the farmhouse. And his immediate reply followed by a passionate kiss told her it wasn't why he accepted. While not regretting her career and the focus she rightly gave the cloud storms, thoughts of the relationships she had kept at a distance harassed her. They'd always been there. Now, in the short time she had left, she listened to them.

On her sixth day at home, the morning sun shone through the windows to light the old farmhouse. Michelle tried to forget that deep voice, its ominous warning of a final storm to end everything—as far as humanity was concerned. Sitting in her living room with Mom tending to Dad and Bobby carrying on about something or other, Michelle felt no fear or worry about the final weeks, days, or hours. Not knowing where she left it or if its battery had died, she hadn't checked her phone in over a day.

Unlike the malevolent alien singularity, Michelle finally found the balance between her individuality and her "collective," the ones she loved and chose to be with now. Snuggling up to Brian, she felt the warm comforts of *home*. As they peered out the window, Michelle tightened her grip on his interlocked fingers and said, "The darkened clouds are here."

Mom had prepared tea, and they just started sipping when Dad rose up, said those infamous words, and headed toward the door. Michelle pulled herself from the sofa, but not to stop her father. Smiling at her Superman, she handed everyone a pair of color-spectrum-enhancing glasses the government had graciously provided in appreciation for her service.

"Come," she said to Mom and Bobby and Brian. "Let's gaze upon the darkened clouds and see the beauty my dad sees in them."

Thank You!

I hope you enjoyed this race against climactic Armageddon and related to the struggles of the main characters. While I love a "happily ever after" as much as the next, endings like this one resonate with us, making us ponder the consequences and outcome long after reading.

A brief review helps others find this story and takes only a few seconds. Scan the QR code.

As a thank you for reading (and to connect via my newsletter), I have a gift for you. In this bonus short story, we follow Michelle as the dark clouds first arrive, and she begins work on her storm warning system.

Claim your copy at: go.glassauthor.com/clouds

P.S. You may find a gift within a gift at the end of the story...

Also by

books.glassauthor.com

Finding Idyllium: Earth's Stolen Future

EARTH IS DYING. HIS daughter is dying. The parallel world of **Idyllium is her only hope.** Marc must make her end justify his means. A covert mission to save Earth's billions clashes with the fate of a pristine parallel world. From politician to soldier to civilian, ethical lines blur. Loyalties are challenged. The order to assassinate Idyllium's key political leader forces Marc to take desperate turns, dividing members of his team.

Sci-Fi Shorts: Speculative Fiction, Alternative History, UFO Throwback Satire

1 – A desperate time jumper must find a way to bend the laws of physics to avoid being torn from the family he irresponsibly created.

2 – President Kennedy survives his assassination attempt, only

to discover that fate itself is now his greatest enemy, and the price of his life is being paid by others.

3 – In a satirical homage to a cult classic, discover the backup plans to "Plan 9 from Outer Space" and find out just how badly an alien intervention can go.

Overlap: The Lives of a Former Time Jumper

What if you had the power to redo your life, and it only made things worse? Marcus repeatedly relives his life when he discovers the overlap. In "normal time" he lives alone, grief and regret his constant companions. Now, Marcus unveils the dark secrets of time jumping to a reporter who holds revelations of her own that could shatter his understanding of reality—again.

The New Europa trilogy

Gift Ojo is relentlessly optimistic. As gnawing doubts are stirred by conspiracy theories and whispers grow into a deafening din, discontent sprouts sabotage, threatening New Europa. When the world expands into something Gift and her friends never imagined, with the marvels come new and horrific tests of their humanity. Gift's journey brings her to the brink of all-out war. Will she have what it takes to stand against her people and find her choice?

About the author

Reading is a passion. Writing is an obsession.

Born and raised in Brooklyn, NY, I live and write in Milan, Italy. As an independent author, I invest in my writing by working with coaches, using beta readers, polishing every manuscript with professional human editors, and finishing with a proofreader. Added to my passion for crafting stories, this offers you quality books that are an enjoyable read and often provide a thought-provoking experience.

I love to expound stories that are driven by relatable characters on meaningful journeys. Drawing from personal experiences enriches the writing process and leaves readers feeling like they know the characters they spend time with in a story. That human connection between my characters, readers, and myself, fuels my drive as an author.

Optimistic views of the future through art always interest me, as I believe ours will be bright.

glassauthor.com

9 798990 748446